"Sharon Randall's legion of fans, who've
paper column for years, have a new rea.   ...ıc—her
first novel. Talented writers who are als   ͜ ͜ ͜ tellers are rare,
but Sharon is in that elite club. *The World*   ͜ *nen Some* is storytelling
at its finest."

—Thomas Walton, Retired Editor,
Monterey Herald, California; *Toledo Blade*, Ohio

"Sharon has the gift of writing about what everyone wants to read—everyday life! Readers laugh with her, cry with her, and smile with her as
they reminisce about situations in their lives that mirror hers. That is
exactly why she sells out events with the mention of her name! The audience feels as if their best friend is coming to town."

—Nancy Brown, Executive Director, Hands to Hands
Community Fund, Wichita Falls, Texas

"To hunker down with the works of Sharon Randall is like spending qual-
ity time with a poet, and then learning that the poet is the sweetest
person on earth."

—Joe Livernois, Editor, Voices of Monterey Bay,
www.vomb.org

"Sharon has a way of connecting to readers unlike anyone I have ever
known. Her life experiences are expressed in a way that touches your
soul."

—Steve Snider, Publisher,
Carmel Magazine, California

"Sharon makes me feel like I'm a member of the family, so when the joys of life give way to the pain, I never feel alone."

—Mike Konz, Enterprise Editor,
Kearney Hub, Nebraska

"Sharon writes in the authentic voice of one who knows where people live their lives, the snapshots of joy and the quieter moments to reflect on what it all means. Her writing is full of knowing observations, but beneath it all is a generous and open heart that hears the stories of others. Life is made of moments—a child's party, a phone call with bad news, a visit with an old friend—and she captures their meaning framed with grace, grit, and hope."

—Jeff Fox, Executive Editor, *The Examiner*,
Independence, Missouri

THE
WORLD
and
THEN
SOME

A NOVEL

Sharon Randall

Design by Elina Cohen
Cover design by Laura Duffy Design
Title and part title photo from Shutterstock by Yarygin

978-1-7358011-1-7 (TR)
978-1-7358011-2-4 (ebook)

Library of Congress Control Number: 2020918632

Published by Hummingbird Books
Carmel Valley, California

Printed in the United States of America

THIS BOOK IS DEDICATED TO FAMILY

To my grandmother, who inspired it; to my father and mother
and sister and brothers and others, who sewed the seeds for the characters
that fill its pages; to my husband and children and grandchildren,
who nagged me to finish it, and who give me reason to laugh, love,
and wake up every morning just to see what will happen next;
and finally, to my family of readers and friends, who have encouraged me
in all my years as a writer to "never stop writing." You know who you are.
Please know I am grateful.

Who is she that looketh forth as the morning, fair as the moon, clear as the sun, and terrible as an army with banners?

—Song of Solomon 6:10

PART I

1898–1930

1

Deliverance

$\mathcal{L}$aurel Lacy never saw the snake that bit her. She wasn't even sure it was a snake. In the end, it didn't matter. What was done was done. She had never been one to waste time casting blame. And she had finer things to think about than a snake.

On that day—August 17, 1898—Laurel took a notion to go walking in the cornfield. It was late afternoon, sweltering hot, a few hours before sundown. But soon it would be the cool of the evening, her favorite time of day. She needed some time to herself to settle her mind and pray for strength for what lay ahead.

Supper was done. Her family was fed. Harlan, her husband, had finished the milking and left the buckets on the kitchen table. Laurel skimmed the cream from the milk and sent Edward, the eldest of her three boys, down to the creek to store it in the cooler. Tomorrow, she thought, if she were able, she'd churn it into butter.

Something caught her eye and she turned to smile at a small crystal vase that once belonged to her mother. It sat on the ledge of the kitchen window, catching rays of light from the sun and spitting little rainbows around the room. It never failed to warm her heart.

Harlan sat in the rocking chair in the front room reading to the boys a passage from the Gospel of Mark. John the Baptist was about to lose his head and the boys lay sprawled on the floor, bug-eyed with anticipation. Laurel waved to Harlan as she slipped out the front door. He paused mid-verse, to watch her leave, then continued to read.

Out on the porch, the August heat washed over Laurel in a wave of nausea. She waited. It passed. Then she climbed the hill beyond the barn to stand on the ridge and look out across the wide green valley that had cradled her family for five generations.

In the distance, the French Broad River glittered like a silver necklace across the landscape, winding through the farms, the fields, the pastures, past the church, along the road into town. The red clay earth lay baked and steaming, fragrant as a skillet of corn-bread fresh from the oven. A breeze from the creek carried the scent of butterscotch and rotting leaves and rushing water.

To the west, the Blue Ridge Mountains rose and fell in waves, smooth and round as a mother's breasts. An egg-yolk sun was slid-ing slowly down the sky above Mount Pisgah, sending long, languid fingers of buttery light rippling along the corn rows, beckoning her to follow.

She walked slowly, trailing her hands along the corn stalks to hear the rustle of the leaves, counting her steps to time the min-utes between contractions. They had started that morning as she chopped wood, the familiar clenched-fist tightening in her belly that had always marked the onset of her labors. Ten minutes apart now. Getting stronger. They meant business. No mistaking it. Her fourth child—a girl this time, Laurel felt sure of it—had decided to come a bit early.

The thought of a baby girl made Laurel smile and cradle her belly with her hands. She adored her boys. They were as fine and good as the man who fathered them. But she longed to have a daughter. As a child, she had watched how the women in her family talked and laughed and cried together, how they carried one another's burdens. There was something important about the company of women. She couldn't name it, but she could feel it. She treasured the women she knew as neighbors and friends, especially her dear friend, Ada. But she saw them mostly at church or socials. A daughter, she told herself, would be her friend for life.

Near the end of a corn row, Laurel noticed a clump of weeds, a thick, tangled vine that would choke any green thing in its path. She hated that vine. Reaching down with one hand, holding her belly with the other, she tried pulling it up by its roots. When it held firm, she gave it a yank, and was surprised to feel a sharp pain on the inside of her wrist.

Puzzled, she stared at the marks—two tiny wounds, oozing blood, on either side of the vein. Fangs? Quickly, she kicked the weeds with her boot. Nothing moved. Her mind raced. What could it have been? Just a black snake, probably, nothing to fear. There was no warning, so it couldn't have been a rattler—could it? What if it was a copperhead?

Laurel's cry came out a strangled whisper: "Harlan!" She turned and ran stumbling to the house, holding her belly, sucking her wrist, spitting out blood.

Ada Shields was nursing her youngest when she heard shouting in the distance. Her baby, Grady, rolled his eyes toward the sound and sucked harder. Ada pulled him from her breast and laid him on a quilt on the floor just as nine-year-old Edward Lacy burst through the door.

"Miz Shields!" Edward was dripping sweat, gasping for air. "The baby's fixin' to come and Mama . . . she got snake bit!"

Ada mopped Edward's brow with her apron. "Catch a breath, boy. Is your daddy home?"

"Yes, ma'am, he sent me to fetch you. Please, Miz Shields, my mama's hurtin' bad."

Grady started bawling. Ada shushed the baby, then took Edward's sweaty face in her hands.

"Listen to me, son. Go on down to the barn and fetch Mr. Shields. Tell him I said to hitch up the wagon. We'll need to take a lantern. It'll be dark in another hour."

The Shields' place was two miles by wagon from the Lacy farm, less than a mile on foot through the woods. Edward didn't wait. He found John Shields forking hay at the barn, begged him, "Please, sir, hurry!" Then he ran off barefoot in the gathering dusk with one thought in mind—a thought so powerful it would not be swayed by stones or thorns or total exhaustion: He had to get home to his mother.

The waning light in the western sky cast long shadows through the window, sending starry shapes from the pattern in the old lace curtains dancing across the bed where Laurel lay. Harlan loosened a tourniquet on her arm and used it to dry the sweat, first from her face, then from his.

"It's not swelling much," he said. "I think I sucked out all the poison."

Laurel's labor was going quickly, despite the throbbing in her wrist. Her water had burst an hour ago as she ran from the cornfield, and on the last contraction, she had felt an urge to push.

At Laurel's mention of needing to push, Harlan's face had gone as white as a trout's belly. "No, darlin'," he said. "Please. We ought to wait for Ada."

Laurel managed a weak laugh. "Try telling that to this baby."

"We have to wait, Laurel. I don't know what to do. God help me, I'm . . ."

"Mama?" Edward stood in the doorway, his bloody feet smearing tracks on the worn pine floor. Laurel looked at her firstborn and smiled at him with her eyes.

"I'll be all right, son. You go see to your brothers for me."

Edward rubbed his mouth with his fist and looked to his father for direction.

"Did you tell Miz Shields we need her quick?" Harlan asked.

"Yes, sir, I did. Mr. Shields is bringing her in the wagon."

"Well, go on then, see to your brothers. Put some liniment on those feet."

As the boy turned to go, Harlan called after him, "And light a lantern! It's gettin' dark."

Laurel waited until Edward was out of sight, then reached for her husband's hand.

"Hear me, Harlan," she said, looking into his eyes. "I don't need Ada. I need you."

He started to speak, but stopped. Who could argue with such fierceness of heart?

A contraction swept over Laurel and she gripped his arm, clenched her teeth, and bore down with all her might. When the pain eased, she leaned back and closed her eyes.

"That was a good one," she said softly. "Won't be long now."

Harlan didn't answer. He was staring at the bed. On the piece-work quilt beneath Laurel's hips, a crimson stain was slowly blooming like a rose.

On the next push, the child slipped from her mother's body into her father's waiting hands. Harlan was shaking. "A girl, Laurel! We've got us a girl!"

The baby began to wail, and Laurel tried to lift a limp hand to reach for her.

"Give her to me, Harlan."

He placed the infant face down across Laurel's chest, and began tying off the cord with a piece of twine. The afterbirth came with an awful gush of blood.

Laurel's voice was thick. "I want to name her . . . for my mama."

Harlan had slaughtered pigs and butchered deer but he had never seen such blood as he saw now. He pressed a pillow between Laurel's legs and prayed the bleeding would stop.

It didn't.

"Harlan?"

"I'm here, darlin'." Wiping her blood from his hands on the hem of his shirt, he leaned over his wife and child and pressed his face in the hollow of Laurel's neck. He could feel the warmth of their baby's wet body, the bird-like beating of the child's heart, cradled between their own.

Laurel turned her lips to Harlan's ear and whispered. "Tell her, Harlan."

He lifted his head. "Tell her what?"

She combed her fingers through the baby's tangled wet curls, traced the downy curve of her spine, and felt the spaces between each of her toes.

"Tell her that her mama said she was worth it."

Laurel's voice was barely a whisper. Harlan leaned close, straining to hear.

"Worth what, darlin'?"

"Everything," she said. "The world and then some."

Harlan raised his head and stared into Laurel's eyes. Her hand slid from the child's back and fell limp on the bed. The wound on her wrist had stopped bleeding. He pushed her hair back from her forehead and cradled her face in his hands. Finally, he sat beside her, on the same bed where he had held her every night for twelve years, and watched the light in her eyes fade away.

When the angels came to claim her, Harlan fought them. He had wrestled angels before, but never as fiercely as he fought them now for Laurel. He was a big man—solid as a hickory and as strong as he was good—but in the end, he was outnumbered. They knew better than to come for Laurel short-handed. Gabriel himself could not have taken her from him alone.

Somewhere in another world, Harlan heard an awful wailing. At first, he thought it came from the child, but no, it was his own. He lifted the infant from her mother's body, pressed the child to his chest and together, father and daughter, they wept for their loss. Moments later, he felt a hand on his shoulder. Ada Shields stood behind him holding a lantern, her face shining wet with tears. The baby had fallen asleep, sucking on Harlan's neck. He wrapped the child in her mother's blue shawl and handed her to Ada.

"She's hungry," he said. "I'd appreciate you feeding her. I'll tend to her mama directly. But first I need to go talk to my boys."

The child would be called Cora for her grandmother but her middle name would prove more telling of her nature. It was the last word Laurel spoke as she lay bloody and dying, a benediction for one life, an invocation for another. Harlan heard it in the ragged sigh of Laurel's final breath.

One sweet word: "Grace."

2

MAMA

*L*ike Laurel, Ada Shields had always wanted a daughter. She'd had high hopes for Grady, her fifth boy, counting two who were stillborn. The day Grady arrived, pale and hairless, like a fist with eyes, Ada tasted disappointment bitter as bile. She'd been fighting the blues ever since.

But losing Laurel, her dearest friend, had wrapped her in a gloom that she feared she might never escape. Some things in life seemed almost too much to bear. Why should a fine woman like Laurel be taken so soon, leaving a good man like Harlan to raise four children alone? And why—after giving birth to five boys and suffering the agony of losing two—had she herself been denied the daughter she longed for? Where was the justice in that? Ada knew she shouldn't question, but she couldn't help it. Why couldn't she have just one girl? She promised herself that someday, when she got to Heaven, the Good Lord was going to have some explaining to do.

It shamed Ada to admit it, but she was glad—happy beyond all singing—when Harlan asked if she could find it in her heart to take his child to her breast. She didn't ask John. Grady would be weaned soon. She had plenty of milk. The Lord taketh, Ada told herself, but He giveth, too.

For five days after Laurel's death, Ada stayed on the Lacy farm to nurse Cora and help out as best she could. Grady stayed, too, pulling at his mother's skirt and trying to climb in her lap when she sat in the rocker to feed Cora. At night, Ada and Grady slept in a back room, sharing a bed with five-year-old Horace, with Cora in a cradle on the floor beside them.

Two days after Laurel was laid to rest, John Shields grew weary of tending his boys while trying to run a farm. So he hitched up the wagon, loaded the boys into the back, and rode over to the Lacy farm to collect Ada and Grady. When Harlan saw John's wagon, he came hurrying up from the barn to meet him at the porch.

"John!" he called, reaching out to shake his hand. "I'm glad you're here. Come on in the house and help me eat some of this ham that we've got left from Laurel's service. Folks brought enough food to feed Gideon's army!"

John took off his hat, scuffed his boots on the steps, and followed Harlan inside. Ada was in the kitchen trying to decide what to do with the leftovers. Grady sat on the floor by the stove, taking considerable delight in rocking Cora's cradle. Edward was seated at the table shoveling green beans and ham hocks into his three-year-old brother's mouth. Buster was old enough to feed himself, but would rather starve than try. Horace was busy catching bugs out in the yard.

"Ada," Harlan announced, "look who's here!"

Ada turned and locked eyes with her husband.

"Sit down, John," Harlan said quickly, pulling two chairs out from the table. "Ada, would you fix John a plate? I've got something I need to say to you both."

Ada took a plate from the cupboard, heaped it with ham, collard greens, and potatoes, with a generous side of cobbler, and set it on the table in front of John. Then she stood behind him, letting her hands rest lightly on his shoulders, while the two men conversed in the farmer's tongue of weather and crops and hope.

After John scraped the last bit of cobbler from his plate, Harlan pushed back his chair and pressed his palms together, as he did when he was about to preach.

"John," he said, "I want you to know how much I appreciate all you and Ada have done for me and my family. I never meant to take Ada from you and your boys. My word, how long has it been? Four days? No, five! I had no right to ask it of you. But I have to tell you, I don't know what we'd have done without her."

John looked at Ada. She stood by the door with Laurel's shawl covering her bosom, nursing Laurel's motherless child. In the silence of the room, Cora sounded like a newborn pig.

Wiping his eyes with the back of his hand, John rose to leave.

"I'm glad we could help you, Harlan," he said. "It was our blessing more than yours. I'm mighty sorry for your loss."

The two men shook hands, then John picked up Grady and turned to his wife.

"We'll be in the wagon, darlin', when you're ready to go."

Ada took her time. She sat at the table with her back to Harlan, nursing Cora, feeling the tingling in her breasts as the milk let down and began to flow. When the child finally fell limp with contentment, Ada placed her in the cradle and covered her with the shawl. Then she rose, buttoned her dress, smoothed her hair, and turned to face Harlan.

"Hear me out," she said. He looked up at her, blinking.

"Harlan, this baby is going to need feeding day and night, around the clock. How exactly are you going to manage that?"

She waited. Harlan studied his hands, pondering Ada's question, the same question he'd been asking himself for the past five days.

"Let me take her home with me, Harlan, and keep her at our place—just until she's weaned. You and the boys can visit anytime."

Edward stopped feeding his brother. Buster waited with his mouth wide open.

"Don't do it, Daddy," Edward said. "Don't let Miz Shields take Cora. She's our baby. She belongs with us. I can look after her. Mama wouldn't want you to send her away."

Harlan laid a hand on Edward's neck, then combed the boy's hair with his thick fingers. Finally, he turned to Ada and gave a quick nod.

"All right," he said hoarsely. "Just 'til she's weaned."

Ten-month-old Grady, scrawny as a runt, had been sleeping through the night for almost two months when Baby Cora showed up in his life. He woke one night in his makeshift crib (that his daddy had built for Ada's first pregnancy with scrap lumber salvaged from an old outhouse) to see Cora fussing like a hen and trying to find her fist. Grady didn't know what to make of her.

Ada heard the wailing and ran to the crib to find Cora red-faced and furious, with her fist planted under her chin. Grady lay beside her patting Cora's head. He watched as Ada picked Cora up, settled into a rocking chair and nursed her back to sleep. When Ada slipped Cora back into the crib, Grady lifted his arms to his mother. Ada shook her head. Grady knew only three words: baby, mama, and milk. He lifted his arms higher and said all three at once.

"Ba-bee-ma-ma-milk?" Ada rolled her eyes. But she picked Grady up, nursed him back to sleep and tucked him in beside Cora.

Then, for a while, she stood barefoot by the crib, drinking in the sight of two sleeping babies, curled up as one, bathed in silver moonlight. She would probably never stop questioning God and his wisdom. But there were moments, such as this, that swelled her heart to near bursting and made her think that maybe she ought to just wait and trust God for the answers.

The next night, Ada heard Cora begin to bawl. Then suddenly the child grew quiet. Ada crept to the crib and found Grady grinning with his thumb stuck in Cora's mouth. Ada couldn't resist waking John to tell him about it.

"Isn't that the sweetest thing?" she said. "Grady absolutely adores her!"

John grunted, thinking, "Or he wanted to shut her up and get some sleep."

That fall, Laurel's death lay heavy on the valley like a cloud of smoke, refusing to lift. Harlan saw it every day, every place he looked. It was on the faces of his boys as they sat at the table trying to swallow their father's cornbread while pretending not to notice their mother's empty chair. It was in the silent nods of strangers and the warm embraces of friends; in the kindnesses of neighbors who left food at his door; and in the all-seeing eyes of his beloved congregation as he stood before them each Sunday struggling to preach the mercies of a just and loving God.

Most of all, it was in the mirror, in the awful reminder that he was alive, while Laurel, the love his life, was not. For the first time in his memory, he could not bear the sight of his own face. He found it nearly impossible to shave. Day after day, he could think of only one reason to get out of bed: everyone, especially his children, seemed to expect it of him. The first Sunday after Laurel was laid to rest, Edward woke him at dawn.

"Get up, Daddy. Go shave. We've got to get ready for church. You need to preach today."

He could feel his boys' eyes on the back of his neck, studying his every step in this dance of despair with the same wide-eyed trust they had always shown when he taught them how to plow or hunt or fish or find obscure verses in the Bible. He was their father. They were counting on him to show them the way. He had no choice but to find it.

He also had his faith, what was left of it. It had drained from his soul, gushing out of him with every drop of blood that poured from Laurel's body. What remained was not a lot. Yet it was finer somehow, surer than before. The irony astounded him. All his life he had longed for a deeper faith, one of feeling, more than theology—a faith like Laurel's, born in the heart and the soul, more than in the mind. Now that he no longer wanted it, there it was, undeniable.

There are gifts that come with loss. The greater the loss, the greater the gift. Harlan's gift in losing Laurel would be the kind of faith he had always longed for. The faith of a broken heart, with no pretense, no illusions, no false hopes of deliverance or gain. Just a strange, abiding certainty that, come what may, God is God and He is good. Harlan finally understood what Laurel had often told him: "All is grace, all is gift, even faith itself."

Grace would deepen not only Harlan's faith, but his preaching. He was an educated man, an eloquent speaker with a resonant voice that could recite the poetry of the Old Testament as it was meant to be heard, or boom like thunder to rouse a work-weary congregation. But the profound grief of losing Laurel brought to his sermons, and to his soul, a depth of honesty and humility and a kind of genuine humanity that had not always been evident in his words. It tore him from his pedestal and brought him to his knees. To his congregation, he was no longer simply their preacher. He was one of them. And they welcomed him with open arms.

But Harlan's greatest comfort in the wake of his wife's death was the fiery-haired baby that would light up like a sunrise at the sound of her daddy's voice. A lesser man might've blamed the child for taking Laurel from him. But even in his darkest moments, Harlan knew it was wrong to blame a child for anything, in the same way that it is wrong to blame a snake for being a snake, or to blame God for being God. What truly ended Laurel's life? Harlan would never be sure.

Once, when they were first married, he'd asked Laurel if she ever questioned why her own mother had to die so young. He still marveled at her answer.

"Some things can't be explained," she had said. "It's like picking up a hot skillet bare-handed. You can't make sense of the pain. You just have to choose. Hold on to it, or let it go. One choice makes you better. The other makes you burn."

Harlan was on fire, consumed by a hunger to explain and forgive Laurel's death. He prayed for strength to let it go, and his prayer would be answered in time. Strength would come and it would help. But what helped him most was love. He fell head over heels for his baby daughter. And in that love, he realized one of life's sweetest mysteries: a child is powerful medicine, sufficient to bind any wound, heal any hurt, forge any strength necessary.

Once a day, or sometimes twice, Harlan would drive the wagon over to the Shields' place to see Cora. On Sundays, after preaching, he brought his boys along with him to visit their baby sister. He never came inside the house, even when it was raining. He didn't want to impose on the Shields' kindness or intrude into their lives any more than he felt he had already. He'd take a seat on the porch and wait for Ada to bring Cora out, bundled up in Laurel's shawl.

"There's my pretty girl," he'd say, taking her in his arms, "and don't you look just like your mama?" Then he'd tuck the child's head beneath his chin, rock her to and fro, and sing, "O they tell me that He smiles on His children there, and His smile drives their sorrows all away . . ."

He did this instinctively, the way a dog licks its wounds to ease pain.

Ada would stand in the doorway watching. At the sound of Harlan's voice, Cora would grow still, molding her body to her father's barrel chest, lacing her tiny fingers in the graying threads of his beard. At the end of the hymn, Harlan would fall silent and sit for a spell studying his daughter's face as if it held within it the sun and moon and stars. Finally, he'd kiss her forehead and hand her back to Ada.

"You're a good woman, Ada Shields. I'll be forever in your debt."

Then he'd climb back in the wagon and snap the reins to spur the mule. Ada would wait until he rounded the bend before baring her breast to Cora. As her milk trickled out the corner of Cora's mouth, Ada would watch the wagon's dust cloud settle in the distance and say, "Harlan Lacy, I will be forever in your debt, too."

At two months, Cora began to smile, lighting up at the sound of her father's voice and quivering like the leaves on a poplar. Harlan could hardly bear to leave her. At six months, she began sleeping through the night without waking to nurse. At eight months, she could wrestle a leg of Ada's fried chicken out of Grady's hands and gum the meat cleanly off the bone.

One day, while sitting in her father's lap, Cora reached out with her chubby arms for Ada and spoke her first word: "Mama."

The next day, when Harlan came to visit, he squared his shoulders, as if about to preach, and announced, "Ada, I believe it's time for Cora to come home."

"Home?" Ada looked stricken. "You mean to your place? Are you sure, Harlan? It's so soon! Grady . . . he will miss her something fierce!"

Grady sat on the floor sharing a blanket with Cora, who lay belly up, waving her appendages like a June bug on its back. The boy could walk if he wanted, but seemed entirely content to sit, hanging onto Cora's toes. At the mention of his name, he looked up at his mother and grinned. Ada didn't smile back.

Harlan was surprised. He had expected Ada to be glad to be relieved of the trouble of caring for a baby, even one as winsome as Cora. Instead, she seemed grieved. It always amazed him to see the depth of a woman's heart—women like Laurel and Ada—how quick they always were to shoulder a neighbor's burden, especially when the burden was a child.

Harlan had thought long and hard about it. He would move Heaven and Earth to care for Cora Grace and her brothers. But he could not imagine doing it alone. He needed Ada's help. Money wasn't a problem. His salary from the church depended on donations from a small congregation of generous-hearted mountain folks, most of whom lived meagerly off the land. It wasn't much. But his parents had left him a large tract of timberland and a lumbering operation that provided a good and steady income. If need be, he could sell off some of the land. Whatever it might cost, Ada's help would be both a godsend and a bargain.

Harlan cleared his throat. "Ada, I know you've got your hands full with your family, but if you could come over once a week or so to look in on Cora, maybe do a little cooking, I'd pay you what it's worth. If it's all right with John, of course."

Ada knelt down and pulled Cora's foot out of Grady's mouth, wiping the toes dry with the corner of her apron.

"Apples," she said finally.

"Beg your pardon?"

"I won't take your money, Harlan. You can pay me in apples from your orchard. John would let me join the circus if he thought I'd bake him a cobbler."

"John's a lucky man, Ada."

"And don't try to take her until she's weaned. Another month or so, at least."

Harlan knew better than to waste time arguing with a woman who had made up her mind. And so the deal was struck. Two months later, when she was finally weaned, Cora Grace would go home to her family. In years to come, Ada would show up at the Lacy farm twice a week to do the wash and cook a meal and make the Lacy boys take a bath.

Mostly, she spent time with Cora, brushing her hair, teaching her rhymes or letting her help pick beans in the garden. Grady always came, too. If Ada tried to leave him with John, he'd run after her crying. Soon he was going on his own, trotting a mile through the woods every day, longing to be near Cora. It was a longing that, try as he might, Grady would never outgrow.

3

The Right Hand of God

The hemlock on the hill stood forty feet tall, a silent green sentry keeping watch over the Lacy farm. When Cora was little, she'd hide beneath its canopy, covering her mouth to hold her snickers, while her brothers ran about, shouting her name, pretending not to know she was there.

As she grew older, she learned to climb the tree's branches, counting its limbs, one by one, to mark her distance until the tree would rustle and sway in the wind, bidding her to stop. That's far enough today, child, tomorrow you'll go higher.

Then she'd perch for a while to sing hymns with the birds, straddling a limb and pressing her back to the trunk, a scabby-kneed princess on a scratchy throne surveying her kingdom below: the farmhouse, the barn, the pasture, the creek, the Shields' place across the hollow. The church where her daddy preached on Sundays. The cemetery where her mother lay buried. A dog she loved sleeping under the porch. Rolling mountains. Sky above. Earth below. Home.

Some, more than others, feel a kinship to the Earth—to rivers and oceans and mountains and plains—that is as real and as bind-ing as anything they will ever feel for flesh and blood. Cora, like the mother she never knew, was born a daughter of those mountains, a child of that land. Just to be there, for her, was to never feel alone.

Twice a week, when Ada came to cook and clean with Grady in tow, and on other days, when the boy showed up at the farm alone, Cora would grab his hand and pull him up the hill to try to make him climb the hemlock. Grady would swear he wasn't scared, he didn't fear anything except the Good Lord and snakes. He just preferred to keep his feet on the ground.

"Too bad," Cora would say. "Here, I'll give you a leg up."

In the end, he always climbed it, looking back over his shoulder to be sure Cora was behind him. Ada would watch them from the porch, shaking her head. "If Cora told that boy to jump off Mount Pisgah, I swear he'd be gone for good."

They were eight years old, walking home from school on an early spring day when the Barnette brothers caught up with them. Leroy Barnette was almost ten, but he was big for his age, dumber than a doorknob, and thought for some reason he could make up for it by being mean. His brother, Harold, was barely nine, but did whatever Leroy said.

At the start of that school year, Leroy had homed in on Grady the way a hawk trains its eye on a quail chick. Grady was slow, everybody knew it. But Leroy loved to broadcast it, as if calling attention to Grady's shortcomings could somehow distract from his own.

Cora would not tolerate the slightest mistreatment of the timid boy who hung on her heels like a shadow. More than once, much to her brothers' amusement, she had stood up to Leroy, like David in a cotton dress staring up at Goliath, and caused him to back off on teasing Grady.

Leroy hated being cowed by an eight-year-old girl, but he knew better than to incur the wrath of her brothers. So he waited and watched for a chance to catch Cora and her shadow alone. Most days, Cora and Grady walked home with her brothers. But on this day, Leroy heard Cora begging Edward to let her stay late to help their teacher, Miss Harrison, dust the chalk off the erasers. Leroy knew, if Cora stayed late, Grady would stay late, too. So he grabbed Harold by the strap of his overalls and pulled him aside to make a plan.

"Leroy?" Harold was hunkered down next to Leroy on the side of a winding gravel road in a patch of reddish colored shrubs. "This ain't poison oak, is it?"

"Hush up, Harold, here they come!"

In the distance, two small heads came bobbing up the hill, one mousy brown, the other fiery red. Both were covered in chalk dust. They were singing "Jesus Loves Me." Grady thought it sounded good, but he always thought that when he sang with Cora.

The first rock hit Grady square between the eyes. He turned to look at Cora and saw her jaw drop in disbelief as a trickle of blood rolled down his nose and dripped on the ground. The second rock hit him hard in the chest, and Grady fell to his knees, gasping for air.

Cora screamed, and the Barnette boys came roaring up out of the poison oak patch and began beating on Grady with their fists. Cora jumped on Leroy's back, yanking on his greasy hair. He whirled around, trying his best to shake her loose, but she held on hard. Finally he flung her off into a ditch, knocking the wind from her lungs and cutting a gash in her knee. When she didn't get up, he turned his attention back to Grady.

Cora lay in the ditch, trying to breathe, listening to the thumps of the Barnette brothers' fists on Grady's body. She heard Grady whimpering like a fox caught in a steel trap. She could taste blood on her tongue. When her lungs finally filled with a great whoosh of air, she sat up just in time to see a sight she would never forget: Jubal Avery was running hard up the road, coming to their rescue like the right hand of God.

Barely twelve years old, Jubal was just a boy, but he was strong and fierce-hearted like his daddy. Walter Avery had been sheriff for as long as most folks could remember. He'd taught Jubal how to fight—never start it, never walk away—and to choose his battles carefully. As Jubal saw it, there wasn't much choice in this fight.

He grabbed the Barnette brothers, one in each hand, by the straps of their overalls, pulled them off Grady and drew them up close to his face.

"Leave him be," he said. He flung them headfirst back into the poison oak patch. They scrambled to their feet, stumbling and falling, then ran off down the road.

Jubal called after them, "Hey, Leroy? If you ever lay a hand on Cora Lacy again, you won't need to worry about me. Edward Lacy will kill you!"

When Cora tried to stand, her knee stabbed with pain and blood ran down her shin. She hobbled over to Grady and began wiping his face with the hem of her skirt. Grady stopped whimpering and sat up, pushing Cora's hands away.

"I'm fine, Cora, leave me alone!" One of his eyes was swollen shut. With the other eye, he squinted at Jubal. "'Preciate the help, Jubal, but 't'weren't needed."

Jubal nodded. "I know, Grady. You had the best of them. I just finished it up."

Grady insisted he could walk, but Cora was limping badly, so Jubal hoisted her on his back to carry her home. She wrapped her legs around his waist, buried her face in his hair, and tried to put a name to the sweet smell of his neck. Oh, that was it. Salvation.

"Jubal?" Grady's pie-shaped face was a pitiful mess of blood and sweat and snot and tears. "Maybe we ought to go after them boys and give 'em a real ass-whuppin'."

"Grady Shields!" Cora laughed. "Watch your tongue!"

Jubal grinned. "Don't worry, Grady. The poison oak will take care of that."

That was the first time Jubal came to Cora's rescue. It would not be the last.

At school on Monday, Leroy and Harold looked as if they'd been doused with kerosene and set on fire. They claimed they were trying to catch a possum when they tripped and fell in a patch of poison oak. But they were known for lying, even when the truth would make more sense, so nobody believed them.

Cora made Grady swear not to tell a soul, especially her brothers, how she skinned her knee.

"If you do," she said, "Edward'll kill Leroy and go to jail and I'll never speak to you again."

Meanwhile, she spread the word about the attack on Grady and how, with just a little help from Jubal Avery, Grady had made quick work of the Barnette brothers. Grady pulled himself up tall and wore his black eye like a badge of honor.

Jubal, when asked to comment, would say only that he had never seen anything quite like the way Grady Shields had stood his ground.

The Barnette brothers were no wiser for the experience. They would keep their distance from Cora and Grady, but their bullying ways weren't quite done.

People knew—as they always know, in small, gossip-hungry communities, the most closely guarded of secrets—that Leroy and Harold had learned how to be mean from their daddy. He would often beat them with a stick for any reason, or no reason at all. That didn't excuse their behavior. But it helped somewhat to explain it. Harold would never overcome it. But in years to come, Leroy would realize—thanks to the guidance of his mother's brother, a man who went to prison for his own misdeeds and came out the better for it—that regardless of how we are raised, we all get to choose how we will live our one sweet life. For Leroy, that choice would make all the difference.

4

Hell Hath No Fury

1912

$\mathcal{D}$espite her best efforts to be a mother to Cora, Ada often wondered if Cora missed the mother she'd never known. Cora had been a happy child with a sunny and agreeable disposition. But as she eased her way from childhood and began, at fourteen, to bloom into a striking young woman, her nature turned a bit more serious. Lately, Ada had noticed, more than once, a faraway look in Cora's green eyes.

"What's troubling you, child?" Ada asked one day when she saw Cora staring at nothing. Cora laughed and waved off the question.

"I'm not troubled, Addie, just daydreaming."

"From the look on your face, I'd say it's a nightmare. Tell me about it?"

"Nothing to tell," Cora said brightly. "If I needed to talk, you know I'd pick you to listen."

"Promise me you will do that."

"I will," Cora said. "I promise."

Cora didn't want Ada to worry. She knew Ada would worry anyhow, because worry is what mothers do. But if she told Ada what was on her heart, Ada might insist that she tell Harlan, too. Cora loved her father, and she could talk to him about most things. But she couldn't bear the thought of embarrassing him, or worse, making him part of something that people would whisper about at church.

The church had always been her second family. For the first few years of her life, while her father preached his sermons, she was passed from lap to lap around the congregation, shared like a box of candy by good people who adored and delighted in her. Even now, in her teen years, she never felt anything less than loved by God and all His people.

The one exception was the Reverend Winslow C. Bradley.

As Harlan slowly healed from the devastation of losing Laurel, his preaching took on a new honesty and clarity and depth. His sermons spoke the truth, holding nothing back. Thirsty souls were drawn to that truth, like weary travelers to a well. As his reputation as a preacher spread throughout the mountains, and his congregation began to grow, he was often visited by other men of the cloth who came not just to hear him preach, but in the hope of being invited to "say a few words" from the pulpit. The visits occasionally lasted more than a week, during which the visiting minister would be a guest in the Lacy home, and Ada would spend three days, instead of her usual two each week, helping Cora—who at fourteen, was becoming a fine cook and fair housekeeper—with the cooking and the wash.

Most of those guests were unassuming, gracious men who seemed genuinely grateful for the hospitality they were shown, and in particular, for Ada's fried chicken. Rev. Bradley had visited on several occasions, staying a bit longer each time. It was not his fault that he did not like chicken. Ada had never heard of such nonsense, but she might have forgiven him for it, if only he had not been so rude.

"What do you mean he doesn't eat chicken?" she said. She was taking off her coat in the Lacy kitchen, breathless from her rush to get there in time to help Cora prepare the noon meal.

Cora stood at the sink peeling potatoes. A stray lock of hair fell across her eyes and she curled her lower lip and blew the lock back with a puff of air.

"That's what he told me last night after supper," she said. "Actually, what he said was, 'Tell your cook I do not eat chicken.'"

Ada went rooster-wattle red in the face. "He called me your cook?"

Cora laughed. "When he said that, Daddy looked at him like he'd taken the Lord's name in vain. Said, 'Sir, I beg your pardon. Miz Shields is not our cook. She is our friend who cares for us out of the goodness of her heart. If not for her kindness, my children and I would perish.'"

Ada hooted. "Your daddy is a smart man. What did the old fool say to that?"

Cora set the pot of potatoes on the wood stove and wiped her hands on her apron.

"He didn't say a word. He just waited until Daddy went down to the barn, then he handed me a big pile of his wash and said to tell you he likes extra starch in his shirts."

Ada squinted so hard her eyes disappeared in their sockets. When they grew wide again, she laughed. "Well, we'll just have to be sure Rev. Bradley gets exactly what he asked for."

That Sunday at church, Harlan announced that Rev. Bradley had asked to share a message the Lord had laid on his heart about the Biblical call for tithing. Everybody knew what it meant. Some put a tenth of their income in the offering plate every week. But most only wished they could. A tenth of not enough is not much. One thing they all agreed on—tithers and non-tithers alike—was they didn't appreciate an outsider making them feel less Christian because they didn't have more money to give to the church. A murmur rumbled across the room like a growl from a hungry gut, and in the back rows, a few folks got up and left.

An hour later, after Bradley gave the final amen, Ada elbowed her way through the crowd to shake his hand and get a closer look at his neck. She had taken great delight in watching him as he preached, tugging repeatedly on his collar and scratching himself as if he had fleas.

"Oh my!" she said, peering closely at his throat. "Is that a rash? I hope I didn't overdo the starch in your shirt! You poor man! I'll stir up a batch of liniment . . ."

That's when she first noticed it, the gleam in his eye. He wasn't looking at Ada, wasn't hearing what she said. Something had caught his interest. Ada turned to see what he seemed so taken by, and felt her breath catch in her throat.

He was staring at Cora. Suddenly, Ada knew what Cora had refused to tell her. She couldn't believe she hadn't seen it before. Had Harlan been aware of it? Surely not. He would never allow anyone to hurt Cora. No matter. Ada would deal with it on her own.

Most Sundays after church, Ada went home to tend to her family and left the Lacys to fend for themselves. Not today. She told John to go on home with their boys and serve up the pot of pinto beans that she had left simmering on the back of the wood stove.

"Grady can bake you a pone of cornbread," she said, "but send him over to the Lacy place before dark to fetch me. I need to help Cora fry a chicken for Rev. Bradley."

John was hoping for some fried chicken himself, but knew better than to argue.

"Come on, boys," he said, "your mama's up to something. Let's get out of her way."

Harlan was surprised at Ada's offer to cook for them on a Sunday, but he welcomed her help. When he saw the platter of fried chicken that she dropped with a loud thud on the table, he smiled to himself and passed the platter to Rev. Bradley. After the meal, while the men went out on the porch to smoke and joke and solve the problems of the world, Ada and Cora stayed inside to clean up the mess.

As always, when they worked together, they talked and laughed and sang to make the time flow like summer wind through a cornfield.

When the dishes were done, Ada dried her hands on her apron and placed them on Cora's shoulders to look her squarely in the eyes.

"Tell me the truth," she said. "Has that man touched you?"

Cora turned her face and looked away.

Ada cupped Cora's chin and pulled her back to look in her eyes. "Has he hurt you, child?"

Cora shook her head. "No, Addie, he hasn't hurt me. He just . . . he's always trying to hug on me when nobody's around. And the way he looks at me . . . it just feels so . . . wrong!"

Cora shuddered like a dog shaking off muddy water.

"That old goat!" Ada said, punching the air with her fist. "I ought to have seen it sooner!"

Cora grabbed Ada's arms. "Addie, you can't tell Daddy or the boys! Promise me you won't! You know what Edward would do! I couldn't bear it!"

She began to cry and Ada pulled her close, rocking her to and fro.

"Hush, baby. I won't tell a soul. Leave it to me. I'll take care of it."

Moments later, Ada stepped out on the porch, patting her hair. Harlan and Rev. Bradley were deep in conversation, sitting in rocking chairs with their feet propped on the porch rail.

"Pardon me for interrupting," Ada said smiling. "Rev. Bradley, I was so taken by your sermon today that I'm hoping you'll enlighten me a little further." She held out her hand. "Would you be kind enough to permit me to show you the pond?"

Bradley beamed, rose to his feet, and offered Ada his arm.

Harlan sat on the porch, too stunned to speak, watching them stroll arm in arm across the yard toward the path that led through the woods to the pond. At the edge of the clearing, they stopped and turned to face each other. Harlan saw the Rev. Bradley stiffen like a fence post.

Ada stood with her hands clutched in fists at her side, speaking quickly with obvious passion, but too softly to be overheard. After a bit, Rev. Bradley raised his hands as if in surrender, then slumped his shoulders and hung his head. When they finally turned to walk back to the house, Ada did not take his arm.

That evening, when Grady came to take Ada home, Harlan stopped her on the porch steps. "I'm curious about your talk with Rev. Bradley," he said. "Is there something I should know?"

Ada glanced over her shoulder to see if Cora was nearby. Then she turned and studied Harlan's face. "All right," she said finally. "I'll tell you on one condition: you can never breathe a word of it to your daughter or her brothers or anyone in our church. You can discuss it with Rev. Bradley, and with pastors of other churches that he might visit. Actually, I hope you will do that. But keep Cora and her name out of it. I promised to spare her the humiliation of becoming the subject of idle gossip. I need your word that you will help me keep that promise."

Harlan's heart was pounding in dread of what Ada was about to say. But he knew he needed to hear it. He gave her his word. So she told him everything that Cora had told her. When she finished, Harlan closed his eyes and clinched his fists. From the kitchen came the sound of Cora singing. Harlan cleared his throat and looked at Ada.

"What did Bradley say when you confronted him?"

"He tried to deny it," Cora said, "but I was not about to let him do that. Finally, he just gave up and said, fine, he'd be gone by sunrise and won't come back."

Harlan nodded and wiped his eyes.

"Thank you, Ada," he said, resting his hand on her shoulder. "You saw what I ought to have seen, and you did what I wish I'd done. Laurel would've done it, if she were here. I suspect, in some way, that she did it through you. Cora is blessed to have you in her life. We all are."

The following Sunday, Harlan announced that Rev. Bradley had been called away on a personal matter and would not soon be returning. Several members of the congregation started to clap, until they remembered that they were in church.

Opening his Bible, Harlan began, "Our sermon today is from

the Gospel of Matthew, chapter eighteen. The disciples asked Jesus, 'Who is the greatest in the Kingdom of Heaven?' To answer them, our Lord called a child out of the crowd, set the child in their midst, and said, 'Unless you become like little children, you will not enter the Kingdom of Heaven.'"

In a row near the front, Harlan saw a young boy look up at his father and grin.

"Yes!" Harlan said, beaming at the boy. "Jesus wants us to be more like you!"

Laughter rippled around the room, and Harlan continued.

"Then Jesus issued a warning. He said anyone who harms a child would be better off to have a stone tied about his neck and be drowned in the depths of the sea."

A hush fell over the room and Harlan waited to let the words settle in. Then, for the next forty minutes, he poured out his heart. He recalled the agony of losing Laurel fourteen years ago. He described the comfort and joy that his children had brought to him. He said that God had sent an angel to be a mother to Cora and her brothers, and a helping hand for him, and that the angel's name was Ada Shields. Folks who knew Ada nodded in agreement, but smiled at the notion of her wearing a halo. Ada studied her hands in her lap.

To the children in the room, Harlan said, "If you are worried or afraid, what should you do?" He waited, but no hands were raised. "Well, I'll tell you," he said. "You should talk to God about it. Tell Him everything. He already knows it, of course. He just wants to hear it from you. But be sure to tell your parents about it, too. They're not as smart as God is. They want you to think they know everything, but they don't. They need you to tell them what's on your heart."

To the adults, he said, "Friends, we need to listen to our children, to all they say, and most especially to what they don't say. We need to be tender-hearted in all the ways that we treat them, and forever vigilant to guide and protect and keep them safe from all harm."

In the second row, Cora raised an eyebrow and turned to look at Ada sitting beside her. Ada stared hard at Harlan.

"We all have children," Harlan said, closing the Bible, "whether they come to us by birth or as my children came to Ada, by heart. We will be judged by how we treat them. They are gifts from God. And they are worth everything . . . the world and then some."

As always, to end the service, Harlan raised his hands to Heaven and gave the altar call, inviting anyone who felt in need of forgiveness or prayer to come forward and be blessed. Three souls answered the call: twelve-year-old Elizabeth Daley committed her young life to Jesus and asked to be baptized; Bill Mason gave thanks for the birth of his son, Robert, and asked for prayers for his wife, Lois, who was recovering slowly from a difficult birth; and to everyone's surprise, Lester Pierce broke down sobbing, begging the Lord's forgiveness for Lester's many cruelties, both to his wife and his dog.

Finally, they passed the offering plate and sixty-some voices sang as one, "We shall come rejoicing, bringing in the sheaves."

After the service, when head deacon John Shields counted the offering, he felt sure he was mistaken. He counted it again—every dollar, every nickel, every last red cent, plus a plug of tobacco that some fool had apparently dropped in the offering plate by accident and was now probably patting his pockets to find it. On the third count, John laughed and shook his head. He could hardly wait to see what Ada would say when he told her the news that today's offering—in the wake of Rev. Bradley's sudden departure—had far exceeded any in the church's history.

5

Edward, Jubal, and Frank

On summer breaks from high school, Edward worked for his father's lumbering operations, felling and hauling loads of timber to the mill to be processed into logs. It was hard work, and dangerous, but it paid pretty well, and Edward—like other young men who hired on with the crew—took pride in being a part of it.

Harlan had studied to be minister at Wake Forest College, and hoped Edward might follow in his footsteps. But Edward, like his father, was no follower. Harlan knew it and didn't argue.

The day after Edward finished high school, he signed on full-time with Lacy Logging. The men all knew he was the owner's son. But he had earned their respect in the summers he had worked with them. He never expected or received any special treatment. He worked hard, never missed a day, never complained. The foreman, George Bishop, often bragged to his wife, "If I had a few more like Edward, I could fire the rest."

Three years later, when George's wife finally decided he was too old to keep dodging falling timber, George surprised Harlan with his recommendation for a replacement.

"Are you sure?" Harlan said. "He's a mite young to head the crew."

"He's young," George said, "but he's good. Best I've seen. Edward's your man."

As the new foreman, Edward wasted no time expanding operations. He began hiring reliable young blood, including his brothers. Horace and Buster would work summers, as Edward had, through high school. While George had hired men mainly for their physical strength, Edward was more selective. Physical strength was a necessity, he said, but it wasn't enough. He wanted men of character, the kind that you could count on. No drunks. No liars. No hotheads.

"Daddy," he said, "good men don't come cheap. We need to raise pay. Not much, just a little. It will cost some, sure, but it will pay off in the long run."

Harlan studied on it for a minute. Finally, he nodded.

"George was right about you," he said. "You know what you're doing."

Edward laughed. "If I knew what I was doing, why did I hire Horace and Buster?"

Jubal Avery was a few years younger than Edward, but they had grown up together, hunting and fishing and becoming the kind of dependable young men that others turned to when hard decisions needed to be made. Jubal was an only child and had spent near as much time at the Lacy farm as he did at home with his parents. Cora had come to think of him as one of her big brothers, and he, in turn, loved having a "baby sister" to boss him around.

But something happened on Cora's sixteenth birthday. Surrounded by all the people she adored—her father and brothers, Ada and John, Grady and Jubal—Cora leaned down and blew out a candle on the apple cake Ada had baked for her. But before raising her head, she rolled her eyes up at Jubal and gave him a smile he would never forget.

With that one smile, God help him, Jubal realized he was in love. For two years—and for too many years afterward—he would try to deny it to himself, and especially to Edward, who began teasing him mercilessly about it. But in the spring of 1917, Jubal would make a fatal, or fated mistake.

After high school, Jubal had signed on to work for Edward's logging crew. His father, the local sheriff, hoped his son would one day replace him as sheriff. But that day was still years away. In the meantime, Jubal needed to work. And felling timber would be good experience for enforcing the law on mountain boys who didn't take kindly to being told what to do.

One Saturday, on his way home from the mountain, Jubal stopped in at the Long Branch Cafe for a cup of coffee and a plate of fried chicken. He was sitting at the counter, inhaling the chicken, when he heard a voice next to him say, "You look like a logger."

Jubal looked up, holding a chicken leg in midair, and saw a young man about his age, with steady brown eyes and sandy blond hair.

"I'm Frank McCallum," he said, shaking Jubal's hand, "and I'm looking for work."

They exchanged basic information, before moving on to talk at length about more interesting subjects, like fishing. On Monday, Jubal introduced Frank to Edward. Edward looked at Jubal, who gave a quick nod. Jubal's approval was all Edward needed. He hired Frank on the spot.

It took no time for Jubal and Frank to become friends. Neither were much for words, but they found enough to talk about. Fishing, mostly, and hunting. Soon, when they had time off from logging on the mountain, they'd end up casting a line together on the Davidson River, silently solving the problems of the world.

It was only natural for Jubal, who had rarely in his life missed a Sunday in church, to invite Frank to join him for a service. Growing up, Frank had never been taken to church. His experience was limited to a series of funerals for his father, then his mother, both when he was small, and then, as a teenager, for his grandmother, who had raised him. At his father's funeral, his mother held him and wept for her husband. At his mother's funeral, his grandmother held him and wept for her daughter. And at his grandmother's funeral, no

one held him or wept at all. Those were memories he would rather
not revisit. So he politely declined all of Jubal's invitations, insisting
he wasn't much of a churchgoer. But Jubal kept working on him. Finally Frank agreed to be Jubal's guest, not at a Sunday service, but
at the annual church picnic.

"You'll like it," Jubal promised. "The food's good, there's plenty
of it, and it's free."

Frank couldn't argue with that. Never in his life had he seen such
a spread. He was working on his third plate when he heard a sound,
a laugh that made him think of falling water. Years later, he would
tell his boys that it hooked his heart like a fishing barb snagging a
trout.

She was sitting at a picnic table with Grady Shields and Edward
Lacy and two of Edward's buddies, telling a story that had them
laughing, hanging on her words. Her auburn hair was tied back
with a blue satin ribbon the color of the flowers in her cotton summer dress. One hand fluttered like a bird about her face, fanning
back curls that fell onto her forehead. As she spoke, her green eyes
glittered like sunlight rippling on a pond. When she felt Frank's
gaze on her face, on her mouth, on the curve of her neck, she stopped
mid-sentence and slowly turned to stare back at him . . . until Grady
finally yanked on her sleeve.

Jubal thought Frank had swallowed a chicken bone.

"You all right, Frank?"

Frank didn't answer. When Jubal turned to see what Frank was
staring at, he felt his heart drop like a rock down a well. What in
God's name had he been he thinking, inviting Frank McCallum to
that picnic? He took a deep breath, held it, then let it out in a long
heavy sigh.

"Her name is Cora Lacy," he said, flatly. "She's the daughter of the
preacher, and the sister of the man who happens to be your boss. But
I doubt you'll let that stop you. Come on, I'll take you to meet her.
Watch what you say around Edward."

"Wait," Frank said, holding up a hand. "I'm not ready yet. Let's
go pitch some horseshoes."

They joined a match in progress with two men, both young fathers teaching their children—three boys, ages six to nine, and one girl, about five—the basic points of the game.

Jubal was good. Frank was better. They took turns throwing. Frank threw ringer after ringer, until Jubal raised his hands, laughing, and gave up. Then Frank started working with the little girl, showing her how to hold the horseshoe, how to size up the stake, how to wind up and let the shoe fly free. After several tries, when she finally, nearly, almost nailed a ringer, the child jumped up and down and hugged Frank's neck. And every soul at that picnic cheered. Including Cora, who had watched from the corner of her eye, every move Frank made.

When the game broke up, Frank grinned at Jubal. "I guess I'm ready now."

Jubal figured, what the hell, if he didn't introduce Frank to Cora, somebody else would.

"Miss Cora Lacy," he said, with a quick bow, "I might live to regret it, but allow me to present to you this no-good newcomer who claims his name is Frank McCallum and seems, in my opinion, a mite too eager to make your acquaintance."

Frank turned beet red. Everybody within hearing distance laughed, except Edward, who raised an eyebrow and gave Jubal a hard look. Cora held out her hand.

"Pleased to meet you, Mr. No-Good Newcomer," she said, smiling. "Will you join me on a walk by the river and take me away from all these no-good locals?"

Frank glanced at Jubal and whispered, "I owe you."

Jubal looked at the ground.

Cora took Frank's arm and led him away, and every eye at that picnic, the birds in the trees, the rabbits in the bushes, and the fish in the river, watched them go.

Late that night, alone in bed, Jubal lay in bed thinking. Some things couldn't be helped, no matter how much they hurt. They were just meant to be. Like losing his mother to pneumonia when he was nine, and seeing his dad miss her every day.

He recalled, at the picnic, watching Cora and Frank, how their eyes met and lingered and locked on each other. It brought to mind one of his most treasured memories, seeing his parents look at each other that exact same way. Turning over in bed, alone as always, Jubal closed his eyes. Cora and Frank, he decided, were a "meant to be" thing. He was almost happy for them.

6

SUNDAY DINNER

SUMMER, 1917

If asked to explain his popularity as a preacher, Harlan would always say, "It's simple. I try to end my sermons by noon. Most folks, including me, like to get home for Sunday dinner, and I've learned it's best not to keep them waiting."

On Sundays, women would wake before dawn to prepare most of the noon meal, storing it in warming compartments on the back of the wood stove, or chilling it in an ice box. Then they'd make breakfast for their families and dress in their Sunday best to get to church on time.

In the years after Laurel died, Harlan made breakfast for his children every morning—ham and eggs and sometimes what he called "a poor excuse for biscuits." On Sundays, it was usually just oatmeal. They were often invited to Sunday dinner at the home of another family after church, or they ate leftovers that Ada, on her twice-weekly visits, made sure they had in good supply. But as Cora grew older, while her father and brothers shared the farm chores, she insisted on taking over the cooking. Meals were often interesting. But they ate what she put on the table and seldom dared to complain.

On the first Sunday after the church picnic, Cora woke earlier than usual to start cooking. Harlan heard her banging pots in the kitchen, but thought nothing of it. After church, instead of visiting with folks on the steps, she stood waiting, tapping her toe by Harlan's pride and joy, a brand new Model-T. He had justified the purchase by saying that the time it would save on travel could be devoted to the work of his ministry, and that if the Good Lord had wanted him to keep riding in a wagon, he would have made it a lot more comfortable.

When they got home from church, instead of changing her dress, Cora went straight to the kitchen, threw on an apron, and started slicing the tomatoes she had picked the day before.

Harlan had always insisted that to honor the Lord's Day, they would limit Sunday chores to the basic necessities—food for themselves and their animals. Cows had to be milked, and eggs needed to be gathered. But anything that could wait until Monday, had to wait.

Edward and his brothers were usually happy to limit chores. But on the way home from church, Edward had spotted a fence that was down on the south end of the pasture. Fences couldn't wait. They had changed into work clothes and were heading for the pasture when Edward stopped to ask Cora, "How long before we eat?"

She kept slicing. "I'll ring the dinner bell when it's ready."

Harlan had just changed out of his best Sunday preaching suit when he heard a knock at the door. He thought Cora would answer it, but looked out a window and saw her in the garden gathering vegetables out back. He hitched up his pants and headed downstairs.

Opening the door, he was surprised to see the young horseshoe player who had spent so much time talking with Cora at the picnic.

"Rev. Lacy, I'm Frank McCallum. How are you, sir?"

Harlan looked down at the hand the young man offered, and finally shook it.

"I am, uh, fine, son. What can I do for you?"

"Well, sir, with your permission, I'm here to see Cora."

Harlan blinked. "My daughter? Is she expecting you?"

"Yes, sir, I believe she . . ."

Cora came rushing in from the garden, out of breath, holding a tomato.

"Daddy! Where are your manners! Ask Frank to come inside! He's staying for dinner!"

Tucking the tomato into her apron pocket, she took Frank's arm and led him into the parlor, motioning for Harlan to follow.

"Have a seat, Frank. I'll get the biscuits out of the oven," she said, rolling her eyes at Harlan, "while Daddy talks your ear off."

When she left them, Harlan cleared his throat. "All right, son. Tell me about yourself."

"Not much to tell, sir."

"Well, tell it anyhow."

Frank stared at a hummingbird that was hovering just outside the window, staring back at him as if waiting to see what he would say. Turning his hands palms up, Frank looked at Harlan.

"I'm from Haywood County, sir. Lost my daddy to a logging accident when I was four. My mama never got over it. She died in the mental hospital in Raleigh. I was eight. My grandma raised me. She took good care of me until she got feeble, then I took care of her. She died three, no, four years ago. I've been on my own since. She made me promise to finish high school, so I did. Then I hired on with a logging crew. I like logging. I heard about your operation, heard it's a good one, better than most. So I quit that job and came over to Brevard to ask around. Then I met Jubal Avery. He took me to meet Edward and Edward put me to work. That's about it."

As a preacher, Harlan knew all the right words and verses to comfort a grieving soul. But Frank's litany of loss seemed to deserve more than words and verses. Harlan had learned that sometimes the best we can do is to say nothing and let our presence speak for our heart.

He studied Frank's face. When their eyes met, he gave a quick nod. Frank nodded back.

In the kitchen, Cora stood by the door, listening.

"So, sir," Frank said. "Tell me about yourself. I'd be honored to hear it."

Cora covered her mouth to stifle a laugh. Then she went out on the back porch and rang the bell to signal her brothers to quit the barn and wash up for dinner.

When Harlan heard the bell, he rose to his feet and winked at Frank. "I believe it's time to go see what our Miss Cora has cooked up."

On the long family table in the kitchen, Cora had placed an old lace tablecloth that had been crocheted by her mother's mother, for whom Cora was named. It was used only for special occasions, but somehow Cora had a feeling this could be one of the most special occasions of her life.

She had carefully set the table with six places, instead of the usual five, using the fancy china handed down from her father's family. (She skipped the teacups because her brothers always complained the handles were too small for their fingers.) In the center of the table, she had placed her favorite keepsake—a small crystal vase that had belonged to her mother—filled with a mix of marigolds and zinnias and petunias from the garden she tended by the creek.

"What's the big occasion?" Edward said laughing, as he walked in and spotted the table. Then he saw Frank and stopped mid-laugh.

"We have a guest," Harlan said. "Frank, these are my boys—Edward, my eldest, Horace, and Buster. I'm sure you all know each other from logging together."

Frank reached across the table and shook hands with each of them.

"Well," Cora said, "glad we got that out of the way. Let's take our seats. Daddy, you're at the head of the table, of course. Frank, will you please take a seat at the other end?"

Edward always sat at the end, and started to say so, until Cora stopped him with a look.

"Horace and Buster," she said, "take your usual seats and try to show some manners. I'll sit next to Frank. And Edward? You can consider yourself blessed to sit between Daddy and me."

While the men sat as directed, Cora filled the table with platters of fried chicken, corn pudding, creamed spinach, sliced tomatoes and cucumbers, and biscuits with butter and molasses. She gave her father his usual glass of buttermilk, then handed Edward a pitcher of cold sweet tea and told him to pass it around. Taking her seat, she smiled in a way that brightened the room, first at Frank, then at her brothers, and finally, at her father.

"My darlin' girl," Harlan said beaming at the food, "once again, you have outdone yourself."

They joined hands and Harlan prayed, "Oh Lord, for this fine food and all thy many blessings, we give you praise and eternal thanks. In Christ's name, amen."

The talk turned quickly to logging and farming and weather. They ate until they couldn't eat any more. Then Cora served her specialty, peach cobbler, along with Ada's specialty, apple cake.

"Addie knew Frank was joining us for supper," she said, glancing at Harlan, "so she sent this cake over to us with Grady. I had told her we wouldn't need it, but being Addie, of course, she insisted."

"I'm glad somebody knew," Harlan said. The room fell silent. Then everyone laughed.

"Especially Ada," he added. "I could almost be tempted to renounce my religion for a slice of her apple cake. If I could serve it for communion, we'd have a full church every Sunday."

Frank was not Cora's first suitor. Harlan had often seen other young men come calling for his daughter. Cora would respond politely, but coolly, offering each hopeful a chance to sit with her on the porch, but never inviting them inside. Harlan would watch at a window, laughing and shaking his head as, one by one, the young men gave up and left, never to return.

Frank was different. Giving up was something he had never learned to do. That summer, at Cora's invitation, Frank became a regular at Sunday dinner. He'd hitch a ride on the main road from town, then walk a mile up the mountain on a gravel road to the Lacy farm, arriving just after the Lacys got home from church. He'd stay for dinner, but always left before supper. While there, he'd insist on making himself useful, helping Cora clear the table after the meal, and rolling up his sleeves to dry the dishes as she washed them. They worked effortlessly together, talking and laughing, letting their hands touch lightly in the course of the work.

In the parlor, pretending to nap, Harlan would watch them through the door to the kitchen. They looked, he thought, like they were dancing. He remembered dancing in that kitchen with Laurel, holding her close, moving in time to music that played only in their heads. He wanted Cora to have the kind of happiness he and Laurel had known. But he wasn't sure just yet if she could ever be that happy with Frank McCallum.

One Sunday, they were doing the dishes when Edward ran in and grabbed a shotgun from over the mantel. On his way out, he yelled two words: "Rabid dog!"

Frank dropped a towel and ran after him, with Cora and Harlan close behind. On the porch, Buster was hanging on to Harlan's beloved hound, Blue, who was baring his teeth and growling. Out in the yard stood a stray—a mange-covered mongrel that looked half dead, but was baring its teeth and growling back at Blue.

As Edward raised the shotgun, Frank laid a hand on his shoulder. "Wait."

"That dog's rabid," Edward said.

Frank shook his head. "He's not rabid. He's hurt."

Easing off the porch, Frank held out his hand, speaking softly to the stray.

"Hey, boy. It's all right. Let me look at you."

The dog kept growling, but Frank kept coming. When he knelt to rub the dog's head, it began to whine and lick his hand. Frank looked at the dog's front paw and called up to the porch.

"He's got a thorn. Looks infected. If you'll get me some pliers, I'll get it out."

Edward went inside to put away the shotgun and fetch the pliers from the basement. Meanwhile, Frank picked up the dog and carried it down to the creek to wash its paw.

Edward brought him the pliers, and Frank said to the dog, "This is gonna hurt, buddy, but it will make it better."

When he yanked out the thorn, the dog yelped, but licked Frank's face. Then Frank picked up the dog again, eased it down into the creek, and began washing its matted coat.

"If you've got some pine tar," he said, "I could treat some of this mange."

Edward trotted off to fetch it.

An hour later, Cora and Frank sat in the porch swing, talking and swinging. The stray lay at their feet, sleeping in the sun next to Blue.

"I'd take him with me," Frank said, leaning down to scratch the stray's head, "but they won't let me keep a dog at the boarding house."

"He can stay here," Cora said. "Blue's an old dog. We'll be needing another one soon."

"We probably ought to give him a name."

"That's easy," Cora said. "All our dogs are named Blue. We'll call him Blue Two. When Blue's gone, we'll drop the Two."

Frank looked at her and frowned. "That's a sorry name for a good dog."

"He'll get used to it," Cora said, laughing. "Just like I'm getting used to you."

7

ALREADY GONE

The following Sunday, after dinner, Edward surprised everyone, including himself, by insisting that he would do the dishes. Horace and Buster headed to the barn to do the milking. Frank offered to help, but Cora said no, she wanted to show him the pond. Harlan started to ask to go with them, but thought better of it. Instead, he sat on the porch with Blue and watched as they walked arm in arm into the woods, with Blue Two trotting along after them.

Leaning down to scratch Blue's ears, Harlan said, "I guess they'll manage without us."

It was late afternoon, hours before dark, but a pale crescent moon was wide awake, looking down on them from on high. The pond had always been Cora's favorite place on the farm. As a child, she was forbidden to go there without her brothers. The boys had dammed the creek to form a respectable swimming hole. Edward taught Cora how to swim there, and how to dive from the top of the waterfall where the creek fell into the deepest part of the pond. When they grew older, she helped her brothers build a small cabin by the water, and a two-seater outhouse a safe distance away.

When they reached the pond, Frank knelt at the edge and ran his fingers through the water. "It's crystal clear," he said.

"And full of fish," Cora said. "Edward takes pride in keeping it stocked."

She watched as Frank held his hand out just above the surface of the water, waiting. Then slowly he reached in, barehanded, and pulled out a trout.

Cora laughed. "I can't believe you did that! Edward would be so jealous!"

Frank grinned, dropped the trout back in the pond, and dried his hand on his britches. Together, they climbed the steps to the cabin's porch.

"I could live here," she said as they ducked inside the door.

Frank bounced on the floor, checking for sway. The place needed work, but it was sturdy. "Mosquitoes might eat you alive," he said.

She laughed. "It would be worth it to watch the moon climb over the mountain and come walking across that pond. It's quite a sight. I wish you could see it."

Frank turned to look in her eyes. Brushing a lock of hair from her forehead, he took her face in his hands and traced her features with his fingers—the curve of her brow, the cleft of her chin, the fullness of her lips.

"Someday," he said, "if you will have me, we'll swim in that pond at midnight and watch that moon rise together. I promise you that. But all I will see is you."

In that moment, Cora knew in her heart, where all the deepest truths are known, the answer to the question she had asked, day and night, in the months since they first met. The answer was simple: Yes. She and Frank McCallum belonged together.

A tear slid from her eye and Frank dried it with the back of his hand.

"I'm hoping that tear means yes."

"It does," she said, sniffling. "Absolutely."

They laughed so loud birds took wing and fish darted to the bottom of the pond. Frank lifted her hand and kissed the inside of her wrist. Then he led her back to her family.

When they reached the farmhouse, she grinned up at him. "I

can't wait to see the look on Edward's face when I tell him you caught a trout with your bare hand."

>>>

For three days, Harlan pondered what he should do. He had spotted it immediately in both Cora and Frank the evening they came back from the pond—the smiles on their faces, the light in their eyes, the way they could hardly stop looking at each other. He hoped it might fade after Frank left to walk back to town to the boarding house. But it only grew more evident.

Cora kept right on walking on air, humming happily to herself, day in and out, seemingly oblivious to the puzzled looks from her father and her brothers.

Harlan dreaded telling her what was on his heart. She would be furious with him. But he knew he would rather face his daughter's rage than remain silent and risk seeing her suffer.

On the fourth evening, at supper, midway through a pork chop, Harlan put down his fork and reached over to take Cora's hand.

"I like Frank," he said. "You know I do. I find much in him to admire. But I see how much you care for him, and it worries me. There are some things I need to say to you."

"Speak your piece, Daddy," Cora said, pulling her hand away from his.

Harlan took a long breath and let it out with a sigh. "Frank's a fine young man," he said, "no doubt about it. But he comes from hardscrabble dirt, and it's not easy to wash it off. Darlin' girl, you need to ask yourself: do you want to be with a man who is not your equal?"

A silence fell, and the Lacy boys studied their plates.

Cora buttered a biscuit, took a bite of it, and swallowed.

"Daddy?" she said, raising an eyebrow. "When did you start judging people by the kind of dirt they come from? I thought you taught us never to do that."

Harlan wiped his forehead with a napkin and cleared his throat.

"I'm not judging Frank, Cora. I am merely stating a fact that he is not your equal. He never sets foot in church. You know that. Are you prepared to spend your life with a godless man?"

Cora leaned on her elbows and locked eyes with Harlan.

"Does going to church make us godly, Daddy? Is that all it takes? Lester Pierce shows up every Sunday and you said yourself he's the meanest sumbitch in this county. He shot his own dog just to spite his wife. He'd have shot her, too, if he thought he could get by with it. Frank McCallum may come from hardscrabble dirt, but he is the mirror image of you. He's a good man, Daddy, and he will come to church when he's damn good and ready!"

Cora rarely used profanity. When she did, Harlan had learned it was best not to correct her.

The clock on the mantel in the parlor began striking the hour, six loud gongs that seemed to go on for days. On the last strike, Edward swallowed a mouthful of pork chop.

"Baby Sister?" he said. "If that fool tries to take you, we'll just shoot him. Won't we, boys?"

He winked at his brothers and they laughed.

Cora rolled her eyes. Harlan was not amused. He reached over and touched Cora's arm. "If you leave us, child," he said, "we will be . . ." His voice broke and he turned away.

Suddenly, Cora knew. It wasn't Frank that her father feared. It was simply the thought of losing the daughter that reminded him so much of the woman he had loved more than his own life. Cora took his face in her hands and turned it, the way she had done so often as a child, to demand his full attention.

When their eyes met, she smiled. "You'll be fine, Daddy. I'll make sure of it. You will never lose me. But as for Frank McCallum? My heart is already gone."

The following Sunday, for the first time in his twenty-one years, not counting funerals, Frank McCallum stood on the porch of an old country church, trying to muster the courage to step through the door. An early morning rain had sweetened the air, brightening colors and deepening the scent of dogwoods and azaleas and wild mountain laurel that bloomed in spring's profusion in the surrounding woods. In the distance, he watched a red-tail hawk dip and glide on the wind.

One step, he thought. Sometimes it all comes down to that. Forward or back, it's a choice, and once it's done, there's no undoing it. In years to come, Frank would look back on this day and smile to see the hand of God. But he wasn't smiling now.

Just as he turned to run like hell, the congregation began to sing, "Blessed assurance, Jesus is mine . . ." And a fine harmony of some sixty voices—Harlan's baritone, Edward's bass, Ada's alto, Grady's tenor—came swirling out the door to settle on his head like pats on the rump of a skittish horse.

Frank stopped to listen and was surprised to hear one voice clearly above all the rest. It was her voice. The woman he loved. That was all it took. Squaring his shoulders, he removed his hat, stepped through the door, and walked down the aisle to take a seat beside the preacher's daughter, right there in front of her daddy, her brothers, the congregation, and God and all His angels.

"Blessed Assurance" had been Laurel's favorite hymn. In the years since her death, Harlan had refused to have it sung in church. He could not bear to hear it. He had no idea why he chose it that morning for the opening hymn. He had watched Cora take a seat next to Ada in the second row, as always. He saw her glance at the door at the back of the room, and then place her Bible beside her on the bench, as if to save a seat for someone.

She had smiled up at him, looking so much like her mother. Next thing Harlan knew, he was leading the congregation in "Blessed Assurance." And then, there came Frank McCallum, strutting down the aisle to claim a seat beside Cora.

When the hymn ended, a hush fell over the room like a dusting of snow, and all eyes shifted from the back of Frank's neck to the look on Harlan's face. Harlan took a moment to compose himself, shuffling through his sermon notes to hide his total befuddlement. Finally, he stopped, gave a nod, and set the notes aside. When he spoke, the words came tumbling forth like sparks of light in a waterfall, not from his notes, but from his soul.

"My beloved wife Laurel departed this world nearly nineteen years ago. Those of you who were blessed to know her will recall that she was a woman of great kindness and unquenchable faith. Most of what I know about God's tender mercies I learned firsthand from her. She never hesitated to set me straight."

His voice broke, and he waited for it to steady.

"She still speaks to me sometimes in the laughter of our children, the rumble of thunder, or the singing of a hymn. She still sets me straight, and did so, just now. I had planned to preach today about— well, no matter, it can wait. Instead I want to talk about the gift that we call 'woman'—the blessing that she is in the lives of those she loves, and the obligation that we have, a holy trust, to treat her as our treasure. I will begin with a verse from the Song of Solomon."

Harlan opened his Bible to find the verse, but instead, smiled down at his daughter and quoted from memory: "Who is she that looketh forth as the morning, fair as the moon, clear as the sun, and terrible as an army with banners?"

Ada Shields glanced over at Cora and Frank, shook her head, and chuckled.

After church, Frank offered to walk to the Lacy farm, but Harlan said, no, it looked like rain, he could ride with them. So they all squeezed into Harlan's Model T and rode home to Sunday dinner: a glorious meal of fried chicken, boiled potatoes, cream gravy, pole beans canned from last year's garden, and biscuits so light Edward swore he had to weigh them down with butter and molasses to keep them from flying off his plate.

When they sat down to eat, Harlan turned to Frank.

"Son, will you do us the honor of giving thanks?"

"Sir?" Frank blinked as if he had sawdust in his eyes.

"Daddy," Cora said sharply, giving Harlan a look. "I would like to say grace. Dear Lord, we thank Thee for all Thy many blessings, in Jesus name, amen. Edward, pass the chicken."

The following Sunday, when the last crumb of peach cobbler had been scraped from the pan, the Lacy boys headed down to the barn to do a few chores. Cora rose to start clearing the table with Frank, but stopped short when she heard Harlan invite Frank to join him out on the porch.

Frank looked down at the stack of plates he was holding.

"Leave the dishes," Harlan said. "Cora can manage without you for a while."

Out on the porch, Harlan eased into the swing. Frank took the rocking chair beside him. They sat in silence, watching a storm flash lightning as it rumbled over the mountain. Harlan lit his pipe, but let the silence linger. He wanted to wait and watch Frank sweat. Finally he took pity on him. "Son, if you've got something to say, you might as well spit it out."

Frank pulled at his collar, rose to his feet, and locked eyes with the man that some people ranked close to a saint. Neither of them blinked.

"Rev. Lacy," Frank began, reciting the words he had rehearsed for days, "I respectfully ask your permission to ask your daughter, Cora Grace, to be my wife."

A crow cawed in the distance, and the wind rustled branches of the hemlock. Cows mooed and voices drifted on the wind. Down at the barn, Edward said something and Horace and Buster laughed.

On the porch, Harlan spit over the porch rail into the hydrangeas.

"Sorry, son, I can't help you. You're asking the wrong person. Cora hasn't needed my permission to do anything since the day she was born and wrapped her fingers around my thumb."

Frank shifted his weight from one foot to the other.

"No, sir, I'm not asking for Cora. I know she speaks for herself. I'm asking for me. I don't have much to offer, but I'm a hard worker. I've been logging almost six months now with Edward and your other boys and Jubal and the rest of the crew. If you ask any one of them, I think they'll vouch for me. Main thing is, I'll do right by your daughter. Like you said in your sermon—she will be my treasure," he said, stopping briefly to swallow hard. "You've got my word."

Harlan drew on his pipe and looked out across the valley. Summer was waning. Soon leaves would turn, bringing a glorious fall and yet another winter.

"Sit down, son," he said. "I'm going to say some things just this once, and you need to be sure you remember them. I know about your raising. I know you've been on your own most of your years. Those days are over. When you marry Cora, you will marry her family. You will be one of us for the rest of your life. Her brothers will love you like a brother, though you may not always like it, and I will love you like a son. If you need help, we will help you. If someone hurts you, they hurt us. Nothing you can do can change that. It's like the grace of God, a gift. The one exception is this: if you ever harm my daughter, or the children she may bear you, I, and her brothers, will make you regret it. You can strike me down, but my blood will flow on the ground and follow you. Her mother will hunt you down from Heaven. And Ada Shields will beat you with her rolling pin. In this family, we do not tolerate meanness of any kind. Are we clear on that?"

Frank pondered for a moment, then nodded. "Yes, sir," he said, "crystal clear."

Harlan leaned back in the swing and put his pipe back in his mouth.

"All right, then. You'd best get on down to the barn. I expect your soon-to-be brothers are laying wagers right now on whose chores you're going to get."

Frank rose and held out his hand. "Thank you, sir. You won't be sorry."

Harlan took his hand and nodded. "Well, son, I hope you won't be, either."

When Cora heard Frank's boots leave the steps, she went out on the porch and sat in the swing next to her father, resting her head on his broad shoulder.

"Were you hard on him, Daddy?"

Harlan laughed and kissed the top of her head. "No harder than you'll be, baby girl."

8

A Moonlight Promise

They were married September 1, 1917, on a dazzling blue day that Cora would long remember as the finest day of her life. She wore a white cotton dress that Ada had hand-stitched with rows of tatted lace across the bodice. Draped about her shoulders, she carried her mother's blue shawl. She pinned up her auburn hair in a twist at the nape of her neck. And as she stepped off the porch to leave for the ceremony, her father picked the last bloom of the season from the gardenias her mother had planted before Cora was born, and tucked it behind her ear.

Her only other adornment, besides the gardenia and the light in her eyes and the smile that would not leave her face, was a simple gathering of wildflowers tied up with a satin ribbon—Queen Anne's Lace, purple Asters, pink Milkweed and white Clematis—hand-picked and left at her door that morning by Grady Shields.

When Frank asked Jubal to stand up with him, Jubal had been slow to answer. For half his life, he had carried a torch for Cora, but never found the words to speak of it. He feared that it might show in his face, but in the end, his friendship with Frank won out. He told Frank he'd be honored to stand up with him, and in the end, honored was how he felt.

Customarily, weddings took place in the church, but Cora wanted a grander cathedral. She announced to her father that the ceremony would take place on the hill behind the church with a sweeping view of the valley. As with most things she wanted, Harlan didn't argue.

For the wedding march, Cora asked Grady to play his fiddle. "Play something you like," she said. "If you like it, I will, too. But keep it slow, so Daddy won't trip walking me up that hill."

Grady knew exactly what to play. He'd written a waltz, an achingly beautiful tune he called "Cora's Song." It had no words, but needed none. The music would speak for itself.

At the ceremony, Grady played his heart out. Harlan and Cora walked arm in arm to the top of the hill where Frank stood waiting with Jubal and Cora's brothers and a beaming congregation. Cora hugged her father and he kissed her cheek. Then she turned and took Frank's arm.

Harlan stepped past them and turned to face his flock. Taking a moment to find his voice, he began paraphrasing First Corinthians, chapter thirteen, changing the word "charity" to "love": "Love bears all things, believes all things, hopes all things, endures all things. Love never fails . . ."

At the close of his sermon, Harlan bowed his head and asked for God's blessing on Cora and Frank, the children they would bear and the life they would share, amen and amen and amen. Then he pronounced them man and wife.

Frank leaned down and kissed Cora's mouth, and the congregation roared. Above all the laughter and shouts of rejoicing, Ada Shields could be heard bawling like a newborn calf.

The reception took place in the church hall, a long, light-filled, high-windowed room that Harlan had built one summer with the help of his boys and five-year-old Cora, who carried the nails from one hammer to the next. Others in the church had helped, too, including John Shields and Walter Avery and their boys. Harlan had insisted it was a labor of love, and that everyone had done their part. But the congregation had voted unanimously to call it Lacy Hall.

Food for the reception was a feast. The women outdid themselves, bringing their best covered dishes, fried chicken and pork chops, green beans and corn, stewed tomatoes and okra, collard greens and ham, candied yams, boiled potatoes, biscuits and cornbread. Ada brought four of Cora's favorite apple cakes, with fresh strawberries and clotted cream for topping.

At the end of the meal, as the men pushed their chairs back from the tables and the women cleared dishes, Frank found Grady eating a chicken leg, and whispered in his ear. Grady looked up at him and grinned. He took a last bite off the chicken leg and wiped his hands on his britches. Then he picked up his fiddle, tuned it, and once again began to play "Cora's Song."

Frank held out his hand to his bride.

"Miz McCallum?" he said. "Will you do me the honor?"

Cora blushed beet red, but took her husband's hand. With everyone watching—men looking sheepish, children snickering, women smiling wistfully—they began to waltz.

They danced slowly at first, looking only at each other, moving through the crowd as if no one else were there. Then Grady picked up the tempo and they laughed, keeping step.

Cora threw back her head and her auburn hair came undone, tumbling down her back in a beautiful mess. They danced across the room, out the door, and onto the lawn. The children ran after them and the older guests followed, craning their necks and smiling.

Dusk was gathering fast. In the west, the sun sat low on the mountain, staining the sky a deep molten red. Fireflies glittered in the woods. And in the east, like an actress poised to take center stage, the full moon looked down and shone her face upon them.

Frank pulled Cora close.

"Cora McCallum, I will dance with you under every full moon all the days of our lives."

"Promise?" she said. And he did.

There are some promises we make that are not ours to keep. Frank would keep his promise to Cora for eleven years, until the day that he would break her heart.

9

THE WORLD
AND THEN SOME

At Harlan's insistence and Cora's pleading, Frank agreed that they would make their home on the Lacy farm, in the cabin by the pond a hundred yards below the farmhouse. It was there, two years later, on a blistering hot glorious Sunday in September, that Cora gave birth to their first child, a boy, they named Frank Jr.

Ada served as midwife, while Harlan sat on the porch praying silently for God's tender mercies and grace. Out in the yard, Grady tuned and retuned his fiddle, while Edward and his brothers tried to keep Frank distracted with a half-hearted game of horseshoes.

At the first wail of the infant's cry, the men froze in place, holding their breath, until Ada whooped, "It's a boy and he's a beauty!" Then a cheer rose up from the yard loud enough to be heard in Heaven, as the baby's uncles surrounded the new father to shake his hand and pound his back and rough up his hair. Grady broke out a brand new tune, playing the notes that came pouring from his heart. On the porch, Harlan fell to his knees, praising God and weeping for joy.

Hearing the celebration, Cora smiled up at Ada and kissed her hand.

"Thank you, Addie," she said, "for everything you are to me."

Ada shook her head, overcome. "I just wish your mother could've been here."

"She is," Cora said. "I can feel her."

Harlan had told Cora, time and again, the last words her mother had spoken to her. Cora loved those words. She had been waiting her whole life to say them to a child of her own. But until this moment, she'd had no idea how truly and deeply she would feel them.

Looking at her newborn, she pressed her lips to his tiny ear and whispered a message that, unbeknownst to Cora, had been spoken for generations by the women in her mother's family.

"You are worth everything to me," she said. "The world and then some."

One by one, within two years, Cora's brothers left the farm. Buster, like his father, went off to Wake Forest College to become a minister. After college, he pastored a church in Charlotte, where he met, fell in love with, and married the daughter of the church's former pastor.

Edward became hopelessly smitten by a young woman from Brevard, who had no interest in being the wife of a farmer or a logger. Given a choice between marrying the woman of his dreams, or to keep milking cows and dodging falling trees, he picked her. They married and moved to Asheville, where Edward opened a furniture store and convinced Horace to come to Asheville and help him run it.

Harlan agreed with Edward's advice to make Frank the new logging foreman. The decision might've been more difficult had Jubal still been on the job. Jubal was older and more experienced than Frank, and Harlan thought highly of him. But Jubal had left the crew a year ago to replace his father as sheriff, after Walter Avery succumbed to a heart attack. Jubal had never thought of himself as cut out to be sheriff. He generally preferred to mind his own business and let others mind theirs. But he liked helping people who needed helping. Being sheriff let him do that. The job was growing on him. And it gave him more time for fishing.

Frank took over seamlessly as foreman. He got on well with all the men and had no problems with any of them, as long as they showed up on time and worked at least half as hard as he did.

After her brothers moved out, Cora worried about Harlan spending so much time alone. She still cooked his meals and took care of the farmhouse, where, as always, they still shared Sunday dinners as a family. Running two households and looking after Frank Jr. kept her busier than she needed to be. But she and Frank loved the cabin at the pond. They had worked hard fixing it up to make it their home. They didn't want to leave it. But in August of 1922, Harlan suffered a stroke and could no longer tend to himself. So Cora and Frank and three-year-old Frank Jr. moved from the cabin up to the farmhouse to be with him.

Frank Jr. proved to be good medicine for his grandfather. Harlan slowly rallied from the stroke well enough to walk and hold a fishing pole. He taught the boy how to dig worms and bait a hook and gut a catfish. They fished together at the pond most every day except Sundays, accompanied by Blue Two, the stray that Frank had stopped Edward from shooting. The old Blue, Harlan's beloved hound, had died the same day Harlan had his stroke. Harlan missed Blue but liked the way Blue Two always followed them to the pond. He told Frank Jr. that he had never in all his born days seen a dog that liked to fish as much as Blue Two.

Harlan continued to preach on occasion, when he felt up to it, filling in for the young preacher who had replaced him. And he often spent hours on his knees praying, especially during each of the three times Cora went into labor. James Harlan was born six months after Harlan's stroke. And two years later, Andrew Lacy entered the world, bottom side up, kicking and bawling something fierce.

One cold morning, an early frost, when Frank Jr. was almost seven, Frank Sr. was milking at the barn before heading up the mountain to meet the logging crew. In the kitchen of the farmhouse, Cora was frying a pan of eggs at the stove when she felt something, a strange chill, as if a cold hand had brushed the back of her neck. She looked over at her boys. The older two were seated at the table studiously eating oatmeal. Andrew, the baby, sat in the high chair gumming a biscuit. He grinned at his mother, and she smiled back.

"Frank Jr.," she said, flipping the eggs, "will you please go tell your grandfather to kindly come join us before you and your brothers eat his breakfast."

Moments later the boy came back.

"Mama?"

Cora picked up the pan to slide the eggs onto a plate, but stopped when she saw the look on Frank Jr.'s face. "What is it, son?"

"I shook Grandpa hard. He won't wake up."

Cora dropped the pan of eggs and ran down the hall to her father's room.

The boys stared at the mess on the floor until they heard their mother's scream.

"Frank Jr.! Go to the barn and get your daddy! Tell him to hurry!"

Frank Jr. ran out the back door and clattered down the step. James Harlan covered his eyes with his fists. And Andrew spit out his biscuit and began to wail.

Harlan Lacy's funeral was the largest local gathering in anyone's memory. Preachers came from far and near to take part in his eulogy. The church was filled to overflowing with mourners who came to pay their respects to a man who had so often brought them comfort and hope through his sermons, his frequent visits to their homes, and the way he lived his life.

After two hours of eulogies finally ended, Cora and her brothers lifted their father's coffin on their shoulders and led the procession of mourners to the cemetery. Frank carried Andrew, who had fallen asleep sucking his thumb. Frank Jr. and James walked beside them, hand in hand.

When Cora stumbled under the weight, Frank handed Andrew to Jubal, and stepped to Cora's side, putting his arm around her waist to steady her.

On a dazzling carpet of fallen leaves, they walked up the hill, bareheaded in a light autumn rain, and lowered Harlan's coffin into a grave next to Laurel's.

Cora held her tears until she saw Grady. He was standing alone under a blazing red maple, tuning his fiddle. Overcome by grief, he had shied away from the service, but showed up at the burial to play Harlan's favorite hymn.

Stepping forward, Edward picked up a handful of wet earth and scattered it on his father's coffin. Others followed, one by one. When all had taken a turn, Cora took a yellowed gardenia from her hair, the one she had worn on her wedding day, and placed it on the grave. Then Grady began to play and they all joined hands to sing as one voice the words they knew by heart: "Amazing grace, how sweet the sound, that saved a wretch like me . . ."

For three days after Harlan died, Blue Two refused to come out from under the porch. Frank Jr. finally coaxed him out with a piece of ham.

"Mama?" said the boy, watching the dog devour the ham. "Can't we just call him Blue now? He's the only dog we've got. Daddy says Blue Two is a sorry name for a good dog. And Grandpa won't care if we change it 'cause he's up in heaven fishing with his old Blue."

He looked at his mother and reached up to touch her face. "Don't cry, Mama."

"They're good tears," Cora said, smoothing Frank Jr.'s hair with one hand, scratching the dog's ears with the other. "You're right, son. We'll call him Blue."

Harlan's handwritten will left no doubt about his wishes. As in the past, one-tenth of all profits from the logging company would continue to go as a monthly tithe to the church. The remainder would be divided equally between his four children. Frank, as foreman, would distribute the funds and continue to receive his salary with annual raises beginning immediately.

But Harlan left the farm and its twenty acres and all its livestock entirely to Cora. Her brothers never questioned it. They loved the place, but knew their baby sister loved it best. And they felt indebted to Cora and Frank for the way they had cared for Harlan in his last years.

Cora could hardly believe it. More than a place to live, the farm and those mountains were her home. In some ways, they were the mother she never knew. Cora couldn't imagine giving them up, especially after losing her father. Harlan made sure she wouldn't need to.

She and Frank and their children would continue to have a roof over their heads, a garden for vegetables, cows for milk, chickens for eggs, hogs for pork, and land to call their own. Cora would churn butter to sell in town, and Frank would earn a decent wage as foreman. Thanks to Harlan, they could sleep easy at night, certain they'd spend all their days together living simply, working hard, wanting for nothing, being happy. That feeling would last for almost two years.

10

Fly Away

1928

Cora stepped out on the back porch to ring the bell to call her family to supper. The summer heat had been insufferable for days, and she took a moment to lift her chin and let the breeze from the creek cool her neck. Frank was down at the barn milking, but should be finished by now. And the boys had gone to the pond supposedly to fish, but more likely, they were skinny-dipping. She wasn't worried. They were all good swimmers, and growing like weeds.

Frank Jr. was nine, tall and handsome, a hunter like his daddy. James Harlan was only six, but with a little help from his mother, he had taught himself to read. When he wasn't reading, James liked to fish. Sometimes, he did both at once. And four-year-old Andrew—Drew for short—was a constant source of frustration and delight, his brothers' clown, his father's "boy," and the apple of his mother's eye.

Cora smiled to herself, thinking about them. Then she heard boots on the steps.

"Hey, Cora!"

"Hey, Grady! Supper's almost ready. Can you stay?"

"Ma's cooking up a pot of beans. I'd best go home and help her eat it. Is Frank around?"

"He's at the barn. I'll ring the bell and he'll come up."

"Uh, can you hold off for a little while? I got somethin' to ask him."

"Well, all right, go on down the barn. I'll ring the bell to call the boys, but tell Frank I said he can come eat whenever he's ready. And, Grady, be sure to say hey to your mama for me!"

A half hour later, at the supper table, Frank told Cora that Grady had asked him for a job.

"Doing what?" she said.

"He says he want to be a logger. I'd like to help him, but I've got my doubts."

Andrew grinned. "Grady's no logger, Daddy. You ought to hire me."

His brothers laughed until Cora snapped, "Boys, eat your supper! Andrew, I mean you!"

She looked back at Frank. "What are you going to do?"

"I don't know. Grady is . . ." Frank hesitated, glancing over at the boys.

Cora set down her fork.

"Grady is Grady," she said. "He's our friend. He and Addie barely make it on what John left them. He needs to work. Most of all, he needs to know that you think he can do it."

Getting up to clear the table, she gave Frank a look. "And you can tell anybody who doesn't take kindly to him to go find another job for half the pay!"

Two days later, when Frank kissed Cora goodbye and headed out to the pickup to drive to work, Grady was waiting with a flour sack of food and a wooden box he'd hand-built.

"'Morning, Grady," Frank said. "Ready to do some logging? What's in the box?"

"I'm ready!" Grady said, grinning. "This here's the case I built for my fiddle. I thought the crew might like me to play a few tunes for 'em when we take a break to eat."

At supper that night, Frank told Cora, "I wish you could've seen it. The men liked Grady playing so much they started making requests. I thought I'd never get 'em back to work!"

Three months later, in the fall of 1928, the crew was felling timber on a ridge a few miles from the farm. The men who were working that day would later swear they were certain Frank heard the warning and saw the tree, a thirty-foot Fraser fir, falling straight as an arrow. He could have cleared out of its path, they were sure of it, if not for one reason: Grady Shields.

Grady was as slow as Frank was quick. Everybody said so. And he spent too much time making up songs in his head, they said, instead of paying attention to what was going on around him. He should've seen the tree or heard the warning, but no.

It happened fast, and then it was done, and there was no undoing it. In the twinkling of an eye that it took for Frank to shove Grady to safety, Frank's skull was crushed.

They stood for a moment, every man on that crew, blinking in the grim light of death, in the silence of the forest, feeling thankful that they'd been spared, and ashamed for feeling it.

Grady tried to pull Frank out, but it took the strength of eight men to lift the limb that pinned Frank to the ground. When they finally freed his body, they knew there was nothing left to do.

Grady went alone, muddy and broken, to bear the news to Cora.

She was kneeling by the creek, washing the silks off a dozen ears of corn when Blue came running out from under the porch and started howling like he'd been snakebit. Then she heard Grady. He was coming up the road, moaning. At first, she thought he was singing. Shading her eyes from the sun, she suddenly recognized what he was carrying in his hands, held out before him like an offering plate bound for the altar: Frank's bloody cap.

Cora rose to her feet, letting the corn tumble from her lap and fall splashing into the creek.

"No," was all she said.

Grady fell to his knees at her feet, pouring out the awful story, pleading for forgiveness. Cora stood with her hand on Grady's head, watching the corn silks swirl on the currents in the creek. She waited until they washed downstream out of sight. Then she wiped her hands on her apron and pulled Grady to his feet.

"Get up," she said, brushing the mud from his face as if he were her child.

"I've got no quarrel with you, Grady. Frank's always had a mind of his own. He did what he thought was right, and neither you nor I nor God and all His angels could have stopped him."

She looked down at the barn. Andrew stood by the fence, sucking his thumb and staring up at the loft, where his brothers liked to hide from him.

Grady followed her gaze, then wailed, "Them boys don't have a daddy 'cause of me!"

"Hush, Grady. It was Frank's doing, not yours. I've got three boys to raise alone and there's nobody to blame for it but their daddy. I can't even blame him because . . ."

She put a hand to her throat and whispered, "God help me, he's gone."

The day of Frank's funeral, Cora woke at first light, as always, to fire up the wood stove and fix breakfast—oatmeal, biscuits, sausage gravy, scrambled eggs, and country ham—the same meal she served up most every morning.

She bowed her head and offered grace, thanking God for his tender mercies and asking that her husband's soul would find eternal rest, in the name of Jesus, amen. Then she looked around the table at her boys.

"Your daddy was a good man," she said. "You'll be just like him. Now eat your breakfast while it's hot."

Frank Jr. and James Harlan stared at their father's empty chair.

Drew looked at his brothers. "I'll be a better man than them boys, won't I, Mama?"

Gravy dribbled from his mouth and dripped off his chin.

His brothers snickered and kicked him under the table.

Cora shook her head and sighed.

Frank would be laid to rest near the hill where he and Cora were married, in the family plot of the church cemetery where Cora's parents had been buried, side by side—her mother, twenty-five years ago, and her father, less than two.

For the service, Cora wore the white cotton dress she'd worn for her wedding, the one that Ada had hand-stitched for her with ribbon and tatted lace. Folks could say what they wanted about a widow wearing white to bury her husband. Cora didn't care. Frank loved that dress, so she would wear it, with her mother's shawl wrapped around her shoulders. She dressed the boys in their Sunday best, warned them to mind their manners, and told the older two to hang onto Drew and try not to let him suck his thumb.

Edward drove over from Asheville with his wife, Beulah, and their three children. Horace and Edna, his bride of six months, came with them, riding in back under the children. Edward told Beulah the experience would make Horace and Edna think twice about becoming parents.

Buster, in Charlotte, sent his deepest regrets. Eleanor, his wife, was due with their first child and Buster didn't want to leave her. Frank's only living kin, besides Cora and the boys, were a few distant cousins in Haywood County, and Cora knew no way to contact them. The gathering for the service was mainly neighbors and friends, Frank Jr.'s teacher from the one-room school, and the men from the logging crew. Grady Shields stood in back, hanging his head.

They were Scots-Irish dirt farmers, simple mountain folk. Many of them had buried loved ones in that same hallowed ground. They knew firsthand the God-given need in times of grief to be sur-rounded—propped up—by family and friends and neighbors. So they stood together in the cemetery, shoulder to shoulder, forming an unbreakable circle around Cora and her children as Frank's body was laid to rest and his soul was committed to God.

Cora pulled her boys close beneath her arms the way a hen hides its chicks under its wing, and stared at the gravesites.

"Three graves," she whispered. "My mama's. My daddy's. My darlin's."

She felt empty and weightless, and feared, at any moment, that she might leave her body there on the mountain, and fly away up into the clouds to find Frank.

Her boys seemed to sense it. Frank Jr. locked his fingers around her wrist. James Harlan clung to her shawl. When the first clod of dirt hit his father's coffin, Andrew hid his face in his mother's skirt and sucked his thumb. And no one, not even his brothers, tried to stop him.

That evening, after the last of her neighbors had paid their respects, told all their stories, and said tearful goodbyes, Cora tucked her boys and their cousins in bed in the boys' room. She had apologized to Beulah for the limited sleeping arrangements, and suggested they might sleep better in the cabin down by the pond. But Beulah had insisted they all needed to be together under one roof.

"Oh, honey," Beulah said, "this is nothin'! I grew up sleeping in one bed with nine sisters, five at the top, five at the bottom, and most of 'em snored!"

Cora kissed all seven faces, then gave a long hug to each of her boys, taking her time, breathing in the sweet, wet-dog scent of their hair.

"Say a prayer for your daddy," she told them.

She turned to leave the room, but stopped to look back.

"Andrew McCallum? If you think for one minute that I don't

know you're pinching your cousins under those covers, you are fooling yourself!"

Closing the door behind her, she pretended not to hear their snickers.

Cora threw a quilt on the sofa for herself and insisted her brothers and their wives take the remaining beds—one she'd slept in as a girl, and the other in which she'd spent every night for eleven years in the shelter of Frank McCallum's arms.

Bidding Beulah and Horace and Edna goodnight, Cora poured two glasses of sweet tea and took them out to the porch. Edward sat in the swing. His cigarette glowed red in the dark.

"Hey, baby girl." He slid over to make room for her. "Come have a seat with your favorite brother. Unless you want to go out dancing?"

Cora handed him the tea, then sat beside him in the swing.

"I came out here because I need to see something."

Edward grinned. "Can't blame you, darlin'. I'm damn good-looking."

Cora rolled her eyes. Her brother could never seem to resist teasing her at inappropriate times. It was one of the many things she loved about him.

"Not you, Edward Lacy. The moon. I want to see if it will still rise."

Edward looked away from his sister's face and stared out across the farm. Clouds were gathering in the west beyond the mountains, backlit by flashes of lightning. Thunder rumbled in the distance, deep and rolling. On the roof of the smokehouse, a dark, feathery shape drew itself up and took wing across the pasture. In the east, the sky was cloudless, cluttered with stars. No sign of a moon.

Edward cleared his throat. "It will rise," he said, "if you give it enough time."

Cora leaned back and rested her head on her brother's shoulder.

"Maybe you can tell me, Edward. How much time is enough? It's been two years since we lost Daddy, and I still grieve for him every day. How long do you think I'll grieve for Frank?"

Edward gave the swing a push with his toe the way he did in their childhood, when he was a boy big enough to hold a plow, and she was a skinny little girl with legs too short to reach from the swing to the floor. They swung in silence, watching the night parade of stars and planets and fruit bats and lightning bugs, all backed up by a chorus of tree frogs and cicadas and the ripple of the creek and thunder over the mountain.

Edward stopped the swing. "What are you going to do?"

"About what?"

"I've been thinking, Cora. If you and the boys move to Asheville, it would be easier for Horace and me to look after you."

Cora shook her head. "You and Horace have got your own families to look after, Edward. You don't need four more mouths to feed."

"You're going to need help."

"I've got the farm," Cora said. "I know how to work it. My boys are young, but they're smart and strong. They'll learn. Grady's offered to come do the milking twice a day and take care of some chores. He says he'll never . . ." she closed her eyes, ". . . go back to logging."

Lighting flashed on the mountain and a breeze brought the first smell of rain.

"I can pay Grady. He'll refuse it, but I'll make him take it. Thanks to Daddy, I'll have money every month from the company. Don't worry about us, Edward. We'll be all right."

Edward took a drag on his cigarette and let the smoke out in a sigh.

Cora touched his arm. "I know you and Horace are making a good living in Asheville. You're cut out for it, and I'm proud of you. If something happened to me, I'd count on you to do right by my boys. But I can't picture myself living any place in the world but on this mountain. I wouldn't know how to breathe. I've got to stay here—just like our daddy and our mama and Frank—until the day I die."

Edward pushed the swing and it banged against the porch rail.

"You're a stubborn woman, Cora McCallum."

"I've been told that," she said.

"You've got no need to worry about your boys. We're family. They're our boys, too."

Cora closed her eyes. "You're a good man, Edward Lacy. Not good-looking, mind you, but good."

Edward's laugh roused Blue under the porch. In the same way that the dog had grieved two years earlier for Harlan, he was grieving now for Frank, and he did not want to be disturbed. Rising up on his haunches, he growled up at Edward through the floorboards of the porch. Then he turned in a circle, flopped down in the dirt and went back to chasing rabbits in his dreams.

"Sister," Edward said, pointing at the barn, "look yonder."

Cora looked. The swing rocked slowly, back and forth. Finally, she nodded.

A fingernail moon was climbing over the barn breaking free from the limbs of a giant hickory.

11

FISHING

$\mathcal{F}$or weeks after Frank died, Cora barely slept. She lay awake most nights counting rhythms: the ticking of the clock on the mantel, the drumming of the rain on the tin roof, the rushing of the creek outside her window, the snoring of her boys down the hall.

Her face took on a pallor, her copper hair lost its shine, and the shadows under her eyes deepened into pale lavender hollows that would never completely go away.

Sometimes, after the boys fell asleep, Cora would pull her mother's shawl around her shoulders and walk in the moonlight down to the pond to sit on the porch of the cabin where she and Frank started their marriage. She would sit there watching stars dance on the pond, and recall hot summer nights before their boys were born, when Frank would take her hand and lead her down to the water's edge. They'd strip and swim, laughing like children, until their bodies felt cool and clean and new. Then they'd spread a quilt on the ground and lie for hours tangled up in each other's arms. Cora worried at first about snakes. But Frank would make her forget her fears. He would made her forget everything—the ground beneath them, the mountains around them, the rumble of thunder overhead—until all she could think of, or taste, or ever want, was the sweet, salty pleasure of their love.

Cora remembered the night, the very moment, Frank Jr. was conceived. She had felt it at once, not a physical sensation, but a certainty, a wave of peace and joy and trepidation. For some reason, she kept it to herself. She didn't tell Frank until two months later when she got the morning sickness. She wished now she had told him right away. It's a hard lesson, she thought, learning to hold nothing back.

She recalled other things about those nights, things that made her smile and shake her head. Mosquito welts as big as walnuts. A poison oak rash that somehow found its way onto Frank's private parts. A barn owl that sat on a hickory limb watching them and calling for its mate. And the deer—a buck that came crashing out of the woods one night as they lay spent and naked and half asleep. Cora had been mortified, sure it was one of her brothers, maybe Horace, who'd been in the basement of the farmhouse sipping 'shine and maybe had gotten lost in the dark on his way to the outhouse.

She told Frank she'd sooner get trampled by a deer than have to listen to Horace at Sunday dinner cracking jokes about them and the pond. Frank had laughed like it was the funniest thing he ever heard her say. Then he'd reached over and pulled her to him again. More than anyone she had ever known, Frank McCallum had made her feel smart and funny and beautiful and wanted—all the things that she could not imagine ever feeling again.

After he died, she went to the pond late at night to remember him and all the ways he had made her feel. But mostly, she went there to grieve. It was the one place she felt free to weep. Her boys were grieving in their own ways for their father. But they watched her constantly from the corners of their eyes. She didn't want to heap her pain on their heads.

But trying to hide grief is like holding your breath under water. You can smile like nothing's wrong, but everybody can see you're drowning. Sooner or later, you have to come up for air.

Despite nearly thirty years difference in their ages, Ada and Cora had been best friends since the day Cora was born. After Cora and Frank were married and moved into the pond house, Cora cooked all the meals for Harlan and her brothers, and insisted she could do their cleaning and laundry. But Harlan said, no, Ada and John could use the money. Besides, he said, Ada always brought him an apple cake and that was worth more than what he paid her. So on the days Ada came over, Cora would walk up from the cabin and they'd spend the day working together, talking and laughing and singing. Harlan swore that he loved listening to them almost as much as he loved Ada's apple cake. Well, nearly.

In Cora's eyes, Ada never looked like she had aged a day. But the last five years had taken a visible toll, aging Ada severely. First, John, her husband of forty years, had died suddenly of a heart attack. Ada told Cora that losing John had left her homesick day and night, even though she was home. And she found herself wandering around the house, trying to remember what she needed to do.

"Thank the Lord for Grady," she said, "don't know what I'd do without him."

Harlan's death had struck another blow. He was Ada's beloved pastor and friend. She had helped raise his children. There was no one she admired more. But Frank's death, and especially Grady's part in it, were almost too much to bear. Even worse than her own grief was knowing what losing Frank would do to Cora and her children. Ada would rather die than watch them suffer. And she nearly did.

The day Grady came home bawling, with Frank's blood on his hands, and told her the awful news, Ada made him drive her to the farmhouse. She gathered Cora and her boys into her arms and rocked them like babies. She stayed with them for three days, cooking and washing and comforting in every way possible. The day after Frank's funeral, Cora took Ada's face in her hands, smoothed her hair, and said, "Go home, Addie. Get some rest. We'll be all right."

Grady drove his mother home and helped her into bed. The next morning, she could barely walk. Every step was a struggle. Grady had never seen her in so much pain.

"What's hurtin' you, Mama?"

"It's just the rheumatism, Grady. You know how it comes and goes."

But this time, it didn't go away. It grew worse. Grady carved a stick with a vine that twirled from handle to tip, and gave it to her to lean on. By day, she managed to cook a little, and baked cakes for Grady to take over to Cora and the boys. Come evening, to help her sleep, Grady would pour her a small glass of muscadine wine that John had enjoyed and taught him to make and keep stored out of sight. Grady was surprised at how quickly his mother took to it.

Cora and Ada kept in touch through Grady. But for three months after Frank's funeral, they didn't see each other. Ada was in too much pain from the rheumatism to ride in Grady's pickup, and Cora couldn't bring herself to leave the house. She made Frank Jr. and James go to school as usual, and sent all three boys to church with Grady on Sunday mornings. She churned butter each week and had Grady take it into town to sell at the store. But she could not bear to see pity in the eyes of anyone, everyone who looked at her. So she stayed home. When well-wishers brought food and wanted to offer their condolences, she'd send Frank Jr. to the door to thank them politely and tell them that his mother was busy at the moment, but she'd be sure to return their dishes soon and to thank them personally for their kindness.

She even refused to see Jubal. The first Saturday after Frank's funeral, Jubal showed up at the farmhouse just after breakfast. Frank Jr. answered the door.

"Hey, son," Jubal said, ruffling the boy's hair. "How you doing?"

"Doing fine, sir. How are you?"

"Well, I woke up in a mood to go fishing. You and your brothers want to go with me?"

The boy's face lit up. "You mean now?"

"Isn't now always the best time to go fishing?"

Frank Jr. looked away. "Mama might think it's . . . you know . . . too soon."

Jubal nodded. "Tell you what. Go get your mama, and I'll talk her into it."

Frank Jr. grinned and ran to his mother's room. Jubal heard their voices. This Cora didn't sound like the Cora he knew.

Frank Jr. came running back to the door, beaming. "She said to tell you she's sorry she can't come to the door, but we can go fishing with you!"

He turned to go fetch his brothers, but stopped and looked back at Jubal.

"She said to say we surely appreciate your kindness . . . and we surely do!"

For three Saturdays in a row, Jubal showed up to take the boys fishing. He always asked to speak to Cora, but she never came to the door. After that, he stopped asking. He'd just pull up in front of the farmhouse and wait for the boys to come running out. He never had to wait long.

Finally, several Saturdays later, when he brought the boys home, he was surprised to see Cora sitting in the porch swing.

"Look, Mama!" In the back of the pickup, Andrew was jumping up and down, waving a pair of catfish, one in each hand. "I caught two! Frank Jr. and James only caught one apiece!"

Cora laughed and sent the boys down the creek to clean their catch. Then she motioned to Jubal to come join her in the swing.

"I'll stand," he said, as he stepped up on the porch. "I smell like catfish."

She rolled her eyes. "I've smelled catfish before," she said, patting the swing. "Sit yourself down."

He sat. Soon they fell into an old familiar rhythm—push back, release, glide forward, repeat. Swinging reminded Cora of the friendship she and Jubal had shared for years before she married Frank—an easy, effortless pleasure. They had always been able to talk for hours, but sometimes, they just liked to sit together, watch the clouds roll by and swing.

After a bit, Jubal reached over and patted Cora's hand. "How you doin', darlin'?"

"I've been better," she said. "How 'bout you?"

"Yeah. Me, too. I've needed to see you, Cora, to see if I can do anything for you."

"I know. I'm sorry. I haven't been exactly . . . fit for company. But, Jubal, you have given me and the boys such a gift, taking them fishing every week. They love it. And they love you."

"I'd like to do it every Saturday, unless work gets in the way."

"I can't believe you're sheriff now. Your daddy would be so proud!"

Jubal stopped the swing. "Cora, I've got some news."

"What is it?"

"Well, it's like this. I'm getting married."

Cora laughed and punched his arm.

"I'm not joking, Cora. I'm marrying Margaret Whitfield."

"You're marrying . . . wait, Margaret Whitfield? Wasn't she a year ahead of me in school?"

"We been goin' together a while. She thinks it's time to get serious. And I . . . I agreed."

Cora fell silent, searching for words she wouldn't regret saying later. She found it hard to picture Jubal with a wife. She didn't want to admit it. But suddenly she realized that a part of her had been sure Jubal would always care only for her. And maybe some part of her would care only for him. Life was full of twists and turns, disappointments and surprises. Finally, she pressed her hand to his face.

"I'm happy for you, Jubal. And I'm especially happy for Margaret. She's one lucky lady. I wish you both all the happiness in the world."

Jubal nodded, and looked away. "Well, I wanted you to know."

"I'm glad you told me. So, when's the big day?"

"Next Saturday. Shoot! I forgot! I guess I can't take the boys fishing that day."

"It's all right, Jubal," she said laughing. "Believe it or not, some things are more important than fishing."

"Yeah, well, try telling that to your boys."

12

Coming up for Air

*E*very new loss tends to resurrect the pain of old ones. For months after Frank was killed, Cora ached day and night with emptiness. She missed her husband, her father, and even the mother she never knew. But one Saturday, while sweeping the porch, she suddenly realized that she was also missing someone else: Ada.

Just then, she heard Grady's old pickup come growling up the gravel road. Usually, when Grady came over, he'd walk a mile through the woods rather than drive two miles on the road. But this time, he was making a delivery. He stopped in front of the mailbox, jumped out of the truck, and ran around to the other side to open the door.

Waving at Cora, he yelled, "I'll be back to git her!" Then he drove away.

Ada came hobbling up the walk, leaning on her stick, carrying a sack and beaming.

Cora laughed and propped the broom on the porch rail. "Addie!" she said, throwing her arms open wide. "You're a sight for sore eyes! Even if that's not one of your cakes in that sack!"

Ada chuckled and set the sack down on the porch steps. "I thought you and the boys could use a little something sweet."

Then she pulled Cora close and began to sob.

Cora watched the birds fly, startled from the feeder. Closing her eyes, she rested her head on Ada's ample bosom. "Addie," she said, "I don't want you to worry. We don't need anything, not even one of your cakes. We just need you."

"Speak for yourself, Mama!" Andrew stood on the porch, grinning and holding the sack with the cake.

Ada hooted. "Get over here, boy, and give this old woman some sugar!"

Andrew dutifully handed the sack to his mother and tried not to make a face while Ada pinched his cheeks and kissed the top of his head.

"Drew?" Cora said, to spare him further kissing. "Go find your brothers and tell them Miz Addie is here. And make sure you tell them she brought us a treasure!"

The boys were not fond of Ada's affections, but the mention of her cake would bring them running.

As Andrew ran off to fetch his brothers, Cora took Ada's arm and helped her up the steps.

"How's the rheumatism treating you, Addie?"

"Honey, it gets worse ever' day. Thank the Lord I've got Grady and his muscadine wine."

Cora laughed. "Addie, what would folks at church say if they knew you drank that stuff?"

"You know I don't give a whit what people say. Jesus drank wine, and made it, too. It's in the Bible. You can look it up. If it's good enough for Jesus, it's good enough for me. Besides, if folks at church got a taste of it, they'd be lining up at our door to buy it. And don't think I haven't thought of selling it. Maybe I ought to take a jug to the next social and let 'em try it!"

An hour later, after they'd all had their fill of Ada's pound cake, Cora sent the boys out to play and began clearing the table. Grady would be back soon to fetch Ada and do the milking. Cora was about to say how much she appreciated Grady's help, but Ada spoke first.

"Sit, child," Ada said, patting the chair beside her. "We need to talk, and you need to listen."

Cora set the dishes in the sink, wiped her hands and took a seat at the table.

"What's on your mind, Addie?"

Ada studied Cora's face. Finally, she said, "Grady tells me you're not sleeping."

"And how exactly would Grady know that?"

"Your boys told him. They tell him all sorts of things they would probably tell you, if they thought you would hear them."

Cora looked out the window. The boys were throwing rocks in the creek. Andrew threw a big one that splashed his brothers. When he laughed and ran, they took off after him.

"What else did Grady say my boys said?"

"They said you don't talk to anybody. Not even to them. You don't go to church, or answer the door when folks come to call. Cora? Are you listening? Your boys are worried about you."

"I'm listening, Addie. But I also seem to recall how you suffered after John died."

Ada blinked. "Yes," she said, "I suffered. I loved John Shields. I always will. When I lost him, I thought I lost myself. I didn't sleep. Didn't eat. If Grady needed me, I didn't care. One night, I looked in a mirror and could not see my face. That's when I knew what I had to do. I had to be alive. Only one of us was dead, and it wasn't me."

Ada reached over and lifted Cora's chin.

"Child, you look like a corpse. Your children have lost their daddy and now they're scared they'll lose their mama, too. They need you, Cora."

Cora turned to face Ada. Then, for the first time in weeks, she broke down and wept.

Ada held her tight and rocked her to and fro. Cora cried until she had no more tears. Finally, she drew a long, deep breath and rested in Ada's arms.

"I don't feel like doing anything, Addie. I don't want to talk to anybody . . . not even my boys. I see them looking at me across the table, like they're waiting for me to tell something important that they need to hear. I try, but I can't think of what to say. I don't feel . . . anything."

Ada combed Cora's hair with her fingers. "Life is full of things we don't feel like doing, honey. You know that. We do them, not because they feel good, but because they're part of being alive. Sometimes we've got to get out of bed and go through the motions of doing what we need to do, and wait for the feelings to come back."

"What if they don't come back, Addie? What if I never feel anything again?"

"That's how it works. Just when you think you'll never feel again, life will come back to you."

Cora gave it some thought. "Well," she said, "I can go through the motions. I can, and will, do whatever my boys need. But I cannot for the life of me make myself go to sleep. I try, Addie, but sleep won't come."

"I know," Ada said. "Don't worry, honey. I've got a cure for that."

Cora sat up to look at her. "Addie? I'm sorry. I can't stomach your muscadine wine!"

"You don't need wine, child. You need to crochet."

"I need to . . . what?"

"Crochet," Ada said. "Like I taught you when you were little. Don't you remember? Do you still have the hooks and yarn that I gave you?"

"I remember. It was hard, 'cause you're left-handed and I'm right-handed and everything was backwards. I'm sure those hooks are somewhere. But how's that going to help me sleep?"

Ada laughed. "Trust me. If you crochet long enough, it'll put you to sleep. It worked for me. It'll work for you. You can make doilies and tablecloths and counterpanes, if you want. And I'll bet Horace and Edward will be only too happy to sell them for you at their store in Asheville."

They heard little-boy feet stomping up the stairs off the kitchen. The door flew open and Andrew announced, "Grady's at the barn trying to tell Frank Jr. and James how to milk a cow, like they don't already know how. Miz Addie, Grady said to tell you to finish up your visiting 'cause the milking's almost done and he'll be ready to go home directly."

Cora looked at Ada. "Will you and Grady stay for supper? I've got beans on the stove. I'll bake cornbread and we can finish off the rest of your pound cake."

"I'd love it," Ada said. "And Grady will be over the moon."

Supper was good. Grady ate three helpings of everything and looked around for more. When he and Ada finally left, Cora made the boys help her clear the table. She washed the dishes in the sink and handed them to Andrew, who rinsed them in a bucket and passed them to James, who dried them and gave them to Frank Jr. to stack in the cupboard.

The work went fast. Finally, she wiped her hands and said, "Come on, boys, let's read."

That was what she used to say most every night before their daddy died, before the world turned upside down. They were so happy to hear her say it again, they whooped. She chose one of their favorites, O. Henry's "The Ransom of Red Chief," and read aloud for an hour. Then she shut the book, pulled them close, tucked their heads beneath her chin, and drew a breath.

"I am here," she said, "and I'm not going anywhere. There is nothing we can't do together." Then she looked at Andrew and added, "With the help of God."

Later that evening, when the boys were asleep, she spent a half hour searching and finally found the crochet hooks Ada had given her long ago. They were on a shelf in the bedroom closet, along with a few skeins of cotton yarn. She took them down, then undressed and climbed in bed, propping herself up on feather pillows against the iron bars of the headboard.

She started slowly, awkwardly, trying to recall the stitches Ada had taught her. And then, to her amazement, it started coming back to her, as if her hands suddenly remembered what her mind had long forgotten. Soon, she stopped thinking about it at all and simply watched her fingers moving in time with the hooks, pulling one loop through another, again and again, forming intricate patterns, finding order in chaos, making something new from something old.

The next morning, when she woke at sunrise, still holding the hook with her fingers tangled up in the yarn, she was surprised to see that somehow she had completed the centerpiece for what could, with enough time, become a doily. Or a tablecloth. Or, yes, even a counterpane.

She smiled. Ada would be proud. Then it hit her: for the first time since Frank died, she had slept through the night. Cora looked over to the dresser at a photo of her and Frank, smiling with such joy on their wedding day.

"Well, Frank," she said. "I guess I'm coming up for air."

13

CATFISH, PITY, AND ONE-TRICK MULE

1929

"*M*ama! Come look!"

Cora stood at the sink plucking pin feathers off a chicken.

"I'm in the kitchen, Drew!"

A summons from her five-year-old could mean anything from "Mama, come look, I picked you a flower" to "Mama, come look, I cut my toe and it's bleedin' like a sumbitch!" The boy liked to swear and Cora couldn't seem to break him of it.

"Andrew?" She waited, staring into the chicken's dead eye.

Bam! Drew loved to slam the screen door. It made him feel big like his brothers. He came huffing into the kitchen, barefoot and shirtless, with one strap of his overalls hanging off his shoulder, red-faced and sweaty, dragging a wooden bucket.

"Mama, look! Somebody left us some catfish . . . and they still swimmin'!"

Cora gasped. "Andrew McCallum! Don't you dare drop that mess on my . . . !"

Before she could say "clean floor," two gallons of pond water, four live catfish, and a five-year-old boy went sloshing across the linoleum. Cora slipped on one of the fish and came down hard. The chicken landed with a splat. Drew crowed with delight.

Cora was not amused. She lay sprawled on the floor watching Andrew's corn-husk curls quiver like birch leaves as he chased catfish around her kitchen. Suddenly, she was struck by the boy's likeness to his father. Same stubborn chin, same belly laugh, same spark of the devil in his eyes. Frank Jr. and James Harlan looked a lot like their father. But Andrew, her baby, was his daddy's mirror image. When did that happen? How could she have missed it?

"I got one, Mama!" Drew held a catfish up like a trophy. The fish wriggled from his hands, smacked his face with its tail, hit the floor, and skidded out to the front room. When he started after it, Cora caught the strap of his overalls, pulled him down and buried her face in his curls.

"Mama?"

"What, baby?"

"We stink like catfish, don't we?"

When Frank Jr. and James Harlan came home from school, they found their mother scrubbing the kitchen floor.

"Hey, Mama. Where's Drew?"

"Sleeping."

The boys exchanged a look.

"Is he sick?"

"No, Frank Jr., your brother is fine."

"Mama," James said, "Drew don't never sleep in the daylight."

"Well, James," Cora said, wringing the mop rag into a bucket, "this floor needed to be cleaned for the second time today, and I needed your brother to sleep."

That evening, while his brothers went to the barn to milk the cows, Drew sat on a rock by the creek watching his mother clean catfish. The stewed chicken would wait for tomorrow's supper. The catfish needed to be fried up and eaten tonight.

Cora slit open a fish belly, spilling the entrails in the creek to wash down stream.

"You want to try your hand at this, Mr. Drew?" Cora held out the knife.

Drew wrinkled his nose.

Cora laughed and slit another belly.

"Mama?"

"What, baby?"

Drew picked up a rock, checked it for gold, then tossed it in the creek, scattering minnows like silver arrows.

"Do people leave stuff on our porch 'cause they feel sorry for us?"

Cora put down the knife and stared at the fish guts on her hands. It had been two years since Frank was killed. That's when it started, after he died. She'd go out to sweep the steps and find something on the porch, just inside the screen door, where Blue couldn't get to it: a bushel of corn, a sack of flour, or a slab of venison. Sometimes she'd see a neighbor, Bill Searcy, driving off in his pickup after dropping off something his wife, Bernice, had sent from her garden or her kitchen or just the goodness of her heart. Nobody ever waited around to be thanked.

"Why would anybody feel sorry for us, Drew?"

He dug a toe into the creek mud. "Frank Jr. says it's on account of our daddy got killed by a tree. He says that's why people leave stuff, 'cause they feel sorry for us. He says they think we're a bunch of damn orphans."

Cora raised an eyebrow. "Andrew, watch your mouth. Your brother said all that?"

"Yes, ma'am," he said, squishing mud between his toes. "More or less."

Cora rinsed her hands in the creek and wiped them on her apron. Then she gathered Andrew's face in her palms and turned it up to meet her eyes.

"Listen to me, son. Nobody has cause to feel sorry for us. They feel bad that we lost your daddy. But they don't leave us things out of pity. They do it because they are good. That's what good people do.

We take turns helping each other. It's our turn now to need a little help. But one day, it will be our turn to do the helping. And when we do, we won't wait around expecting to be thanked, will we?"

Drew grinned and shook his curls.

"All right then. Go on up to the house and wash your mouth out with soap for swearing."

He nodded, and took off up the hill.

When the screen door slammed, Cora closed her eyes. That boy was enough to make a good Christian woman long for a shot of moonshine. Tomorrow she would have him pick a bucket of apples and leave them on the Lathrop's porch. Anna Lathrop had just lost her husband to pneumonia. She could use a little help. And Drew could use a taste of feeling helpful.

It was James Harlan's idea. Andrew would take the credit, and Frank Jr. would assume the blame, but it was James who came up with the plan.

Grady Shields didn't see the McCallum boys come sneaking up through the woods. He had his mind set on other things. His mama, Ada, had been nagging him all week to finish turning over the cornfield.

"It's too wet to plow, Ma. I'll do when it dries up some, come tomorrow maybe."

Ada had rolled her eyes. "Well, it ain't never too wet to play the dang banjo."

In the years after his daddy died, Grady had stayed on the farm to help Ada with all the chores she could never have managed on her own. But he wasn't cut out to be a farmer. As a boy, he had dreams of being a musician. He could play the banjo and the fiddle like nobody's business. Everybody said so. Thing was, while everybody liked to hear a good tune now and again, most folks in those mountains didn't have the money to pay you to play it.

The logging job had been good for him, providing a little extra income, and giving him a chance to play music during meal breaks for the crew. But after the accident that took Frank's life, Grady didn't have the heart for felling trees any more. He thought about leaving, going over to Nashville and getting a job with the Grand Ole Opry. He thought about it a lot, especially late at night when he sat alone on the porch picking and playing his tunes. A man could make good money playing music in Nashville.

But the mountain had a hold on Grady—the mountain and his mama and a woman that he loved. Fact was, he couldn't bear to leave them. So he had stayed to work the farm and play his music on the porch. But sometimes, he still daydreamed about Nashville.

That was the one good thing about plowing. It freed your mind for finer things. He'd spent all morning sweating rivers down the back of his neck and composing a brand new tune in his head while trudging behind Agnes, a slow-witted, broad-rumped, plow mule, turning over row after row of rocky soil like gashes in the belly of the earth.

It was near noon. The sun had climbed to the middle of the sky, beating down on Grady's head like a kerosene fire and shimmering in waves across the field. Ada would have his dinner, the noon meal, ready soon. Time to take a break. He fetched Agnes a bucket of water from the creek and tied her reins around the fence rail. Then he took off his cap, looked up at the sun, wiped his brow on his sleeve, and headed on up to the house to eat.

The boys waited until they heard the screen door slam. Then they set to work. Andrew was posted as the lookout. He begged to do more, but his brothers made it clear: he could take the job or leave it. He took it. Frank Jr. untied Agnes' reins and slapped her rump to pull the plow up close to the fence. James Harlan helped him unrig the plow from the harness. When the mule was freed, James led Agnes down to the end of the field and around the fence to the other side. After several tries, they persuaded her to back her rump up to the railing. Working quickly, they threaded the reins from the plow through the fence rails and re-hitched them to the mule.

Then they hid in the woods, taking turns covering Andrew's

mouth to keep him from laughing, while they waited for Grady to finish eating.

Grady was in no hurry. Despite the heat, Ada had fired up the wood stove to fry a chicken and make gravy and biscuits, Grady's favorite. He polished off the meal with two helpings of blackberry pie. Ada watched him eat, tapping her toe.

"I heard thunder," she said. "It's comin' a storm. If you aim to finish that field in my lifetime, you'd best get a move on. I'll save the rest of the pie for your supper."

Grady took another swig of buttermilk, then pushed grudgingly back from the table, donned his sweaty cap, and headed out the door. Ada heard his boots clomping slowly down the steps. Minutes later, she was clearing the table when she heard him again, clomping back, considerably faster than before. She looked up to see Grady standing in the doorway, holding his cap and scratching his head.

"Ma?" he said. "You are never in a million years going to believe what I'm about to tell you. That thar mule of ours is a whole lot smarter than we give her credit for."

Andrew was not one to keep a secret. His brothers knew this. They had nobody but themselves to blame for letting him in on the prank. That night at supper, he confessed.

"We played a trick on Grady Shields, Mama! I wish you could've seen it!"

Cora looked up from her plate and stared at her two older boys. "You did what?"

Frank Jr. glared at Andrew. "It was my fault, Mama. We were just having fun."

Andrew shouted, "I was the damn lookout!"

"Andrew McCallum!" Cora snapped. "Mind your mouth! And hold your tongue or leave the table! I want to hear what your brothers have to say."

Andrew stuffed a fist in his mouth. Frank Jr. rolled his eyes at James Harlan.

"Well, Mama," James began, "it was like this. You know how Grady is . . ."

The story—despite James' best efforts to do it justice—was not half as comical as the actual events, except to Andrew, who was sent off to bed for laughing hysterically.

"I'm sorry, Mama." James hung his head. "We didn't mean no harm."

"Look at me, son." Cora waited to see the gold in James' eyes. "You made a fool of that man. He may not know it yet, but he'll figure it out soon enough. Or worse, he'll tell somebody and they'll figure it out for him. He's a good man, and he deserves more from you boys than to be treated like the butt of a joke. You can't expect to make fun of a man and not do him harm."

Frank Jr. banged a fist on the table. "Grady Shields don't deserve nothin' from me, Mama. He was the cause of our daddy getting killed!"

Cora reached across the table and covered the boy's fist with her hand.

"Grady Shields didn't kill your daddy, son. Neither did that tree. Your daddy died because of who he was. He knew what he was doing when he pushed Grady out of the way. He always did what he thought was right, no matter what anybody else thought. He was stubborn about it. Maybe I still blame him sometimes for leaving us. But I'm proud of who he was. Blaming Grady won't bring him back. It'll just eat you up inside."

"Mama?" Andrew stood in the doorway. He'd been crying.

"What is it, Andrew?"

"Today, when Grady Shields was scratching his head about that mule, I heard my daddy talking to God about it way up in heaven, and you know what?"

"What, darlin'?"

Andrew's face broke into a grin. "They was laughing their asses off!"

The next morning, Cora marched the boys over to the Shields' place to apologize. Grady laughed and tried to act as if he'd been wise to their joke all along. Frank Jr. and James Harlan spent the day plowing the rest of the field. Andrew helped, fetching water from the creek and chucking dirt clods at his brothers.

At noon, Ada served up a big meal of pinto beans, collard greens, and cornbread. Afterward, while the boys finished plowing, Grady sat on the porch playing his fiddle, serenading the women. Cora tapped her toe, Andrew danced a jig, and Agnes seemed to flick her tail in time to the music.

Even Ada, for once, didn't seem to mind his playing. Grady sounded good. It helped considerably, he thought, to have an appreciative audience.

14

Fire on the Mountain

The summer of 1930 was generally thought to be the hottest and driest any living soul could remember in those mountains. Come late afternoon, thunderheads would gather on the western horizon, roiling up black as pitch and rumbling like they meant business, only to roll on through without sparing so much as a drop. The red earth baked into clay, hard enough to break a plow. Crops withered to dust. Saints and sinners alike prayed fervently for rain. And the old timers who sat on the porch of Pack's Store, swapping stories and spitting tobacco and remembering good times gone by, swore it was the beginning of the end.

When the creek behind the farmhouse slowed to a trickle, Cora's boys, in a selfless effort to conserve water, offered to forego their weekly baths. Cora assured them their situation was not yet that dire, nor would it be as long as she was their mother. Instead, she set them to work hauling buckets of water from the creek to store in barrels in the earthen basement. Four times a day, at meals and bed, she led them in a prayer for rain.

"Mama?" Five-year-old Andrew was trailing his brothers to and from the creek, spilling more water than he carried in his bucket.

"Why don't we do a dance to make it rain? Grady said that's what the Indians did. And you said we're part Cherokee."

"Shut up, Drew!" James was too hot to have patience for idle chatter. "You and Grady don't know what you're talking about! And I'm sick of hearing your mouth!"

Drew whirled in a circle and slung his bucket with surprising aim, barely missing his brother's head, but sloshing water down his back. James ducked like a startled cat, then took off in a fury running after Andrew. Frank Jr. fell laughing in a heap on the ground.

"Boys!" Cora shouted. "Get in this house right now and cool off!"

The fire started with a dry lightning strike on a remote ridge some forty miles east of the farm. Cora smelled the smoke two days before she saw it. When Grady came to milk that morning, he stopped in for coffee, as usual.

"Looks like we got us a fire brewing somewhere yonder," he said, pointing east. "If the wind changes, it could git here pretty quick. Might be a good idee for you and the boys to come over and stay with me and Maw until it burns itself out."

Cora refilled Grady's cup and poured one for herself. The Shields' place was a mile west of the farm. A mile wasn't much, but it was something.

"If it gets this far," she said, "what's to stop it from burnin' your place, too?"

Grady nodded, thinking. "I was in town yesterday, stopped at Pack's Store to get Maw a tin of snuff. Buford Pack said there's talk of gettin' some men together to fight the blaze before it burns up the whole valley. I can't rightly see how a handful of men can stand much chance of stopping a mountain fire from burning whatever it wants. But I told Maw, if need be, I'll be right in there with 'em."

He stopped and took a swig of coffee. "Don't worry, Cora, we'll be all right," he said. Then he looked out the window. "As long as the wind don't change."

Two days later, the wind changed. It came blowing hard out of the east, hot and foul as the devil's breath, sweeping across the valley. Cora stood at the kitchen window watching the smoke boil up in great black clouds that blocked out the sun and rolled over the ridge toward the farm. She knew the flames couldn't be far behind. Where was Grady and why hadn't he showed up yet to do the milking and . . . just then, she saw it, the first lick of flame lapping over the top of the ridge, less than a half mile away.

Lord, help us! Her mind raced. She sent the boys to the barn to start freeing the animals, to drive the cows down to the creek and turn the chickens and hogs out of their pens. She was harnessing up the mule to the wagon, getting ready to take her boys and a few belongings down to the Shields' place, when she heard a caravan of pickups coming up the road. The first truck stopped in front of the farmhouse and a half dozen men jumped off the back carrying axes and picks and shovels and hoes, whatever they could carry to start digging a fire break.

"Howdy, Cora!" Leroy Barnette climbed out of the driver's seat, took one last drag on his cigarette, and stubbed it out with his boot. "Looks like a mighty fine day to fight a fire!"

The last time Cora had seen Leroy was at a square dance a year before she was married. He had finally worked up the nerve that night to ask her to dance, but she had turned him down. She had never forgotten the beating Leroy gave Grady that day walking home from school. Leroy remembered it, too, standing there on the road, seeing the look on her face.

A gust of wind brought the smell of smoke, and Cora held out her hand.

"Leroy, I'm surprised to see you here. I'm grateful to you for showing up."

He took her hand and nodded. "I've done some things I'm not proud of, Cora. Things I regret. But I'm not about to let you lose your home if I can stop it."

Grabbing a shovel from the truck, he turned and headed up the mountain.

Five more trucks pulled up, each carrying a load of men and tools and determination. Jubal arrived with three off-duty deputies from neighboring counties. Finally, Grady came driving up alone, armed with a hoe and a saw and a couple of pound cakes that Ada had sent to share with the men.

"Wait for me!" Grady yelled. "I gotta go milk them cows!"

"Never mind, Grady!" Frank Jr. called. "Me and James already milked 'em!"

Grady looked at him red-faced. "You did? Well, all right then. Maw made me wait for them pound cakes to finish baking and . . ."

Jubal wasted no time getting started, dispatching men in teams of four or five to move up the ridge and start clearing brush and cutting trees, hoping to starve the fire of fuel and force it to burn itself out, or at least, persuade it to move in a less deadly direction.

"Grady!" Jubal called. "I want you to stay with me! Stay close!"

Grady took a step, then turned back to look at Cora.

"Go on, Grady," she said, "I'll be all right." He nodded and trotted up the hill.

Jubal would be the first to admit it. The plan to clear a fire break didn't stand much chance of working. But it was all they could do. And for men like Jubal and the others who volunteered that day to risk their lives defending a neighbor, it was always better to do something, anything, than stand around scratching your crotch.

They chopped and hacked and dug and sawed for eight grueling hours, trading off to take breaks to relieve themselves or wolf down a plate of Cora's cornbread and beans, and drink a few sloshing ladles of cold spring water.

Frank Jr. and James Harlan insisted they were old enough to work alongside the men. They begged Cora to let them help, but she refused to let them go near the fire line. Instead, she put them to work with Andrew, hauling drinking water from the creek for the men.

Andrew was furious at being relegated to what he deemed a menial task. Ten minutes into it, he threw down his bucket and stomped up the steps to the kitchen to voice his complaint.

"Mama, I'm plumb wore out from filling buckets! I can help fight that fire, and you ought to let me!"

Cora lifted a skillet of cornbread from the oven, set it on the stove and pushed her hair back from her forehead.

"Drew, do not test me today. You will go nowhere near that fire line. Stay at the creek, fill the buckets and hand them to your brothers. Do you understand me?"

"Don't call me Drew! Drew's a baby's name! My name is Andrew!"

"Andrew McCallum! I am your mother and I will call you what I please!"

"Fine!"

"I beg your pardon?"

He rolled his eyes. "Yes, ma'am."

She waited.

"Sorry, Mama," he said finally.

"That's more like it. Now get on down to the creek."

He clomped down the steps and started filling buckets and throwing rocks at his brothers.

Two hours later, the fire jumped the line. All day they had fought it, summoning a strength they didn't know they had, in a back-breaking, bone-wearying, beautiful effort, trying desperately to clear a swath of land to stop the fire's advance. Yet it inched ever closer, crawling over the ridge and down the side of the mountain, relentlessly burning its way to the farm.

Before it jumped the line, the fire began hurling embers that flew on the wind like grenades, landing in thickets or trees that moments later would explode into flame, and forcing the men to begin their retreat. Cora spotted a blaze in the yard and hurried over to stomp it out. When the hem of her skirt suddenly caught fire, Jubal came running across the road to throw himself upon her, rolling over her on the ground to tamp out the flames. Then he pulled her to her feet, put his hands on her shoulders, and looked into her eyes.

"It's time, Cora. I'm sorry. We've got to get you and your boys out of here."

Cora stared at him, shaking her head. When a giant cedar across the road burst into flame, she turned and ran back in the house to gather up—what? She took what she could, lifting her skirt like a sack to carry it: three photos—one of her parents, one of her and Frank on their wedding day, one of her boys when Andrew was a baby; her father's Bible, her mother's shawl, and her grandmother's crystal vase from the window sill in the kitchen. She stood for a moment in the doorway, looking back at the only home she had ever known, had ever wanted to know. Then she ran out on the porch, calling for her boys.

Out on the road, the men had started pulling back, climbing into the trucks. Jubal was shouting and waving his arms, trying to direct their sudden retreat.

In the smoke and fear and agony of defeat, no one had noticed the unnatural phenomenon taking place in the heavens above them. On the western horizon, a fierce, black line of magnificent clouds with beautiful, iridescent wings had risen up, as if out of nowhere, soaring silently across the sky to confront the deadly conflagration on the ridge, like an army of God's angels rushing into battle against the demons of hell.

A bolt of lightning split the air. Thunder shook the earth, echoing on the mountains. Cora looked up and felt a cool drop of rain slide down her cheek. Suddenly, the heavens opened and poured out on the Earth a deluge unlike any that anyone could recall, pounding every flame, every spark, every ember, until they hissed and sputtered and died.

The men jumped down from the trucks, dancing for joy, slapping one another's backs, slipping and falling and rolling in the mud like boys at play and shouting, "Thanks be to God!"

No one could explain it. No one tried. Who can explain a miracle?

Cora and Jubal looked at each other, laughing, soaked to the skin, too stunned for words. When the creek began to gush, Cora turned, scanning the bank for her boys. Finally she spotted James and Frank Jr. standing together, buckets in hand, staring drop-jawed at . . . what? She followed their gaze. Then her jaw dropped, too.

On the footbridge over the now raging creek, Andrew was a sight to behold. He had stripped down to his undershorts, painted his face with axle grease, stuck a fistful of wild turkey feathers in his nappy blond curls, and was jumping side to side, round and round, back and forth. With one hand, he wielded a makeshift tomahawk. With the other, he kept slapping his mouth, chanting something Cora couldn't quite hear above the rain and the roar of the creek.

No matter. She knew. "Drew," she whispered.

"Cora?" Jubal squinted through the downpour. "What in God's name is Andrew doing?"

She pushed her sopping wet hair off her face. "I believe, if you ask him, he'll tell you he's doing a traditional Cherokee rain dance."

They stood in the downpour watching Andrew hoop and whirl.

"I saw his daddy do that once," Jubal said.

"What? You saw Frank McCallum dance like that?"

"Yeah. After he'd had a little too much 'shine."

Cora laughed. "Drew doesn't need moonshine. He's wild at heart."

Down at the creek, Frank Jr. and James had thrown down their buckets to mimic their brother's moves, whooping and laughing hysterically.

"Next time we get a dry spell," Jubal said, "let's get Andrew to dance a little sooner."

15

THE WATCHER

On the hill twenty yards from her window, beneath the limbs of a low-spreading hemlock, he sat alone in the dark, in a cold steady rain, smoking a cigarette and watching her read. Earlier that evening, he had huddled beneath the window, straining to hear, as she read aloud to her boys—the two older ones lying sprawled on the floor, the younger one sitting curled up in her lap sucking his thumb and pulling on her ear.

The rain melted her words, so he could barely make them out. But just the sound of her voice, rising and falling on the wind, stirred something inside of him.

An hour ago, she had put the boys to bed. Now she sat alone by the fire reading a different book, head bent low, firelight licking copper strands in her hair.

He liked watching her hands—how she held the book, the way she turned its pages. They were good hands, he thought, a mountain woman's hands, strong as a hickory, tender as snowfall. How would it feel to have those hands hold him?

He heard the clock on her mantel begin striking nine. She stood, closing the book, marking her place. The lantern light moved from room to room as she looked in on the boys in their beds. Then a door opened at the back of the house and she emerged, carrying the lantern aloft with one hand, holding a shawl above her head. He stubbed out his cigarette and watched, hardly breathing, as she made her way down a muddy path to the outhouse.

Seconds later, she was back, hurrying up the steps, stopping at the top to scrape her shoes. Then, as if someone had called her name, she slowly turned and stared up at the hill.

He drew back into the tree, cutting his lip on a limb. The tree shook like a wet dog, dousing him in an icy shower. He shuddered, licked his lips, tasted blood. Water trickled down his spine, bristling the hair on his arms. He blinked to clear his eyes. She was still standing on the porch holding the lantern, peering into the night.

"Blue!"

A hound crawled out from under the porch and ambled up the steps. She opened the screen door and bent down to dry the dog's ears and muddy paws with a rag. Then she stepped back and the dog trotted inside and curled up on the porch.

Minutes later, the house went dark.

He closed his eyes and let out a slow breath. He tried to picture her sleeping alone in her bed, her long copper hair spilling in waves across her pillow. He could almost smell the scent of her skin and taste the sweat on her neck.

What would it be like to hold her—a woman like that? How would it feel to wake up some cold winter morning to find himself tangled up in her arms?

How exactly could a broken man like him ever get to be that blessed?

A drop of water fell from his nose and splashed on his lip, stinging the cut.

Most nights, it was enough just to watch her. He was content with that, for now. But someday, he thought, maybe soon, he just might get the nerve to pay her a courting call.

16

SHELTER

"*M*ama?"

Andrew stood by Cora's bed in his long johns, yanking on her nightgown. She rolled over, squinting. His curls looked like a halo, backlit by the moon.

"Go on back to bed, son. If you're cold, get yourself another quilt."

"I ain't cold, Mama. I'm scared. They's something outside the house."

Andrew had nightmares. They had started soon after his daddy was killed. Sometimes Cora would wake to find the boy curled up against her, shaking like a poplar in the wind, with his thumb jammed in his mouth. It had been two years now, going on three. How long would it last?

"It's just a 'possum, baby. Now go on back to sleep."

Andrew slapped the mattress. "No, Mama, it ain't no 'possum. It's big! Blue was barkin' at it and then he quit. I think it ate him!"

Cora sighed and swung her legs off the bed. Pulling Andrew close, she pressed a hand to his forehead to check for fever. He felt cool to the touch, but the hair at the back of his neck was soaked in sweat. The house had gone cold.

She rose to go out to the front room to stoke the wood stove, then padded back to the bedroom, with Andrew close on her heels. After the fire that summer, the fall had been wetter and colder than normal, as if trying to avoid another dry spell. It had rained so much that Andrew's brothers had started teasing him about doing a "no-rain dance." Andrew hated being teased, but he'd grown weary of the rain, and had been giving their suggestion some serious thought.

Another storm had rolled in around suppertime and Cora could hear the creek rushing nearly out of its banks. Suddenly she stopped and turned her head to listen.

"See, Mama!" Drew hissed. "I told you something's out there! You heard it, didn't you?"

She pulled the boy into the folds of her nightgown and stared into the darkness, letting her senses adjust to the night. Raindrops pattered on the tin roof. In the distance, a barn owl called to its mate. On the hill . . . wait . . . what was that?

Boots on the back steps—heavy soles, trying to tread light.

Where was Blue? Why wasn't he barking?

A board creaked on the porch. Move, Cora. Now!

Andrew started to speak and she covered his mouth with her hand, pressing her lips against his ear. "Stay close to me and don't make a sound!"

The cedar wardrobe that had belonged to her mother stood in the corner of her bedroom by the door. Cora reached inside of it, pushed away her wedding dress, and pulled out Frank's shotgun. She had hidden it there after Frank died, for fear Drew might find it and decide to shoot his brothers. It felt heavier now than she recalled. She turned to take Andrew's hand.

"Wait, Mama," Andrew whispered, patting her arm. "You need the bullets. They're down in the bottom by Daddy's old shoes. I'll get 'em for you."

Shaken from a dead sleep, James and Frank Jr. rubbed their eyes at a sight they would not soon forget: their mother stood beside their bed in her nightgown, her hair loose and wild, holding a shotgun. Drew stood next to her clutching his crotch to keep from wetting himself.

"Get up, boys!" he hissed. "Mama's gonna shoot some bastard!"

Cora grabbed the neck of Drew's long johns and squashed his mouth against her belly. She held him there until he stopped squirming. Then she motioned for the boys to be silent and follow her. The bedroom faced the creek on the east side of the house. She leaned the shotgun against the wall, eased open the window, and turned to Frank Jr.

"Take your brothers," she said. "Go along the creek bank and hide under the hemlock. Do not come back, no matter what, until I tell you to do so. You hear?"

James shook his head. "We ain't leaving here without you, Mama."

From the kitchen came a sound. The back door was rattling on its hinges.

"I'll be right behind you, James, I swear. Now go!" She pushed them toward the window. Frank Jr. climbed through first. James followed. Then Cora lifted Andrew and handed him out to his brothers, pulling her sleeve free from his fist.

"Hurry!" she whispered. The older boys grabbed their brother and ran together half crouching toward the creek. Cora waited, holding the shotgun, watching her boys' shadows in the moonlight until they dropped over the creek bank out of sight. Out in the kitchen, she heard voices, low and urgent. Two men, maybe three.

There was a time in her life when she was sure that she could never harm a living soul, even to save herself. That time had ended eleven years ago, as surely as if it had never existed, the day she was chopping wood and felt deep within her belly a flutter—that wondrous, fearsome, quickening of life. She had stood there with an ax poised above her head, marveling at two revelations: First, she realized that she was with child. And second, she knew beyond a doubt she'd do anything necessary to protect that child. If need be, she would kill with her bare hands.

Cora looked at her hands holding the shotgun. They were shaking. She would need to steady them to . . . Oh god, the bullets! Andrew had taken them with him!

She heard the boots again, heavier this time, coming down the hallway.

God in Heaven, she prayed, tell me what to do! On the dresser in the moonlight, she caught a glimpse of Frank's face staring up at her from their wedding portrait. Hoisting her nightgown, she leaned out the window, placed the shotgun on the ground and climbed out after it, gouging her thigh on the hydrangea. Grabbing the gun, she bolted to the creek and slid feet first down the muddy bank.

For a moment, she lay still, letting the dampness seep into the back of her skull, feeling her heart, like a caged bird, trying to claw its way free from her chest. The clouds suddenly parted, opening like a curtain, and the moon gazed down upon her. Finally, when she could breathe, she rolled over on her belly, prayed again for God's deliverance, and forced her eyes to look back at the house.

Someone had lit a lantern and was carrying it from room to room. She could hear voices cursing and arguing. Doors slamming. Glass breaking.

She looked up the hill at the hemlock. No sign of her boys. Her feet lay ankle-deep in the creek, numb with cold. She pulled them out and tried to dry them on her nightgown. Then she began to crawl along the creek bank, flat on her belly, digging her elbows into the mud, holding the shotgun with one hand over her head, glancing back over her shoulder to be sure she wasn't being followed.

The lowest branches of the hemlock began some six feet from the base, reaching out in a graceful arc, then curving down to touch the earth, forming a thick, fragrant canopy, a haven from wind or rain or harm. Beneath those branches, Cora found her boys. When Andrew saw his mother, he pulled his thumb from his mouth and began to cry. With a muddy fist, he handed her the box of shotgun shells.

Cora cupped his face in her hands. "Thank you, Drew, for keeping them safe."

She passed the box of shells, along with the shotgun, to Frank Jr.

"Load that for me, will you, son?"

He did. As he handed it back to Cora, James caught hold of the barrel.

"Give it to me, Mama," James said.

In the moonlight through the branches, Cora saw the still-water green of his eyes. His face was that of an eight-year-old boy, but his voice and the will behind it belonged to his father.

"Let me and Frank Jr. go down there," he said. "We'll make them sons-a-bitches sorry they ever set foot on our land."

Andrew popped his thumb out of his mouth and shook his head hard. "Don't let him do it, Mama. I saw them bastards. They's bad!"

Cora took the shotgun and placed it on the ground at her side.

"James Harlan," she said quietly, using his full name to make it clear he was not to argue. "Those men and their evil ways would be no match for you and your brother. They'll get their just rewards. But right now, I need you here with me."

She opened her arms and gathered them in, rocking them softly, rhythmically, as she had done so often when they were babies, humming in their ears a hymn she'd learned from her father: "Be still my soul, the Lord is on Thy side."

They huddled there, the four of them, on a carpet of fallen needles that the hemlock had spent its lifetime weaving just for them, while three men desecrated their home. Morning would come soon. They would wait.

"Mama?" Andrew was half asleep, his face pressed into the curve of her neck.

"What, darlin'?"

"When we was running from the house, I called Blue, but he didn't come. Frank Jr. said he reckoned one of them men had cut his throat."

A gust of wind shook the hemlock, spattering raindrops on their heads.

Cora pulled the boys closer, hunching her shoulders to cover them.

"Go to sleep, Drew," she said. She buried her face in the sweet, sweaty smell of his curls and waited, fighting the words, feeling them claw at her throat, until she could hold them back no longer. Sooner or later, truth always prevails.

"Drew," she said finally, "I believe Old Blue has left us. I believe he's gone off hunting with your daddy."

Jubal Avery had lived all his life in those mountains, as had four generations of his family before him. His daddy, Walter, had been sheriff for some forty years until the day Old Walt, as folks liked to call him, tried to wrestle with Bayliss Howard. Bayliss, as usual, was sloppy drunk on moonshine, kicking like a mule and refusing to be locked up. Walt could have used his stick to persuade him, but he wasn't that kind of lawman. He got hold of Bayliss' overalls to drag him into a cell and promptly keeled over dead with a heart attack. When Jubal stopped by the jail to take his daddy a ham sandwich, he found Bayliss on the floor holding Walt in his arms and bawling like a branded calf. Some said Bayliss was guilty of murder, and there was even talk of stringing him up. Jubal wouldn't stand for it. Bayliss was a drunk, he said, and a dumb one at that, but he had meant Old Walt no harm. Stupidity was not the same as malice.

Bayliss was so overcome—so slain in the spirit by such unfathomable grace—that he quit drinking, and instead, started preaching the Word of God, testifying to the grace and the gift of salvation.

Jubal had no interest in being sheriff. But he knew how much it would mean to his father to have his only son follow in his boots. So Jubal had agreed to wear the star that had been pinned on Walt's chest on the day Jubal was born. In his time as sheriff, Jubal had seen his fill of ignorance and meanness—stabbings and shootings and fistfights that almost always involved liquor or jealousy or pride. Men would fight at the drop of a hat over cards or mules or women.

Jubal had seen it all, or so he thought, until this night. He and Margaret had just fallen asleep when they were awakened by a fist pounding at the door.

"Lord have mercy!" Margaret sat up in bed. "Who can that be at this hour?"

Jubal rolled out of bed in his long johns and grabbed his pistol off the dresser.

"Stay here, Margaret. Get the shotgun out of the closet, but don't come out."

Opening the door, Jubal was stunned to see eighty-year-old Albert Collins standing on the porch, gasping for air.

"Put your britches on, Jubal," Albert wheezed, "and bring your pistol. Be quick about it. We need to get on out to the Searcy place."

It was still dark when Jubal and Albert drove up to the Searcy farm. The barn was smoldering, the air thick with smoke. Some neighbors—Albert's wife Lula, and the Adams from across the hollow—were in the house tending to the family.

Bill Searcy lay on the floor, bleeding from a stab wound in his belly. His wife Bernice sat at the table, staring at nothing, with her arms locked around her two little girls, their sobs muffled against her breast. A trickle of blood ran down Bernice's leg and pooled on the floor around her bare feet.

Albert motioned Jubal to follow him out on the porch.

"Lula saw the flames when she got up to go the outhouse. We got here quick as we could. I sent my grandson to get Doc Owens, but I doubt Bill will last until he gets here. Bernice is hurt bad, too. She said the three men that busted in on 'em was wearing stripes like convicts. Bill was going for his shotgun when they stabbed him. Bernice told Lula . . . well, I'll just say it. They had their evil way with her. When they left, she looked out and saw 'em driving away."

"Which direction?" Jubal said.

Albert nodded. "Thataway, toward the McCallum place."

Jubal stared down the road into the darkness, trying not to see what he feared. Then he turned and laid a hand on Albert's stooped shoulder.

"Albert," he said, "I'm deputizing you. Get yourself some good men—no hotheads or fools—just men you can trust. Tell 'em I said they're deputized, too. Then you boys spread out and start looking. I'm going to see about Cora McCallum."

The day they met, nearly fifteen years ago, Jubal had taken an instant liking to Frank McCallum. They had worked side by side on the logging crew, and often fished together when they could. In time, they became more like brothers than friends. When Frank fell hard for Cora, Jubal kept his own feelings for her to himself. Looking back on it now, he had no regrets. He'd been best man at Frank's wedding, godfather to his boys, a pallbearer at his funeral, and he had missed him every day since. On Saturdays he often stopped by the farm, bringing a pie that Margaret had baked for them. He and Cora would visit for a bit, then he'd take the boys fishing, piling them in the back of his pickup along with Blue, Frank's old dog. Blue was a hunting dog, but Frank had taught him to like fishing.

Thinking about Frank's family made Jubal's heart pound in fear of what might have befallen them. Turning onto the road to the farm, he gunned the engine, felt the pickup fishtail on the gravel, and prayed, "Please, God in Heaven, let no harm come to Cora and her boys!"

17

Morning

*A*t daybreak, under the hemlock. Cora woke from a fitful sleep, startled by a distant sound. A car, or maybe a pickup, was coming fast up the mountain, wheels spitting gravel on the road. She sat up and eased herself out of the tangle of her boys' arms and legs. James and Frank Jr. were sleeping, limp as dishrags. Andrew stirred and she helped him find his thumb.

Lifting a branch, she looked out on the dawn of a new day. The farmhouse sat dark and still. Across the valley, the sun's first rays were spilling over the mountain, dimming the last of the morning stars. The moon was a smoke ring on the western sky. Out in the pasture, the cows were ambling up to the barn, hoping to be milked. Birds gathered at the feeder, hungry for Cora's cornbread, chattering like churchgoers at a potluck. She closed her eyes and whispered, "This is the day the Lord hath made. We will rejoice and be glad in it."

Suddenly, headlights swung around the bend, sweeping a beacon across the yard. Cora ran stumbling toward the road, waving her arms. When he saw her, Jubal hit the brakes hard, jumped out of the truck and ran to meet her.

"Jubal!" Cora fell weeping into his arms. "Some men broke in on us!"

"Are you all right, Cora? Did they hurt you? Where are the boys?"

"No, I'm not hurt. The boys are asleep up there," she said, nodding toward the hemlock. "We've been hiding under that tree for hours. We got out of the house just in time before they . . ." She covered her mouth with her hand.

"Are they gone?" he asked.

"Lord, I hope so! I heard a car drive off about an hour ago."

She told him everything, start to finish. Then she broke down again.

Jubal pulled her close and held her, whispering in her ear, "It's over, Cora. You did good. You saved your boys."

When she finally stopped shaking, he checked his pistol and told her to stay by the pickup while he went inside to go room by room through the house.

"Wait," she said. "You'll find Blue somewhere around back. There's a shovel by the basement door. I'd appreciate you burying him before my boys see him."

Jubal nodded and headed to the house. Twenty minutes later, he was back.

"You were right about Blue," he said. "I buried him down by the pond."

They stood for a long moment, looking out across the valley. The sun was hitting the river, lighting it up like a silver thread.

"Cora," Jubal said, "I've got some hard news. It's about the Searcys."

James awoke with a start to find Andrew's muddy foot in his face and realized that his mother was missing. Bolting up, he parted the branches and saw her standing by the road with Jubal. She was crying into her hands.

"Mama!"

Cora wiped her face. "I'm all right, James! Stay up there with your brothers!"

Jubal pulled a handkerchief from his shirt pocket, handed it to Cora, then looked back at the house. "It's a mess in there," he said. "I'll help you clean it up."

Cora shook her head. "No, you go take care of the Searcys. We'll manage."

She gave him back his handkerchief.

"Listen to me, Cora," he said. "Those men escaped from the county jail. They stole a car and we think they're probably headed toward Asheville. But they're not coming back here. That's for sure. We've got half the men in this valley out looking for them. We'll find them. I promise you'll never have to see them again."

Cora nodded and pressed her hand to Jubal's face. "Go on now," she said.

As he started the pickup, she waved for him to wait.

"Jubal?" she said. "I found cigarette butts under the hemlock. They didn't look very fresh, but do you think those men might've left them?"

Jubal looked up the hill. The McCallum boys had crawled out from under the tree and stood side by side, scratching themselves and watching their mother.

Jubal grinned. "Those men were on the run, Cora. I doubt they'd be smokin' in that tree. You might want to ask your boys what they have to say about it."

Cora made the boys wait out on the porch while she walked through the house alone. It wasn't as bad as she feared. Drawers had been emptied and the contents were strewn from room to room. Mattresses were overturned. A jug of moonshine that Frank had kept in a cupboard for special occasions lay empty on the floor.

In the kitchen, a ham hock had been gnawed to the bone and left lying on the floor, like the work of some mongrel dog. On the table, a jar that had held two dozen pickled eggs lay shattered, with no eggs in sight, filling the air with a sharp, sulfurous smell. Cora gagged and threw up in a dishpan. She had always loved pickled eggs. She would never eat them again.

The clock on the mantel had stopped at twenty minutes to three. Cora opened the casing and moved the hands to half past six, waiting while it struck each hour and half-hour. The last time that clock had stopped was the day Frank died. She had stopped it then herself, unable to bear the sound of its ticking until Frank was laid to rest. Now, as then, she tapped the pendulum and watched in wonder as, once again, time began.

"Boys!" she called, "you can come on in now. We've got work to do."

They were hungry, but hunger could wait. Food would taste better without the stench of pickled eggs and evil men in their nostrils.

She desperately needed to reclaim her home, to rid it of every trace of desecration, and restore it to what it had always been for her, a haven of safety and comfort and belonging. She knew her boys needed that, too. So she sent Frank Jr. and James to milk the cows, feed the animals, and gather the eggs. She told Andrew his job was to pick things up and put them back where they belonged. Then she tackled the kitchen, scrubbing the table, the floor, every inch of every space.

"Mama?" Andrew stood in the doorway. "I'm gonna go find Blue."

Cora looked up, then froze. Andrew was holding the loaded shotgun.

"Put the gun down, son," she said quietly, "right there on the floor. Frank Jr. will unload it. Then you can put it in the wardrobe. We won't be needing it again."

Andrew's lip began to quiver. "But I want to go look for Blue! And those men might be out there and I might have to shoot 'em!"

Cora tried to breathe. "Those men are gone, Drew. Put down the gun. Then you and I will go find Blue together."

Two hours later, with their home and their lives back in some measure of order, Cora and her boys sat down to a breakfast of ham and grits, biscuits and gravy.

"Who will give thanks for God's bounty?" Cora asked, as always.

"I will," said Andrew, and his brothers bowed their heads.

"Dear Lord," he began, "thank you for this meal that our mama has prepared. And thank you that she didn't have to shoot one of them b . . . I mean, one of them bad men. Thank you for Blue, for the fine dog he was. That's all I've got to say, God. Amen."

For the first time that day, Cora smiled.

"Thank you, Andrew," she said. "That might be the best prayer I ever heard."

She watched while the boys ate their fill, and then indulged them with extra molasses for their biscuits. Andrew finished first, as usual. When he asked to be excused from the table, she said, "Not yet, son. We need to talk first."

Pushing back her plate, she leaned on the table and studied her boys.

"Those men who broke into our home last night were desperate men," she said, "and they did desperate things. But there are two things you need to remember. First, they were no match for us. The Lord was with us, and we outsmarted them. You boys were brave. I am proud of you. And your daddy would be proud of you, too. The second thing to remember is this: those men are never coming back here. Jubal has a lot of deputies out looking for them. He promised they will find them. And Jubal Avery keeps his promises. We know that, don't we?"

James and Frank Jr. nodded. Andrew kept stabbing a biscuit with his fork.

"So we have nothing to fear from those men ever again," she said. "This is our home. We are safe here. Do you understand what I'm saying?"

All three boys said, "Yes, ma'am." Andrew asked, "Can we go now?"

"One more thing. I want to know what you know about those cigarette butts."

James and Frank Jr. traded a quick look. Andrew bit his lip the way he always did when he was trying not to say something that would get him in trouble.

Frank Jr. spoke first. "Mama, we've been finding 'em up there ever since Daddy died. Once or twice a week. They're rolled the same way Daddy rolled his."

"I saw that," Cora said. "Can you tell me how they get there?"

Drew could not contain himself. "Frank Jr. said Daddy puts 'em there to show us that he's watching over us, but I said, no, ghosts don't smoke 'cause Jesus won't let 'em! I think Frank Jr. only said that about Daddy 'cause him and James like to smoke them butts, but they won't let me smoke 'em, and that ain't fair!"

Frank Jr. narrowed his eyes. "Shut your mouth, you big baby, or I'll bust it!"

"Frank Jr.!" Cora said. "You will do nothing of the kind."

Andrew puffed up like a toad. "I ain't no baby!"

"Not another word from either of you," Cora said. She looked across the table. James was studying his fork. She knew he couldn't tell a lie to save his soul.

"James Harlan?" she said. "What have you to say about this?"

James put down his fork and lifted his face squarely to meet hers.

"It's like this, Mama. We find 'em there, OK? We find 'em, and sometimes we smoke 'em. But we've got no idea about how they get there."

Cora sat for minute, thinking. Then she pushed her chair back from the table.

"All right," she said. "I want you all to hear me, and hear me good. From now on, you are not to go anywhere near that tree. No excuses. Stay away from it. If you test me, you'll see I mean business. Moreover, you are not for any reason allowed to smoke. Smoking is a man's business. It's not for boys. At least, not for my boys. What worries me the most is not the smokin', but the sneakin'. You would never tell a lie to my face. I know that. But if you do things behind my back, it's the same as lying. Your daddy liked to say that a man is only as good as his word. You are good boys. And you come from good people. You don't sneak and you don't lie. Can you try to remember that?"

"Yes, ma'am," they mumbled.

"I will count on it," she said. "Do you have anything else you want to say?"

"Sorry, Mama," said James.

"Sorry, Mama," said Frank Jr.

Andrew glared at his brothers.

Cora raised an eyebrow. "Drew?"

"Sorry, Mama. But please don't call me Drew. My name is Andrew!" He glared at his brothers. "And I ain't no stinkin' baby!"

PART II

1938–1945

18

LORETTA GETS LUCKY

*J*ustine Rollins didn't ask to grow up too soon. Little girls never do. It was forced upon her before she was even old enough to understand what was happening to her, by the men her mother brought into their lives, always hoping to find Mr. Right. They were never right, always wrong. The few that were halfway decent always left sooner or later. Loretta Rollins had a talent for making bad choices and taking up with bad men. She'd be the first to admit it. She liked to say she suffered dearly for it, and that was the truth. But her daughter suffered far more.

By some miracle, Justine survived the nightmare of those years. In time, she learned to turn the terror and pain and the sense of helplessness into a power that she would wield like a sword on everyone around her, though mostly on herself.

Folks were often mystified by the kind of sway Justine held over men and boys alike. Some blamed it on her looks—the curve of her cheekbones, the fire in her eyes, the music that played when she walked—as if it were her fault that God made her beautiful.

Others blamed it on her mama. Loretta had dragged her daughter from one mean drunk to the next. The child never got a chance to sink roots. But roots weren't the whole story. Loretta had been

119

dragged around and beaten on her whole life, too. It was all she knew. Nobody ever bothered to tell her the God's honest truth: she and her daughter deserved better.

By the time Justine was fourteen, weary of running from the sweaty clutches of Loretta's men, she gave up trying to be her mother's savior, and started looking for her own salvation. She would search long and hard in some dark and dangerous places. But the day would come when a light would dawn, and she'd believe with all her heart she had found it—a life worth living—with James McCallum.

In the fall of 1938, Loretta was waiting tables at a coffee shop near Asheville, living with a short-fused breakfast cook named Harold. Harold had a temper, but he was not the worst man Loretta had ever tangled up with. Not even close. In the six months they'd been together, Harold had never once tried to mess with Justine. At least, as far as Loretta knew. She had to give him that. And he hardly ever beat on them, except when he was drinkin', which was mostly just on his days off, when he didn't have to get up and go to work.

But one morning at the restaurant, Harold was taking a break, eating a plate of his own biscuits and gravy, when he made a serious mistake. He took a long sideways glance at the generous backside of a recently hired waitress, Peggy Jo, who had already been getting on Loretta's last nerve. Unfortunately for Harold, Loretta saw him do it, knew exactly what he was thinking, and proceeded to dump a pot of steaming coffee in his lap. In addition to ending their relationship, it got Loretta fired, and put a surefire damper on Harold's manhood.

Justine came home that day from ninth grade to find Loretta red-faced and puffy-eyed, sucking on a Lucky Strike and stuffing her clothes into a flour sack.

"Git yer stuff," Loretta said, "we're movin' on."

"Mama," Justine said, slowly, "I've got school."

"Not for long, you won't," said Loretta. "Not if you want to keep eatin'. Hell, girl, I don't care, suit yourself! Go with me or stay in this hellhole with Harold! Either way, I'm leavin'."

Justine set her schoolbooks on the table and picked up an empty flour sack.

"Where to?"

"Don't know. And it don't matter. We'll find out when we get there."

Loretta had six dollars to her name and some loose change from her tip money. She started rummaging behind couch cushions and in the pockets of some overalls that Harold had left on the floor. Suddenly she stopped rummaging and cocked her head, like a cat ready to pounce on a gopher. Then she ran back in the bedroom and shouted "Hoowee!"

Harold kept a stash under the mattress. He was dumb enough to think Loretta was too dumb to find it. She came out of the bedroom waving a wad of cash like a victory flag.

"This is gonna hurt him a helluva lot worse than that whole pot of hot coffee!"

Harold drove a pickup, but kept an old Plymouth parked in back of the trailer. He said he saved the Plymouth for "special occasions," which, as Loretta liked to say, meant "never."

"He don't need two vehicles." She winked at Justine. "We'll take the Plymouth."

They gassed it up and got out of town twenty minutes before Harold got home from the doctor, where he'd had his private parts treated for third degree burns. Harold was hurtin' bad—about as bad as he'd ever hurt—but mostly, he was hoppin' mad, foaming at the mouth, pulling like a rabid dog on a chain to settle up the score with Loretta.

The first thing he noticed was the missing Plymouth. Then he waddled on up to the trailer and saw that Loretta and Justine had taken, not just their own stuff, but some of his, too. Then he waddled even faster back to the bedroom, making little moaning sounds, to find the mattress flipped off the bed, and all his money gone.

Harold nearly had a stroke over that. The only thing that stopped him from taking off after them like a bat out of hell was the unbearable thought of having to sit on a plastic seat cover in the pickup, possibly for hours, on his third-degree-burnt private parts.

Loretta had hoped the scalding would slow Harold down some, and in more ways than one. In years to come, she would laugh, telling the story to anybody who'd listen, of how a pot of coffee and an old Plymouth had spared her a beating and put her on the road to a better life.

They drove for six solid hours, all the way to Raleigh, putting as many miles as possible between them and Harold before stopping at a diner to order ham and grits. They took a booth by the window to keep an eye out, just in case, in the off chance that Harold's temper might somehow manage to overrule the pain in his privates.

In the next booth, facing Loretta, an older gentleman sat alone dressed in a black suit, as if he had just been to funeral. Which, it turned out, he had.

Loretta struck up a conversation, as she was wont to do, and invited him to come join them at their table. Justine looked down at her plate. She had finished half of the ham and grits. She slid out of the booth and offered the man her seat.

"Excuse me, sir," she said. "Mama? I'll be in the car."

On her way out, she heard Loretta nattering on about being on "vacation."

Justine climbed in the backseat of the Plymouth, pushed a couple of sacks of Loretta's clothes down onto the floorboard, stretched out as best she could, and fell asleep. Two hours later, she awoke with a start when the driver's side door flew open and her mother jumped in behind the steering wheel.

"Jackpot!" Loretta shouted, lighting up a Lucky Strike. "Wake up, Justine, you are never gonna believe our luck!"

His name was William Mason, though Loretta called him Bill. A widower and a retired bank manager, Bill had been to a funeral in Raleigh for his brother, Ted, Bill's last living kin, except for a few distant cousins and a grown son he'd lost touch with some years ago. Bill had stopped at the diner for a bite to eat before going back to the motel next door, where he planned to stay the night before getting up early to drive six hours to home the next day.

"He's just the sweetest thing!" Loretta said, dangling the cigarette from her lips as she backed the Plymouth out and drove toward the motel next door. "He lost his wife to cancer a while back, bless his heart! I forget how long he said it's been. Anyway, you can just tell the poor old feller is all eat up inside with lonely!"

Loretta had told Bill her whole story, she said, except for a few unnecessary details, such as the coffee shop incident and Harold's scalded crotch.

"I just told him I was between jobs, which is basically half true, pretty much, and he didn't ask a whole lot of questions. I think he was just hungry for somebody to talk to. Anyhow, the more we talked, the more we hit it off, and finally, he offered me a deal! Oh, and listen to this, Justine: the man has got money to burn! He picked up the check for our supper, and right now, he's over at that fancy mo-tel next door renting us a room for the night!"

Justine rolled her eyes. "I'll sleep in the car. I ain't sleeping with you and him."

"Are you deaf, Justine? I told you, he's already got a room for hisself. He's gettin' a whole 'nother room just for me and you!"

Loretta squeezed the Plymouth into a parking space in front of the motel and flicked the Lucky Strike out the window. In the back seat, Justine sat in silence, watching her mother's eyes in the rearview mirror as Loretta primped, touching up her blood-red lipstick and fluffing up her tightly permed hair.

"All right, Mama," Justine said, finally. "I give up. What does he want?"

Their eyes met in the mirror.

"He's a man, Justine. What do you think he wants?"

Justine looked away.

"I don't know," she said. "He didn't strike me as, you know, that kind of man."

Loretta snorted. "Why? You mean 'cause he's old? Ha! Honey, that's a laugh! Take it from your mama, old goats are the worst!"

Justine crossed her arms, trying to stop a chill that was crawling up her spine.

"No, Mama, not 'cause he's old," she said. "Just 'cause he's . . . good."

"Oh, now you're the expert on men? Fine, Justine! He's a good old man or whatever the hell you want him to be. Let's just take what we can get and be glad to get it!"

"What kind of deal did he offer you, Mama?"

"Best I've had in a long old time! He needs somebody to cook and clean and keep him company. And we need a place to stay. Hell, Justine! It's a match made in Heaven!"

It was dark now, getting colder. A light came on in one of the motel rooms.

"What's the catch, Mama?"

"There is no catch, Justine! Can't you for once in your life just be happy for me? Now stop your whining and hand me one of them sacks! Which one did I put my red dress in?"

Justine rummaged through two sacks to find the red dress, then pushed both sacks over the seat. "Where, Mama? Where does he live?"

"What? Oh. He's got a real nice house with plenty of room. He said there's a school right up the road that you can go to, if you want. I told him how much you love school. You're always saying how you want to finish, don't you? Well, here's your chance!"

Justine sighed. "I don't mean his house. I mean his town. His state. His country. What planet does he live on?"

"Don't you get smart with me, Justine Rollins! I'll put your skinny butt out on the road and you can hitch yourself a ride and go live with crazy old Harold!"

"Mama, I'd just like to know, if you don't mind, where the hell we're going."

"Well, see, now that's the funny thing about it. Tomorrow morning, we'll be driving back on the road we came today. Not to Asheville, or nowhere near Harold. About thirty miles away from him. Bill lives near Brevard. Some place called Pisgah Forest."

That evening, in his motel room, Bill Mason lay wide-eyed awake wondering what in God's name had come over him? Never once in his seventy years had he ever done anything as imprudent, as flat-out hare-brained, as he had just done in that diner, inviting Loretta Rollins, if that was really her name, and her beautiful, angry daughter to come live with him.

Bill had no idea what made him do it. Was it his brother's funeral? He and Ted had never been all that close, but still. Losing Ted, the last of his family, was just one more pound of grief to add to the truckload Bill had been dragging around for three years, ever since Lois died. It surprised him sometimes how much he still missed her. People always said you don't know what you've got 'til it's gone. He understood that now. It's how he felt about Lois. How he wished that he had told her, while he still had the chance, how much she meant to him.

Before losing Lois, there'd been that riff with his son, Robert, that one final argument that ended it all. Robert had come home from college, all excited to tell them his news: he was quitting school, he said, and going to Nashville to play in a band.

"This is my chance, Daddy. I can feel it. I've got a place to stay and a job washing dishes. If I don't go, I'll always regret it. I'm leaving in the morning."

Bill couldn't believe it. The boy had always wanted to be something other than the kind of man Bill knew he could be. They'd never seen eye to eye on anything. But dropping out of college to go to Nashville to wash dishes and play in a band?

"Well, Robert, you've had some hare-brained ideas, but this one takes the cake. If you leave tomorrow, don't count on a penny or another word from me."

Bill thought that would end it, and it did, but not the way he hoped. The argument, like so many others in their past, caused them both to say things a father and son ought never say to each other. Most anything can be forgiven. But some words, once spoken, can't be taken back. They live in memory, playing over and over, inflicting the same pain, time and again. Robert didn't wait for morning. He stormed out that night, taking nothing but the guitar that his father hated.

For two years, until she grew too weak to walk, Lois would stand at the window, watching for the mailman, praying for a letter that never came.

Lying there that night, miles from home, thinking about Robert, Bill remembered something from the diner. It was the look he saw in the girl's brown eyes, when she slid from the booth to offer him her seat. "Excuse me, sir." She had spoken politely, but he saw it clearly, that flash of fire, that ready-to-bolt wariness of an animal that's been beaten so often it will bite any hand that tries to feed it.

Bill had seen that same look in Robert's eyes countless times over the years. He had never understood it until tonight in the diner, when it saw it in the girl. It was the look of someone who had been robbed of a birthright, something as precious and needed as water to drink and air to breathe: a sense of self-worth.

It pained him to face it, but there was no one else to blame. Bill knew that he had put that look in Robert's eyes, always wanting, always demanding that the boy needed to be different somehow than the way God had made him.

Bill would give anything to go back and change it. He had often written to Robert at the only address he had for him, not in Nashville, but in Chicago, where he had somehow ended up, and asked him for forgiveness, hoping for another chance. But his letters were never answered. It was too late, Bill realized, to change the past.

Too late for Robert. Too late for Lois. Too late for Bill to be the kind of husband and father and man that he ought to have been.

Was that it? Was that what caused him to lose his mind in the diner and open his heart to a couple of strangers on the run? Ever since Lois died, he had been asking himself why that good woman was gone and he was still here, still alive? He didn't deserve it. Somedays he didn't even want it. Why did he keep waking up each day in an empty house with no one to talk to, nothing to do and no place he needed to be?

He'd had a lot of time to think about it and he still didn't have an answer. But what if it wasn't as hard as he'd tried to make it? What if it was all just as simple as this: Some people live longer than others. Those who do, owe a debt to those who don't, not just to live, but to live well—no matter how old or broke or whatever you might be—to take each breath as a God-given gift, and try in return to breathe a little life back into the world.

Bill knew he couldn't change the past. But maybe, God willing, it wasn't too late to change a few things for that poor girl and her crazy mother.

On that thought, he turned his pillow over to the cool side and closed his eyes to try and get some sleep. He had a long, hard road ahead.

19

THE ROAD HOME

*T*he next morning, Justine was surprised to find Bill waiting for them in the diner, just as he had promised. She had halfway hoped, for his sake, that he'd come to his senses while he still had a chance and hightail it out of there without them.

"Good morning," he said smiling, rising respectfully from the booth as Loretta and Justine slid in to join him. "Thought you ladies might like breakfast before we get underway."

They ate sausage and eggs and biscuits and gravy while Loretta chattered nonstop. Justine noted that when Bill picked up the check, he left two dollars on the table, a generous tip. Then they got on the road in a mini-convoy with Bill in the lead in his new black Buick, followed by Loretta and Justine in Harold's old Plymouth.

Ten miles later, when the Plymouth broke down, Loretta insisted on leaving it right where it sat on the side of the road.

"It's been on its last legs too long," she said, batting her mascara-caked lashes at Bill. "Maybe it will help some poor soul who needs it more than I do."

They stopped twice to eat (Loretta had developed quite an appetite) and to gas up the Buick. It was almost dark by the time they pulled into Bill's driveway.

"Oh, my!" said Loretta, "it's a palace fit for a queen!"

It was not quite a palace, but it was, Justine decided, a nice home with three bedrooms, on a hill with a view of the river and the rolling blue mountains beyond.

Bill was proud to show them around. He put Justine and her sack of belongings in Robert's old room, and hauled all of Loretta's stuff into the guest room. Then he fried up some potatoes for their supper, with a can of Spam from the cupboard, and promised that tomorrow they could all go into town together to shop for groceries.

They ate in the dining room, three people at a table for twelve. On the wall behind the table, watching over them as they ate, hung a portrait of Lois that Bill had commissioned from an old photo soon after she died. By the end of the week, Loretta would move it to a more suitable location, in the basement behind a rusted-out wringer washing machine.

After supper, Justine did the dishes while Bill and Loretta sat by the fire, sipping a glass or two of brandy that Bill said he'd been saving for a special occasion. Never in his wildest dreams could he have imagined an occasion as special as this.

Late that night, after they all retired to their respective rooms, Bill was lying in bed reading, as he always did before drifting off to sleep. He had just started a chapter of a Zane Grey novel, *Riders of the Purple Sage*, when suddenly he was stunned spitless to see Loretta show up unannounced, standing at his bedside, wearing nothing but a towel.

"Do you mind," she said smiling, "if I bunk with you? It's cold in that guest room."

Then, as if to prove it, she dropped the towel.

Bill knew he ought to say something, but could not for the life of him speak.

Finally, he just moved over, and Loretta climbed in.

And in the end, he did not mind at all.

After breakfast the next day, while Loretta made a grocery list and hummed a little tune, Bill asked Justine if he could have a word with her. They bundled up against the cold and took a walk down by the river. Bill talked about his family, how he'd grown up in that same house, how his brother Ted had taught him to swim in that river.

Loretta watched them from the kitchen window. At one point she heard a laugh. Was that really Justine? Loretta couldn't recall the last time she'd heard that laugh.

Bill told Justine a little about Lois, what a fine person she was, and how lucky he'd been to have her as his wife. He spoke quickly of the estrangement with Robert, said how sorry he was for failing to be a better father, the kind of father Robert deserved.

Justine just listened and kept walking.

"I hope your room is comfortable," Bill said.

Justine had stopped to watch a flock of geese fly in a V across the river.

"It's fine," she said. "Your boy, he liked music?"

"What?" Bill said, a bit flustered. "Well, yes, he did. How did you know that?"

"I found some old guitar picks in the closet."

Bill nodded. "Robert played the guitar. His mother thought he was good at it."

"What kind of music did he like to play?"

Bill thought for a minute, then his eyes welled up.

"I don't know," he said. "I wish I did. I guess I was just never . . . interested."

Justine shoved her hands deep into the pockets of the wool coat Bill had bought for her at a truck stop on their way back from Raleigh.

"It was probably country."

Bill looked at her, puzzled.

"Your boy probably liked country music," she said. "All the mountain boys I've ever known who loved music, they all wanted to be on the Grand Ole Opry."

Bill nodded. "What about you?" he said. "What do you like?"

Justine looked away.

"I was at a juke joint one time," she said. "They played this old record by a woman, name of Bessie Smith. Somebody said she was colored. I'd never heard a colored person sing before. She was beltin' out this tune, 'A Good Man Is Hard to Find.' And it just climbed up inside of me and dug in deep, right here," she said, knocking her fist on her chest. "There was an old man at the bar listening with his eyes shut, all dreamy-like. I asked him what it was called and he laughed and said, 'Baby, that's the blues!' Never heard nothin' like it, before nor since."

Bill stopped and turned to look into her eyes. "You've been to a juke joint?"

Justine slid her hand over her mouth to wipe off a grin.

"A time or two," she said.

"How old are you?"

"Old enough," she said, and kept walking.

They were halfway back to the house when Bill finally got around to talking about the thing he'd decided that morning was the only right thing for him to do.

"Justine," he said, clearing his throat, "I know this is, uh, sudden and all, but I've given it a great deal of thought, well, in the last day or two. I'd be honored if you could see fit to grant me permission to ask your mother to be my wife."

Up at the house, in the kitchen, Loretta was surprised to hear Justine laugh once again. Only this time, Justine kept it up, laughing long and hard about something, like it was the funniest thing she had ever heard in her whole life.

"Well, I never," Loretta muttered. She hadn't figured Bill to be the kind of man who could make Justine laugh like that.

She stuck her head out the back door and yelled, "Hey, you two! Come on back up here in this house and thaw yourselves out! It's freezin' out there!"

Bill waved real big and Justine busted out laughing all over again.

Loretta couldn't believe it. Bill held out his arm and, of all things, Justine took it. Then the two of them started walking back up to the house together.

In the kitchen, Loretta waited, hands on her hips, tapping her toe on the linoleum the way she did whenever she got that old tingly feeling that said, "Look out, Loretta, something is up!" She was dying to know what was so dang funny.

Two weeks later, Bill and Loretta were married at the courthouse by a justice of the peace. Loretta looked, as Bill said, "resplendent," in a brand-new, spanking white, worsted wool suit, tailored to fit her body like a glove. This was not by a long shot Loretta's first wedding, but it was surely going to be her last, she said, and as such, it seemed only right that she should wear white. She also wore a little white hat with a bit of a veil, pinned to the side of her head with a white silk rose; matching high-heeled pumps that made her a good two inches taller than Bill. And best of all, as Bill put it, she wore a smile that outshined the sun.

Justine stood up for both of them. Afterward they went out to eat at the nicest restaurant in town, where Bill insisted on ordering anything their hearts desired.

They made quite a show: Loretta radiant in her white ensemble, Bill all dignified in his black funeral suit, and Justine stunning as always, in a plain cotton dress.

Other patrons, who didn't know them from Adam, looked at them and smiled, quickly guessing the cause for the celebration. One by one, as they paid their checks, they filed out of the restaurant like a receiving line at a reception, stopping briefly to congratulate the happy couple and share in their joy and wish them all the Good Lord's best.

It was a happy day, the beginning of a lull in the storm that Loretta and Justine had tried to weather all their lives. For the next three years, Loretta would dress in style and pretend to be a lady and make Bill happier than he had ever been.

And Justine would fall asleep each night curled up on the bed, no longer needing to hide under it, thanking God for Bill Mason and the peace he had brought her.

That Monday, after the wedding, Justine started back to school.

20

THE NEW GIRL

$\mathcal{S}$he showed up in tenth grade like a bolt of lightning in a clear blue sky. The boys wasted no time making fools of themselves over her. The girls rolled their eyes and hissed their envy like a roomful of stray cats. Justine didn't care. She was used to it, all of it, male attraction and female revulsion alike. One meant no more to her than the other.

The teacher, Miss Littlefield, welcomed her and told her to pick a seat.

Justine sized up the room, assessing the possibilities. Robert Fields was too short. Danny Perkins was cross-eyed. Delroy Phillips wasn't bad-looking, but he smelled like the pigs his daddy raised, and when he grinned, he was missing several teeth. Charles Holloway looked like he might come from money, but seemed a little too full of himself.

At the back of the room, in a pool of yellow sunlight, James Mc-Callum sat alone, dark-haired and broad-shouldered, solid and still. His hands looked big enough to hold the world. His eyes were downcast, locked on the pages of an old dog-eared book.

Justine placed her hand on her hip, tossed her coal black hair back over her shoulders and sashayed slowly across the room.

"The boy can read," she drawled under her breath, as she slid into a seat in the row beside him. "But can he dance?"

James didn't hear the remark, or the howling that followed it from his classmates. His mama always said, if James was reading, he wouldn't hear Gabriel blow his horn. But what he felt at that moment—what he sensed and would never forget—was the icy thrill of Justine's eyes crawling like spiders across his face, around his neck and down his spine. He looked up and saw her smile.

For three years, James would lie awake at night trying to think of something to say to her. In the meantime, Justine showed him no mercy. She went through pretty much every boy in that school from Robert Fields and Danny Perkins to Charles Holloway and Delroy Phillips, who took up bathing every Saturday just for her. But in the end, it was James.

For Justine, it would always be James.

21

WALTER

$\mathcal{W}$alter Washington could not believe his luck. Ever since he was six years old, barefoot and shirtless in ragged overalls, hardly big enough to fetch a sack of sugar for his mama, he had dreamed of getting a job at Buford Pack's General Store.

Walking home every day from the colored school, Walter would stop by the store to volunteer his services to Mr. Pack. He took great care never to interrupt, never to cause trouble, always to show respect, just like his mama taught him.

Most white folks, she said, generally didn't mind having little colored boys around as long as they behaved themselves and stayed out of the way. Walter made sure to do both. He would stand off at a distance, studying the candy and chewing gum and cigarettes and tins of snuff and all the other wonders on display in the counter. He held his hands behind his back to avoid smearing the glass, and pretended not to listen to all the white-folk talk going on just above his head.

It struck him that white folks seemed to talk about the same things that colored folks talked about—fishing and farming and weather and such. Only difference, as far as he could tell, was that white folks and colored folks seldom talked about such things to one another.

He would time it just right, waiting until Mr. Pack wasn't busy ringing up a purchase or visiting with a customer or entertaining a crowd with one of his tales.

Then Walter would squirm around and shuffle his feet until Mr. Pack looked down to take notice.

"Well, hello, little Walter, how you doin' today?"

"I'm doin' fine, Mr. Pack, sir," Walter would say with a grin, keeping his eyes downcast to show respect. "I was wonderin' if you might be needin' me to sweep the porch for you today?"

Buford would always laugh and repeat the same reply. "Boy, you're not big enough to hold a broom yet, are you?"

"Yes, sir!" Walter would say, stretching his skinny self up tall, like a rooster strutting across a barnyard. "I be big enough and strong enough to do anything you need!"

Walter meant it. He would gladly do anything Mr. Pack needed, from sweeping up to stocking shelves to pulling weeds around the porch. But what he wanted most of all—the thing he'd never admit to anybody, not even to his mama—was this: he wanted to be the money man.

From the corner of his eye, he would watch Mr. Pack take cash from a customer, lay it out in plain view, ring open the register, take out the change, and count it twice—once to himself, and finally, to the customer. Then he'd put the money in the cash drawer and slam it shut.

Walter never got tired of watching money change hands. He knew it was a white man's job. As he grew older, he would realize, maybe that was part of why he wanted it. He figured his chances of ever getting hired for such a job were somewhere between slim and none.

But his mama had always told him, "Walter, God doesn't care if we're colored or white. He made us the way we are and loves us all the same. If you want him to give you the desires of your heart, you need to ask him politely, and then believe that he will."

So every morning, when he woke, and every night before he slept, Walter would pray, "Dear Lord, please let Mr. Pack give me a job at his store, and a chance to work my way up to be the money man. Thank you very much. I am believing that you will."

This went on for years. Walter would volunteer to sweep the porch or pick up trash around the steps or polish the glass on the counter until it shined. In return, Buford Pack would give him a piece of penny candy or a stick of chewing gum or, on occasion, a whole nickel. Walter ate the candy and chewed the gum, but always took the nickel home to his mother.

Finally, on a fine summer day in 1938, when Walter was thirteen years old, and almost six feet tall, Buford had looked at him across the counter, as if he had never seen him before, and realized to his surprise that the boy was becoming a man—big and strong enough to do most anything he needed, from sweeping up to stocking shelves and unloading delivery trucks.

"Walter?" Buford said. "You want a real job?"

"Mama, please, you gotta let me do this! You know we need the money. Daddy drinks up every dime he makes. You work too hard and I see how much you worry. I can help!"

Effie Washington sat at her kitchen table, staring out the window at a storm that was gathering in the west. Every muscle, bone, and nerve in her body ached from scrubbing floors and hanging wash and ironing shirts all day. Finally, she turned to look at her only child.

"All right, Walter," she said finally. "I will let you take this job. Mr. Pack is a good man. He will treat you right. But, son, you have got to promise me two things. Are you listening?"

"Yes, ma'am!"

"First, you cannot let this job get in the way of your schoolin'. I won't hear of it. You understand me? You've got to finish school."

"I'll finish, Mama. You got my word. Mr. Pack says I can work around it."

"The second thing is this. The store closes at six. You'll be walkin' home when it's gettin' dark. I don't want you takin' no main roads. Walk in the cornfields or along the river, but don't you go walkin' by no white folks' place. Some people won't take kindly to Mr. Pack hiring a colored boy. You know what I'm saying? Don't give 'em no reason to do you no harm, you hear?"

"Yes, ma'am," he said, quietly. "I hear."

She drew a long breath, let it out, then cupped his face with her hands.

"All right, Mr. Workin' Man," she said with a grin. "I am so proud of you."

Buford Pack was more than happy to have Walter's help with all the heavy-lifting kinds of work at the store. He knew Walter was smart enough to run the place, if need be, but the last thing Buford wanted was to put the boy in a position that could raise the eyebrows of the wrong kind of people. So he let Walter work out of sight mainly, never behind the counter or directly helping customers, unless somebody needed a hand hauling supplies out to their truck.

This was fine with Walter. To most folks, he was just like any other hired help: invisible. But he noticed how some people, a few, would look at him, as if watching to make sure he never dared to inch a toe across some unseen but clearly-drawn line. He was content, for now, to work in the background and leave the register and customer relations to Mr. Pack. But he never stopped daydreaming about the way he'd do things someday, when he owned his own store.

22

GRADUATION

*O*n a balmy spring day in 1940, James and Justine, along with their classmates, finished high school. After the commencement ceremony that day, they both waited around, scanning the happy gathering of graduates and families, hoping to see each other one last time, yet praying it wouldn't be the last.

Justine waited with Loretta and Bill on the left side of the crowd. James waited far off on the right with his mother and his brothers. Finally, when all was said and done and they could not think of another excuse to keep waiting, they went their separate ways, each to their own separate destinies, wondering if they would ever meet again.

James got a job, along with Frank Jr. and a lot of other local boys, at a pulp and paper manufacturing mill that had recently opened on the Davidson River near Brevard. Andrew was itching to go to work with his brothers, but Cora would not hear of it until he finished school. She had told her boys they could work for the logging company, or even run it for her, if they wanted. They never spoke to her of how they felt about it. But the truth was, they wanted nothing to do with the kind of work that had ended their father's life and forced them to grow up without him.

James loved farming. All he'd ever wanted to do was farming and hunting and fishing. Especially fishing. But farming was changing in those mountains. It was getting harder by the day for a man to make a living pushing a plow and staring at the backside of a mule. James told himself the mill wasn't forever. But it was good for now. Best of all, it meant he'd never need to ask his mother for money.

Justine took a job at the soda shop in town. Bill and Loretta made sure she had what she needed, but Justine didn't like to ask them for help. Besides, the soda shop gave her something to do, kept her from going bat crazy with boredom while waiting for James McCallum to come walking through the door. She knew James was not the kind of man to frequent soda shops. But there were plenty of men who did, and they were only too happy to help her pass the time.

Bill kept offering to pay for Justine to go college, anyplace she wanted to go.

"You're a smart girl," he said. "Just think about it. You could be a teacher or a nurse or do most anything you want to do."

Justine tried not to laugh. Bill meant well, but sometimes he got a little carried away. She told him she surely appreciated his kind offer, and promised to give it some thought. But late at night in Robert's old room, she'd stare into a mirror that had a spiderweb crack from the time Robert, in a rage against his father, punched it with his fist. And she'd find herself wondering: What exactly did Bill Mason—the kindest man she'd ever known—see when he looked at her? It sure as hell wasn't the same person she saw in the mirror.

Justine could not picture herself being a schoolteacher or a nurse or anything else but exactly what she was. And what was that? She had no idea.

Children who grow up being used and abused find it hard to feel their own worth. What Justine wanted, or thought she did, was someone solid and strong, someone who made her feel safe and wanted. Most of all, she wanted someone who—no matter what, come hell or high water—would never leave her.

She had sensed all those things in only one man.

She wanted James McCallum.

23

THE MONEY MAN

*I*t was June, 1941, unseasonably hot and muggy. School was out for the summer and Walter was glad when Mr. Pack offered him a few extra hours each day at the store, mostly to do some long-delayed maintenance. He was working out back, replacing a window casement that had succumbed to a bad case of dry rot, when Mr. Pack came out on the porch in a panic.

"Walter! Miz Pack just called. She sliced her hand bad cutting up a chicken and it's bleedin' somethin' awful! I gotta go take her to Doc Owens to git it stitched up. I need you to come on in here and mind the store while I'm gone!"

Mr. Pack ran back inside and Walter stood frozen, staring at the chisel he'd been using to chip out the dry rot. When Mr. Pack yelled his name again, he shoved the chisel down into the pocket of his overalls and bounded up the steps, brushing wood chips out of his hair.

"I'm puttin' a sign on the door that says I got a family emergency and if folks need anything, you can help 'em. Don't worry, son," Buford said, putting his hand on Walter's shoulder. "You can handle this. And I'll be back quick as I can."

Walter stammered, "I . . . I will pray for Miz Pack's hand to be all right."

With that, Buford was gone, giving sixteen-year-old Walter Washington a taste of something that few of his race in those mountains had ever known: he was in charge. It tasted good.

Soon after Buford left, J.D. Allen and his buddy Ray Brown came stomping up the steps.

"Hey, boy! What's that sign on the door mean?"

Walter was restocking canned goods on the top shelves. He climbed down from the ladder and walked over to the counter, rubbing his hands on his overalls.

"It says Miz Pack cut her hand real bad and Mr. Pack had to go take her to git it sewed up."

J.D. snorted. "He left you runnin' the place?"

Walter studied the floor. "Naw, sir, I ain't runnin' nothin'. Mr. Pack be back soon."

Ray cleared his throat. "C'mon, J.D., get the smokes and let's go."

J.D. glared at Walter, who kept his eyes on the floor.

"All right," J.D. said, finally. "Gimme two packs of Camels."

Walter quickly reached below to get the cigarettes and placed them on the counter.

"That'll be twenty cents, sir."

J.D. picked up the packages. "I ain't payin' you nothin', boy."

Walter nodded. "That be fine, sir. You can leave it on the counter for Mr. Pack."

J.D. tossed two dimes on the counter. They bounced and skipped and rolled across the room. When they stopped, he turned and strutted out the door with Ray following behind him. Walter waited to breathe until he heard the truck spin gravel. Then he whispered "Thank you, Jesus," and got on his knees to look for the dimes.

Mildred Pack's hand was cut bad, but Doc Owens had seen worse.

"Who's minding the store, Buford?" he asked, as he stitched Mildred up.

"I left it with Walter," Buford said. "It was either that or close, and Walter can handle it."

"You mean that colored boy you got workin' for you?"

"That's right," Buford said. "Walter. I've knowed him for years, ever since he was little. He's a good boy, sixteen now, growing up to be a fine young man."

Doc Owens laughed and tied off another stitch. "I 'magine some of your customers might not take too well to having to buy goods from a colored boy."

Mildred made a little whimpering sound as Doc Owens dug in again.

Buford patted Mildred's back. "Depends on the customers."

Three days later, Mildred's hand was on the mend, and Walter's brief tenure as store manager was all but forgotten. A late delivery kept Buford and Walter working an hour past quittin' time, stocking shelves in the storeroom with sacks of flour and cornmeal and sugar.

When they finished, Buford offered to give Walter a ride home.

"Thank you kindly, Mr. Pack," he said. "I'll be all right. You ought to git on home and take care of Miz Pack. My mama said she'll be glad to bring y'all some supper, if you want."

"Maybe tomorrow," Buford said. "Polly Simpson from church brought a rabbit stew over yesterday. It was godawful, but she seemed right proud of it. We ought to try to finish it tonight."

Walter laughed. "I'll tell Mama. She'll fry you up some of her good chicken."

"Oh, my Lord!" Buford said, rolling his eyes. "I can taste it already!"

Buford waved, drove off to the right, and Walter turned left toward home. The day was waning. It was hot and he was tired and
hungry. Just this once, he thought, he'd take a short cut.

J.D. Allen sat sprawled half-lit on his porch with Ray Brown and
a few other drinking buddies he'd hung out with in the ten years
since they all quit high school and went to work at the mill. They
were passing around a half-empty gallon jug of moonshine. The sun
had just set, cicadas were singing and lightning bugs flashed in the
weeds.

J.D. squinted hard and spotted Walter Washington walking up
the road.

"Hey, boy!" he yelled. "Where you think you goin'?"

Walter heard the words, recognized the voice, and knew exactly
what it meant. He took off sprinting, running like he had never run
before. He tried to get off the road, but the brush was too thick. He
thought he could outrun them, make it to a clearing where he could
cut through the woods before they could get in their trucks and
catch up with him. He was wrong.

The McCallum boys had planned to go fishing that morning. The
plan changed when a thunderstorm rolled in at daybreak and lingered until noon. When the storm finally passed, they were still
itching to fish. They told Cora not to plan on them for supper, they'd
eat whatever they could find when they got home. Then they piled
into the pickup and headed off to spend a few blissful hours smoking
and joking and casting lines on the Davidson.

Frank Jr. and James didn't have much luck. But Andrew caught
three good-sized trout, and could not, as usual, resist the temptation
to lord it over his brothers. On the way home, they made him ride in
the back of the pickup with his catch.

Another storm was working its way over the mountain and they hoped to make it home before it hit. The evening air hummed with the rumble of thunder and the chorus of cicadas and the annoying drone of mosquitos. But they rode with the windows down, letting the wind cool their faces and dry the sweat on their necks.

They had just passed the old Allen place, only a few miles to go to the gravel turn-off to the farm, when they spotted two pickups on the side of the road. The trucks' headlights were shining on a circle of men, who were kicking something on the ground. On closer look, it appeared to be the body of a young colored boy.

Frank Jr. was driving. He slowed briefly, then kept going.

From the back of the truck, Andrew banged on the window and yanked his head in the direction they were leaving behind them.

Frank Jr. ignored him and picked up speed.

James stared straight ahead. "You know what's gonna happen back there, don't you?"

"Yes, James, I know what's gonna happen. Maybe it happened already. The boy's probably dead, or will be soon enough."

Andrew banged harder on the window, cussing into the wind.

"We could stop it," James said.

Frank shook his head. "I counted five of them, James, to the three of us. You know J.D. Allen and his drinkin' buddies. They're a bunch of cowards, the lot of 'em. When they fight, they use weapons. Do you want to have to explain to Mama how we got her baby boy killed?"

James glanced back over his shoulder.

"Well, I hate to tell you, Frank, Mama's baby boy just jumped off the truck."

Frank looked in the rear view mirror and saw the back of Andrew's head running down the road. "Aw, hell!" he said, spinning the wheels of the pickup in a U-turn. He gunned the engine, roared past Andrew, and pulled in between the trucks.

"Well, if it ain't the McCallum boys!" J.D. said, as James and Frank climbed out of the pickup. Andrew came running up breathless, and Frank grabbed the back of his shirt to stop him. Walter

Washington lay in a heap on the ground, eyes swollen shut, bruised and bloody, but still breathing.

"Evenin', J.D.," James said, sizing up the other four drunks in the circle. He nodded at Ray Brown, and Ray looked away.

"Evenin', yourself, James!" J.D. said. "What brings us the pleasure of your company? You here to help, or to stick your nose in where it don't belong?"

"I doubt you need much help, J.D. I count five against one. You can probably handle it. But I gotta tell you, it don't rightly seem like a fair fight."

"This ain't about fair," J.D. snarled.

"I can see that."

"I know him, James!" Andrew pointed at Walter. "He works for Buford Pack!"

Keeping his eyes locked on J.D., James said, "Shut up, Andrew."

J.D. laughed. "Yeah, Andrew, shut your stupid mouth or I'll shut it for you!"

Andrew lunged, but Frank twisted his shirt tighter to hold him at bay.

"All right, J.D.," James said amiably, as if choosing sides for a horseshoe match, "this is how it's gonna be. Me and my brothers are gonna take this boy on home to his mama. And you and your buddies are gonna go on back to your porch and get a whole lot drunker. You've done enough here for tonight."

J.D. squinted, studying James' face. When he turned, lifting his boot to kick Walter again, James stepped between them.

"It's over, J.D. Just go on home."

"It ain't over 'til I say it's over!" J.D. drew back his fist at James, but stopped midair.

"You sure you want to do that?" James said, lifting his chin.

For a moment, they just stared at each other. The others just watched.

Finally, like a dog tucking its tail, J.D. lowered his head and said, "Aw, hell, I need a drink!"

When he stomped off to climb into his pickup, Ray and the others followed.

Then they spun out, slinging gravel, and drove away.

Andrew and James helped Walter to his feet.

"Can you walk?" James said.

Walter coughed and spat blood that glistened red on the ground in the moonlight. "I think so."

They lifted him up on the bed of the truck and Andrew climbed up beside him.

Frank drove. When they pulled up in front of the shack, Effie Washington came out on the porch. Andrew hopped down and reached up to give Walter a hand. Walter shook him off. "I can do it. Don't wanna worry my mama."

Then he slid off the back of the truck and collapsed on the ground.

When his mother saw him fall, she covered her mouth and came running.

Andrew and James carried him into the shack and laid him on a cot in the front room.

Effie asked no questions, just got a rag and a basin of water and started cleaning Walter up. But when the McCallum brothers turned to leave, she stopped them.

"I got fried chicken and biscuits," she said. "We'd be proud to have you eat."

Frank and James tried to decline, but Andrew grinned and said, "Thank you kindly, ma'am. We'd be much obliged."

The next morning, Effie left Walter sleeping and drove into town to make a long-distance call at a pay phone. Someday, she told herself, she'd get a telephone at home, but probably not soon. The call went through quickly and rang only once.

Ophelia Sherman was on the cemetery side of eighty, plagued with arthritis and pushing two hundred pounds. She couldn't move like she had when she was young and chasing her babies. But she lived alone these days, and was more than a little lonely. So on the rare occasion when her phone rang, Ophelia moved fast.

"Hello?"

"Hey, Mama."

Effie wrote her mother long letters most every week, but couldn't afford to call often. Ophelia knew the call must be important. They exchanged pleasantries, discussed Ophelia's health and Effie's latest part-time job as a maid. Finally, they got down to business.

"What's troublin' you, child?"

"Mama," Effie said, "it's Walter. He's a good boy, you know that, or I would never ask this of you. I need him to come stay with you. He can be a lot of help to you, Mama. And if he stays here . . ."

Effie's voice broke, and Ophelia waited, praying silently, fearing the worst.

"If he stays here," Effie finally repeated, "he will end up dead. Some white boys have got it in for him. I know them. They won't let it go until they kill him."

Effie told her about the beating, how the McCallum brothers had intervened.

"He won't be so lucky next time. Mama, if you'll take him, you won't have to support him. Walter's a hard worker. He'll get a job and I will send you money every chance I get."

"Don't worry about money," Ophelia said. "We're family. We'll manage."

"You won't be sorry, Mama. I can promise you that. Walter will be a blessing to you . . ." her voice broke again, ". . . in the same way he has always been to me."

They said a long and tearful goodbye, then Effie hurried off to her job. Ophelia hung up the phone, dropped wearily into her rocking chair and studied the photos on her living room wall: her late husband, her grown children, more grandchildren than she could count, all grown up and too busy with their own lives to spend time with their old grandma. She seldom saw any of them any more. The only picture of Walter—a little boy with a big grin—was taken when he was ten, the last time he and Effie came to Memphis to visit her. Would she still recognize him?

Lately, she had been praying for strength and faith and whatever else she might need to live out her remaining days, as few or as many as they might be. She smiled, recalling what her mother used to say: "Be careful what you pray for, Ophelia. You just might get it."

Suddenly, she laughed. Seems God in his wisdom had answered two prayers, two needs, all at once. Walter needed her. Almost as much as she needed him.

It was almost a week after the beating before Walter could walk again. When he was able, Effie drove him to Pack's Store to give Buford Pack his notice and his thanks. Walter made no mention of the beating, but Buford took one look at his swollen eyes and split lip and demanded to know: "Who did this to you?"

Walter shook his head. "It don't matter, Mr. Pack. My grandma needs my help."

Buford insisted on paying him double for his last week of work. When Walter tried to refuse, Buford said, "No, take it. It's the least I can do."

Then he wrapped Walter in his arms and said, "I'm going to miss you, son."

When Walter finally managed to speak, he said, "I'll miss you, too, Mr. Pack."

The next morning, at the bus station, Walter held his mother until she stopped sobbing. Then he picked up a sack of belongings and boarded a bus for Memphis.

Two days later, when he knocked on his grandmother's door,

Ophelia smothered him for several moments in her enormous bosom before allowing him to come up for air. Then she ordered him to take a seat at her kitchen table.

"Supper's almost ready," she said, "but first we need to talk."

Exhausted from five hundred miles in the back of a bus, and intoxicated by the scent of the chicken sizzling in the oven, Walter rubbed his eyes and tried to focus.

"I'm so happy you are here," she said, smiling in a way that assured him she meant it. He knew that smile well. He had seen it often on his mother's face.

"This is your home now and I expect you to treat it as such. Eat when you're hungry. Sleep when you're tired. Clean whatever needs cleaning. Your mother has raised you right, the way I raised her. Her rules and mine are much the same. School comes first. Chores second. Church every Sunday. You'll tell me where you're going when you leave, and be home promptly by ten. No cigarettes, no alcohol, no unbecoming behaviors, and no associating in any way with fools. If you think you can do something behind my back, think again. Make me proud, Walter, and we'll be happy. Make me regret taking you in, and you'll regret it far more than I will. But I want you always to remember this: There is nothing within my power that I won't do for you. We are family. Is that clear?"

Walter nodded.

Ophelia raised an eyebrow. "I want your word, boy, not your head."

"Yes, ma'am," he said, laughing. "You have my word. I'll make you proud."

"One last thing. You need to get a license to drive my old Buick. I recently had a minor mishap. It was not my fault, mind you, but it has convinced me that I no longer care to drive. So you will drive me wherever I need to go, especially to and from church every Sunday. I think that's all for now. Are you hungry?"

At that moment, Walter would have agreed to most anything for a plate of his grandmother's chicken. But he meant what he said about making her proud.

24

HE SPEAKS

$\mathcal{J}$t was August, a scorcher, hot and steamy, despite a downpour from a sudden cloudburst, on the day James finally thought of something to say to Justine.

He was bolting up the steps of Pack's General Store, trying to drop off a batch of Cora's home-churned butter before it got too soft in the heat and lost its shape.

Cora would pack it, pound by pound, into an old wooden mold that had a plunger for stamping the top with two daisy-like shapes. For reasons she never understood, some people seemed to like decorations on their butter. Then she would press the blocks out of the mold, wrap them in wax paper, and send them off with James to Pack's Store, where they sold like hot cakes. Unless they got too soft on the way. Buford Pack insisted his customers wouldn't pay full price for misshapen butter, no matter how good it tasted.

Just as James hit the top step, Justine Rollins came barreling out the door with an armload of groceries, holding a burlap sack over her head to save her hair from the rain.

Buford was standing behind the counter, claimed he saw the whole thing.

"She saw him comin' plain as day," Buford would say in years to come. "She was standing right here at this very counter, paying me for a sack of groceries. I wish you could've seen the look on her face when she saw him runnin' up those steps. She grabbed that sack and took off out the door like a scalded dog. She coulda missed him by a mile if she'd had a mind to. Y'all ask me, that purty girl knew 'zactly what she was up to. Poor ole boy never knew what hit him."

James and Justine collided on the porch like a clap of thunder, the way the sky, when cut by lightning, will pull itself together with a great, rumbling boom, as if God himself had clapped his hands. The impact sent them reeling off the steps, into the mud in a beautiful mess of tin cans and coffee beans and long pent-up stirrings.

James scrambled to his feet, slipping and cussing under his breath. Justine lay in a soggy heap on the ground, the breath knocked clean from her lungs. James fell back to his knees to cradle her head in his hands and brush the muck from her eyes.

"Breathe!" he said. "You have to breathe, Justine! God help me, I love you!"

To his surprise and relief, Justine's eyes fluttered open and she gasped for air.

Then they sat there, looking around like two mud wrestlers taking a coffee break. A crowd gathered on the covered porch to point and laugh. They didn't notice. They were both too busy thinking about the mess they were in, not just the mud, but the same love mess they had been in for years.

Finally, Justine pushed her hair off her face and gave James a long, lingering look. It was a look he had never seen before, not in any other eyes, in any other soul, the kind of look that leaves a man hungry and helpless, longing for more.

Lightning split the air, prickling the hair on the backs of their necks, and the mud tried to suck their clothes clean off their bodies. Suddenly James found the words he'd been searching for since the first day he saw her.

"Justine Rollins," he said, "I have tried for a long time, and I cannot think of any good reason why you would ever agree to be my wife."

Justine took her time, slowly licking the mud from her lips.

"Neither can I," she said. Then she slid up close and threw a long, muddy leg like a lasso around his hip, roping him in. "Except for maybe one or two."

When they laughed, the clouds parted and the rain stopped falling and the birds set to singing and God told the sun to shine down from Heaven and kiss the tops of their heads.

That's how Buford Pack would tell the story, time and again.

It was a good story. People loved it. Which somehow only made it even more of a shame, folks would say, in years to come, to see how it all turned out.

Three days later, after trying for hours to think of some fitting way to announce his intentions to his mother, James just went on and told her.

"Mama," he said, "if you've got no objections, there's somebody I'd like to invite to Sunday dinner. Her name is Justine. I've asked her to be my wife."

Then he hurried out the door and down to the barn to help Grady with the milking, leaving Cora in the kitchen with her jaw hanging halfway to the floor.

That evening, after fielding as many of Cora's questions as he could possibly tolerate, James drove into town to Bill Mason's home, drew himself up as tall as he could reach, took a long breath, and knocked on the door.

Loretta answered, fluffing up her hair.

"Evening, ma'am. My name is James McCallum. I don't know if your daughter mentioned me. I wonder if I might have a word with you and Mr. Mason?"

Justine stood in the hall with her eyes as big as the hubcaps on Bill's Buick.

Bill came out to shake hands and offered James a seat on the porch. Loretta went in the house looking for Justine, who was hiding in the hallway closet where she could hear every word from the porch. Finally, Loretta gave up looking and went out to the kitchen to pour three glasses of sweet iced tea, spiking hers with a generous shot of whiskey, and returned to the porch to join the men.

By then, Bill had already made up his mind. He had known Harlan Lacy, had attended his church for some years before moving closer to town to work at the bank. He had admired him both as a preacher and a man. He also remembered the tragic accident that had ended Frank McCallum's life and left Harlan's daughter a widow with three small boys. Bill recalled years later, when Lois came home from Pack's General Store with a pound of the best butter he ever tasted, and told him Buford Pack said it was churned by Cora Lacy McCallum.

But what Bill saw in James McCallum was more than just the kind of stock the boy came from. Fifty years in the banking business had taught Bill how to look a man in the eye and make a quick, but reliably accurate, assessment of his character. He'd been wrong a time or two, but he would not be wrong about James. One look in the boy's eyes and Bill knew. If James was man enough to try to stand up to Justine, he would surely do right by her.

Loretta was not so easily convinced. She was thrilled at the idea of Justine getting married. At least the girl wouldn't be following in Loretta's footsteps, getting knocked up out of wedlock and, God forbid, expecting Loretta to help her raise the child. And Loretta had to admit, the boy was certainly good-looking, which in Loretta's estimation, never hurt. She had only one hesitation, and it was a big one: James was just a farm boy working in a paper mill. She had much higher hopes for her only daughter than to see her settle for a life as the wife of a millhand.

Loretta also knew perfectly well that it really didn't matter what she thought. Justine would never listen to her advice. She would do exactly as she pleased.

So Loretta knocked back her third glass of whiskey, spiked with tea, and pretty soon, all her hesitations drifted away. She gave James her blessing, with a big sloppy kiss, and started planning the outfit she would wear to the wedding.

James thanked them both and promised he would not let them down. Then he jumped in the pickup and drove off before Justine could crawl out of the closet.

Loretta wanted a big fancy wedding. Justine said no. Cora wanted a Christian wedding. Justine said no. James said he just wanted to get it over with, and finally, Justine said fine.

They were married that September, by the same justice of the peace who had married Loretta and Bill. Justine gave only one nod to tradition: she asked Bill Mason to do her the honor of walking with her into the courthouse on his arm. Still, she made it clear to all concerned that she would give herself away. James asked his brothers to stand up with him. Loretta and Cora sat together and shared a handkerchief, patting each other on the back as they dabbed at their tears. After the ceremony, they all shared a meal together at the local cafe. Bill paid the check.

James and Justine moved into the cabin down by the pond where Cora and Frank had once started their lives together. All was well for almost two weeks.

Cora was out on the back porch hand-feeding a load of wash through the wringer washer, when she heard the screams.

James and Frank Jr. were at the mill. Drew was at school. So she grabbed a walking stick she kept on the porch and took off down the back steps, running for the pond. Halfway there she met Justine running toward her. Justine didn't slow down, just glared wild-eyed at Cora as she ran by and yelled, "Under the bed!"

Cora stopped to call after her, "Justine? What's under the bed?"

In the distance, Justine screamed, "SNAKE!"

Cora was about to ask, "What kind?" but heard the screen door slam on the porch, which meant that Justine was already in the house and wouldn't hear her.

Turned out to be just a black snake. Decent-sized, but nothing to get all worked up about. Cora spotted it up under the bed in the cabin, hovering back in the corner. Justine had probably scared the poor thing half to death. Cora chased it out from under the bed then scooped it up on her walking stick and flung it off into a patch of weeds on the bank of the pond. Then she headed back up the path to the house to finish wringing out the load of wash and get it hung on the line to dry before a thunderstorm rolled in off the mountain.

Justine was in the kitchen trying to drink of mug of coffee, but her hands were shaking so hard she kept sloshing it.

"Did you kill it, Cora?"

"Kill what?"

Justine slammed down the mug. "The snake!"

"No, of course, I didn't kill it. It was just an old black snake. You never want to kill one of them. They eat rats. Besides, they won't hurt you. They're not poisonous."

Justine's face screwed up like she was trying to eat a green persimmon.

"Poisonous or not, that makes no difference! If it can scare me to death, I'll still be just as dead!"

"Sit down, Justine," Cora said. "Drink your coffee. Want something to eat?"

They sat at the kitchen table, not talking, just drinking coffee and eating biscuits with butter and molasses. Justine's hands stopped shaking. Finally, she spoke.

"I hate snakes."

Cora waited.

"When I was little, Mama took up with this crazy old Holy Roller, name of Carl Lee Crawford, the kind of man that's so mean he'd cut off his own nose just to spite his face. Mama only liked him 'cause he was good-looking. She was always falling for good-looking men that didn't have a lick of sense."

Cora smiled and buttered another biscuit.

Justine looked past her, out the door to where a breeze was ruffling the poplars that grew on the hill by the creek, flipping the leaves like silver coins in the sun.

"Carl Lee was a snake handler," she said. "Rattlesnakes, copperheads, cottonmouths, you name it. He'd been bit a bunch of times, claimed it just made him tougher. Right. If you ask me, it just made him dumber."

Justine laughed hard, as if it really wasn't funny.

"He tried to get Mama and me to handle 'em, too. Mama wasn't about to go anywhere near 'em, of course. She wouldn't even let him bring 'em in the house. He always had to handle 'em out on the porch, sitting out there on the steps in his underwear."

"In his underwear?" Cora said, raising an eyebrow. "On the porch?"

"Yeah," Justine said. "Ain't that just a picture to put on the piano?"

They both laughed. Then Justine shook her head, as if trying to shake the memory from her mind. Out by the creek, the breeze was blowing harder, bending the tops of the poplars, making them sway side to side, like a church choir humming an altar call.

"I tried a few times," Justine said, quickly. "I figured if Carl Lee could do it, I could do it, too. I got close to touching one, once or twice, but that was it. At the last second, I always backed out. I couldn't do it. It just . . . it just wasn't in me. You know what I mean?"

Justine waited, studying Cora's face.

Cora looked as if she wanted to say something, but didn't. She just nodded.

Justine leaned back in the chair, and drew a long breath.

"So, Carl Lee, he kept egging me on, trying to get me to hold one. Mama told him to leave me be, and he finally shut up about it. Then one night, I was climbing into bed and out of the corner of my eye, I saw something move under the quilt. So I threw back the covers and, sure enough, there was one of Carl Lee's old snakes, all coiled up and flickin' its tongue at me. Carl Lee swore he didn't put in there, but Mama didn't believe him. They had a big fight over it. Not just about the snake, but a lot of things. We had been there six months, which is about as long as Mama ever lasted with anybody. Carl Lee wasn't looking nearly as good to her as he did at the start. Next morning, we packed up and left."

Justine reached up and pushed her damp hair back from her face.

"Anyhow," she said. "I hate snakes."

The wind caught the screen door and slammed it hard. Out on the porch, Blue—Andrew's latest hound—roused from a dream, turned in a circle, flopped down, and fell back asleep.

"You want another biscuit?"

Justine shook her head.

"Come on, then," Cora said, pushing up from the table. "Let's get this wash on the line before it starts to pour."

They worked well together. As Cora fed the wash through the wringer, piece by piece, Justine caught it on the other side as it came out flat as a board, and shook it out to loosen up the wrinkles. Then they carried it across the creek to the clothesline that was strung between two poplars in a sunny patch on the hill. When Justine started to pin up a shirt, Cora said, "If you'll do the bending, I'd rather do the pinning. Your back is younger than mine."

So Justine bent down, picked up the wash, shook it out and handed it to Cora, who shook it again and pinned it on the line, just in time for Justine to hand her the next piece.

Cora remembered, as a child, helping Ada hang the wash, doing the bending while Ada did the pinning. Cora's boys did their share of the farm chores, but she never asked them to help her hang wash. It had been a long time—too long, she realized—since she had known the pleasure of working alongside a woman.

When they finished, Cora thanked Justine for her help.

"I enjoyed it," Justine said. "I've always done wash alone. It goes faster with company."

They were crossing the footbridge over the creek, one after the other, with Cora leading, when Justine said, "James told me your mama died of a snakebite."

Cora kept walking, didn't look back as she spoke. "My mama thought she got bit, but wasn't sure. She had marks on her wrist, but she never saw the snake."

"Well, if it wasn't a snake, what killed her?"

Cora stopped on the path and turned to face Justine.

"She died bringing me into the world. It wasn't the snake's fault any more than it was mine. She didn't blame me or the snake or even God. That's who she was, Justine. She didn't cast blame where it didn't belong. My daddy said she loved grace more than anybody he ever knew."

Cora turned and started walking to the house. "That's why it's my name."

"What?" Justine said, hurrying to catching up.

"Grace," Cora said. "She named me Cora, for her mama, and Grace, for what she loved."

Justine caught the back of Cora's apron.

"Hold on. Look me in the eye and tell me the truth. You don't hate snakes?"

Cora shook her head. "No, Justine, I don't hate snakes. But I wouldn't handle one if you held a gun to my head. I'm just like you. It's not in me."

Justine looked off down toward the pond, and shook her head.

"I am never going back in that cabin."

"I know," Cora said, resting a hand on Justine's shoulder. Then, as they started up the path together, she said, "You and James can take Andrew's room."

"But where will Andrew sleep?"

"He can move back into his old room."

"What old room?"

"The one he slept in for years until two weeks ago, when James moved out to the cabin to sleep with you. It used to be a good-sized room, before the boys begged me to split it up and put in an indoor bathroom. I have to say, I don't miss walking down to the outhouse in the dark or bathing in a washtub in the kitchen."

"You mean that little shoebox room with the cot? Will Andrew fit in there?"

"Barely. Drew calls it the outhouse."

They climbed the steps to the porch, stepping over Blue, who, as usual, didn't seem to feel any need to move out of their way.

"James won't be happy about leaving the cabin," Justine said. "He keeps saying how much he likes, well, you know, us having the place to ourselves and all."

"He'll get over it," Cora said. "I'll talk to him."

The breakfast dishes sat washed and rinsed on the drainboard, where Cora had left them to dry that morning while she started the laundry. She stacked five plates and handed them to Justine. "Put these in the cupboard for me?"

Justine grinned and took the plates. "I'll put these in the cupboard and hang the wash and do anything else you want," she said, "as long as I never have to set foot back to that cabin."

When James came in from work that day, he went straight to the cabin. Minutes later, he came trotting up the back steps to the farmhouse. Cora was in the kitchen peeling potatoes for a pot of James' favorite potato soup.

"Mama, have you seen Justine?"

"Nice to see you, too, son. Justine is resting in my room. She had a big day. Sit down, James. We need to talk. You need to listen. Would you like some coffee?"

Justine was right. James was not pleased about having to give up their privacy and move back into the big house with his mother and his ever-teasing brothers. The brothers weren't thrilled about it, either, especially Andrew, who was forced to reoccupy the "out-

house." They briefly considered moving down to the cabin, but decided they'd rather stay close to their mother—and her kitchen.

James got over his disappointment at moving back to the farmhouse. And soon life settled into a happy routine for all, with two
women to share the housework, and three men, plus Grady, to share
the farm chores, and five keen minds to make mealtime conversation
ever so much livelier. In years to come, they would look back on that
time, grateful for what they'd had, longing for what they had lost.

25

EFFIE AND LORETTA

"*M*ama, why in God's name would you think you need a maid?"

Justine had stopped by, after leaving a batch of Cora's butter at Pack's General Store, for a quick visit with Loretta and Bill. She was sorely disappointed to find that Bill wasn't home, and that Loretta was cooking up one of her schemes.

"I need help," Loretta said, all huffy. "This is a big house. Besides, Bill can afford it."

"Mama, you don't do anything. Zero. Bill waits on you hand and foot. You mean to tell me you're going to hire somebody so you can do less than zero?"

"How would you know what I do? You're never here! Besides, I already hired her."

"You already hired who?"

"Effie Washington, a colored lady. She needs the work and I need the help."

Justine stared at Loretta. Finally, she started to laugh.

"Who in a million years would ever have thought it?" she snorted. "Loretta Rollins from the backside of nothin' and nowhere, no way, no how, has hired herself some help!"

Loretta grinned, all pleased with herself. "Be nice to me and I might let her serve you tea."

They were still laughing when Bill came in, delighted as always to see Justine.

"And how is our lovely Miz McCallum?" he said.

"Better now, just seeing you," Justine said, hugging his neck.

"What were you two fine ladies laughing about?" he asked.

Justine snickered and Loretta gave her a look.

"We were just reminiscing," Loretta said sweetly, "about the good old days."

Justine covered her grin with her hand.

"I was telling Justine how my back has taken to hurtin' me lately," Loretta said, "and how you were so sweet to suggest that we ought to hire some help."

Bill looked a bit lost, as if he'd come home to the wrong house.

"Why, uh, yes," he said, finally. "Of course. I'll look into it right away."

Loretta jumped up and gave him a good hug.

"No need to trouble yourself, darlin,' I've got it all taken care of! She starts Monday!"

"Monday?" he said, nodding. "Well, I see, all right then."

He turned to Justine and kissed her cheek.

"Lovely to see you, my dear. I trust married life is agreeing with you?"

"Very much so," she said, kissing him back.

"Glad to hear it. Should that ever change," he said with a wink, "you know you always have a home here with us."

"I know it," Justine said, laughing. "I'll keep it in mind."

Then Bill wandered off to do whatever Bill did to keep out of Loretta's way.

Loretta poured another iced tea with whiskey and leaned back in her chair.

"So," she said, "what's it like living with that old woman?"

Justine shook her head. "Cora's not bad. We get along all right. James' brothers feel like my brothers, too. I'd be bored without them.

They keep me laughing. And Cora's no older than you are. She just doesn't dye her hair or paint her face."

Loretta snorted. "I'd be bored spitless stuck up on that mountain."

"Mama," Justine said. "You've been bored spitless all your life. Can't you just be thankful for Bill Mason, and the stupendous fact that you finally landed somebody who can afford to hire you some help?"

"Fine," said Loretta, "go on and make fun of me. See if I care."

Justine kissed her mother's permed head, then drove back to the farm.

Two weeks before Thanksgiving, Bill Mason had his first stroke. He was sitting in the living room with Loretta, reading a Zane Grey novel by the fire, after enjoying yet another fine meal prepared earlier that evening by Effie, Loretta's recently hired help.

Effie had proven to be quite a find—a pleasant soul, a hard worker, and best of all, a great cook. That evening, she had prepared one of Bill's favorite dishes: chicken 'n' dumplings, with English peas, the way his mother used to make it.

After serving the meal, Effie had washed the dishes and stacked them to drain, before bidding Miz Loretta and Mr. Mason goodnight.

She was out the door, halfway to her old car, when she heard Loretta scream.

Effie ran back to find Loretta hysterical and Bill slumped in his chair, unable to speak.

Bill lingered a week through a series of strokes, each leading him a little closer to his grave. When Justine came to sit broken-hearted at his bedside, holding his hand and wiping his brow with a cool cloth, Bill tried his best to rally.

He couldn't speak or make a sound or even lift a hand, but he prayed silently that somehow Justine would see in his eyes what he so desperately wanted to tell her. It was the same thing he wished with all his heart that he had told Robert years ago: "Life is short. Live it well. Be happy. Do what you want."

But all he could do was to look into her eyes and weep the bitter tears of a man who had learned too late to speak his heart while there was time.

Bill was buried, at his request, in a family plot next to Lois. Loretta got the house, the Buick, and an impressive amount of money. She would never in her lifetime feel poor again. He also set aside something for Justine, in the hope that she might one day decide to go to college. The rest of his estate, a sizable sum, was to left to Robert, who surprised everyone, including himself, by showing up at the funeral. Apparently, a distant cousin passed the news of Bill's demise on to Robert.

The service was held in town, at the church Bill had attended in the years after taking the job as bank manager. He was well known in the community, and the church was filled with friends and well-wishers who came to pay their respects. Loretta, at Cora's urging, disregarded any concerns for propriety and wore the outfit that Bill had said made her look like an angel: the form-fitting white suit and veiled hat that she wore the day they were married.

After the service, they gathered at the home for a covered-dish supper supplied by neighbors and friends. Cora helped Effie in the kitchen, working as a team to replace one empty dish with yet another full one. And Effie kept checking to make sure everyone had enough iced tea (and that Loretta's frequent refills always came with a generous shot of whiskey).

Justine leaned close to whisper in James' ear, then left him sitting with Frank Jr. and Andrew. The three brothers watched as she glided across the room to where a tall, bearded man in his late twenties stood alone, looking at a collection of framed photos on the piano.

"I'm Justine," she said, taking Robert Mason's hand in hers. "My mother, Loretta, is your father's wife. Let's take a walk. It's a bit stuffy in here. You look like you could use some air."

She led him down to the river, where she had often walked with Bill. They walked arm in arm along the bank, smelling the musk of rotting leaves, hearing the crickets and the frogs and the lapping of the waves, and watching the clouds billow up above their heads.

"Bill told me you're a musician. You play the guitar, right?"

"Really? I can't believe he told you that. He was always . . . ashamed of it."

"What kind of music do you like to play?"

Robert kicked a pinecone from the path and sent it rolling down the bank.

"I started out playing country, like most musicians in these mountains. We all wanted to go to Nashville and play on the Grand Ole Opry."

She smiled. "So I've heard. Is that where you live now, in Nashville?"

"No," he said. "When I left here—what's it been, about ten years ago?—I planned to go to Nashville. Spent two days trying to hitch a ride. One night it was pouring rain, I was soaked to the bone, miserable. Got picked up by a guy who said he was going to Chicago. I just wanted to sleep. So I said, OK. Never regretted it. Chicago's where I learned to play the blues."

Justine stopped to give him a long look. "You play the blues?"

He laughed. "Yeah. Got a pretty good band, we play a few gigs a week. It's not the big-time, but it's enough to pay the rent and buy another round of beer."

"You ever heard of Bessie Smith?"

Robert laughed. "Sure. The Empress of the Blues. I got to hear her sing live once. 'Nobody knows you when you're down and out.'"

Justine's jaw dropped. "You heard Bessie Smith sing—in the flesh?"

"Yeah. She died some years ago. Car accident, I think. Anyhow, this was a few years before that. I was playing a gig at a club in

Memphis. Somebody said Bessie Smith was in town. I begged my way into her show, stood in back. I'll never forget it. She was something."

Justine shook her head. "I cannot believe you got to hear Bessie Smith."

"Well, good," he laughed. "It's not often I can impress a pretty girl."

She took his arm again and they kept walking.

"So tell me," she said. "After all these years of being so bitter and keeping so distant? Why are you here? What made you want to come to Bill's funeral?"

He stopped for a moment, as if hobbled by the question, then kept walking along the riverbank. "I did it for my mother," he said. "I never came to see her when she was sick. I wanted to come to her funeral, but, well, I had a gig. When I heard he'd died, I knew she wouldn't want me to miss his funeral. I did it for her."

"You were right to come," Justine said. "I'm glad you're here."

Robert stopped suddenly to face her. "I'm not sorry he's gone."

"I know," she said. "But you ought to be."

"And why exactly is that?"

"He loved you, Robert. He told me he did. He wrote you letters every week begging you to forgive him. But they all came back unopened."

Robert looked out across the river and shook his head.

"I never opened 'em. I didn't care what he said. He was a bastard."

Justine tilted her head to one side, just so, the way she'd learned to do long ago, when she wanted to catch a man's eye and make him hear what she had to say.

Robert turned to look at her.

"Bill Mason may have been that to you," she said, "but he was not that to me. If you persist in speaking so disrespectfully of him, I will be quite happy to kick your rude ass into that river."

He looked away from her and grinned.

"Do you think I'm joking?" Justine said.

"No, ma'am," he said. "I absolutely do not."

"That's more like it," she said, taking his arm again and turning toward the house.

"You know, my mother-in-law makes the best biscuits you'll ever put in your mouth. Bill loved them. She made a big batch for today in his honor. Let's go have one before they're all gone, shall we? I guarantee they'll make you feel better."

They started up to the house, where the gathering was slowly winding down.

"I sure do love the blues," Justine said. "I'd like to hear you play sometime."

"Well, if you're ever in Chicago, look me up."

"Maybe I will," she said. "You never know."

Three days after Bill's funeral, Loretta broke down sobbing into her whiskey glass and begged Effie to move into the house and stay with her full time.

"Effie, I can't stand being alone! I've never been alone in my whole life, and I'm not ready to go out and start lookin' for another man yet!"

The truth was, Loretta wasn't sure she'd ever be ready to start looking again. There had been a time she would settle for pretty much any man who caught her eye and picked up the bar tab. Not that she wasn't picky. Loretta had her standards. But they pertained primarily to looks, not to character. Bill Mason had cured her of that. For the first time in her life, a man had treated her like a treasure, and she vowed to herself she would never again settle for anything less.

Thanks to Bill, and the generous sum he had left her, she would never need to have a man in her life again. Unless, of course, she wanted one. She planned to keep an eye open, in the unlikely event that, by some miracle, the Good Lord might drop another Bill Mason in her lap. But for the time being, Loretta felt sure, more or less, her "looking" days were over.

"Please, Effie!" she whined. "I can't take another night in this house alone!"

Effie Washington was no fool. She knew Loretta was half-lit, and would likely change her mind by morning. Besides, Effie had her own life to tend to. It was true that Walter, her only child, had gone to live with Effie's mother in Memphis. But Effie was not to blame for that. The only blame was on some local white boys who wanted to kill Walter for no reason, except for the fact that he was colored. Effie feared more than anything the thought of losing Walter. She couldn't bear it.

Still, she had William, her husband, who worked on the railroad. It kept him gone more than not, and he had never been easy to live with. But Effie loved him. And when he came home from his railroad job for a few days, he wanted her to be there to cook for him and fuss over him and warm his bed.

"Miz Loretta," Effie said, "I have a husband."

"Hell, Effie," Loretta snorted. "He's never around, and when he does come home, he gets drunk and beats on you! Don't try to tell me I'm wrong! I've seen the bruises! You think they don't show, but honey, I'm here to tell you, they do! God knows I've had enough of 'em myself to know what they look like!"

Effie lowered her head and stared at the floor she had scrubbed that day.

"Miz Loretta," she repeated softly, "I have a husband."

Loretta leaned back in her chair and studied Effie's face.

"I'm sorry, Effie," she said. "I meant no disrespect. I've been in the same mess that you're in. I put up with it all my life before I met Bill Mason. God help me, I made my daughter put up with it, too. But I'm not putting up with it any more. Never again. I just want you to know that you're not foolin' me or anybody on this Earth but yourself."

Effie didn't speak. Part of her longed to say that it was easy for a trashy white woman, who had tricked an upstanding old man into leaving her his money, to brag to her hired help about what she would not put up with anymore. But once again, as so often in her life, Effie's fearless side bowed down to her far more cautious nature, and she simply folded her hands and stared at the clock on the wall.

"Thank you, Miz Loretta," she said finally. "Is there anything I can do for you before I go?"

Loretta leaned across the table and covered Effie's hands with her own.

"Listen to me, Effie, will you? Just hear me out. I know what I am and where I come from. I know I didn't deserve Bill, and I sure as hell don't deserve his house or his money or you and your help. But life doesn't always go from bad to worse. Sometimes, whether we deserve it or not, it finds a way to get better. Bill made it better for me. I'd like to make it a little better for you. That's all I'm saying. That and the fact that I hate like hell having to stay all alone in this big house."

Effie sat for a moment, looking at Loretta's red fingernails twined around her wrists like roses on a fence post. Finally, she rose to leave.

"Thank you, Miz Loretta," she said. "I . . . will think on it."

As she started for the door, Loretta called after her.

"Effie? How about just the nights when William's gone? I'll pay you well. If you're fool enough to want to stay with him when he's in town, that's up to you."

"Goodnight, Miz Loretta. See you tomorrow."

James hated working the graveyard shift, but there was no getting around it. After supper, he left Justine and Cora playing checkers in the front room and went to bed to catch a few hours of sleep. He'd need to leave by a quarter past eleven to punch the clock for his shift by midnight. But on this evening, Justine woke him early, at 10:30, kissing the back of his neck.

He pulled her down and buried his face in her neck. "You think you're safe 'cause I've got to go to work? Wait 'til next week when I'm back on first shift."

She laughed. "I'm waking you early so you can drop me at Mama's."

He rolled over and sat up, rubbing his eyes. "Is your mama all right?"

"She's fine, far as I know. But I feel bad about not going to see her this week. She hates being alone in that house. I thought I could go keep her company, stay the night. You can pick me up in the morning on your way home from the mill."

"Won't she be asleep this late?"

"Mama?" Justine laughed. "She's always been a night owl. Besides, ever since Bill died, I don't think she's sleeping much at all. I could call to let her know I'm coming, if we had a telephone. Which, in case you haven't noticed, we don't!"

The lack of a telephone was a sore point, but James couldn't help it.

"We'll get a phone, I swear," he said, "as soon as they run the lines out this far."

An hour later, James pulled up in front of his mother-in-law's house and Justine leaned over for a kiss. "See you in the morning," she said. She waved as he drove off, then she walked around to the back door. Stepping up on the porch, she was surprised to hear voices.

Through the window, she saw Loretta sitting at the kitchen table in a bathrobe, knocking back a glass of whiskey and laughing at somebody across the table out of Justine's sight.

"If that don't beat all," she thought. "Bill's not even cold in his grave, and Mama's already gone out and got herself another man."

It was a new low, even for Loretta. Justine stood for a minute, watching her mother laugh. Then she leaned over the porch rail and threw up into the azaleas.

"Justine?" The porch light came on and Loretta stood in the doorway peering out at her. "What the hell are you doing out there? I almost ran to get Bill's pistol! You're lucky Effie spotted you and stopped me! I could've blowed your head off!"

Justine looked up from the azaleas. "Effie?"

"Yes, of course, it's Effie! Who'd you think it was, John Wayne? Get in here, girl, it's freezin' out there!"

In the kitchen, Effie sat at the table in a pink chenille bathrobe, holding a hand of playing cards and looking as if she'd been caught stealing the family silver.

"Evenin', Miz Justine," she said, keeping her eyes on the cards.

Justine looked at Loretta. "You and Effie . . ."

"We're playing cards, Justine. Is there a law against that? The only thing wrong here is Effie keeps beating me! Effie, I swear, if you win one more hand, I'm gonna dock your pay!"

"Fine," Effie said. "Dock my pay, and you can fry your own chicken."

Loretta laughed and refilled her whiskey glass. Then she looked at Justine.

"Do you mind explainin' what exactly you were doing snoopin' around on my porch at this hour of the night? Don't tell me you've already left that handsome husband of yours."

"No, Mama, I didn't leave James. He dropped me off here on his way to work. I knew you'd be up, and I thought you might like my company."

Loretta took a long swig of whiskey.

"Justine, you know I am always happy to have the pleasure of your company, if you aren't in one of your smart-mouthed moods, as you clearly seem to be now. But I will not sit around waiting for you to take pity on me and show up at my door. So Effie, God bless her, has finally come to her senses and agreed to move in and stay with me full-time!"

"Only when my husband's gone," Effie said quickly.

"Whatever!" Loretta said. "Anyhow. I'm glad you're here, Justine. You're looking a little peaked. I do wish you'd use a little of that nice pot of rouge I gave you. Are you hungry? Effie fried a big mess of catfish for supper. It was delicious! Effie, did we eat all that fish?"

26

FREEDOM

Walter wasted no time making his grandmother proud. He followed her rules, just as she had clearly spelled them out. School came first. He enrolled as a junior in high school in the fall of 1941, never missed a day, or failed to do any assignment.

Chores came next. Ophelia cooked, and Walter cleaned: dishes, laundry, floors, porches, walkways, and yards. And once a week, he washed and waxed the Buick.

He passed the driver's test to get a license and was more than happy to chauffeur Ophelia any place she pleased, including to church every Sunday.

Memphis in the early forties was a boomtown. After the bombing of Pearl Harbor in December 1941, when the US officially entered the war, the War Department built military supply depots in the city and a Naval Air Station opened nearby to train pilots. The city's population grew to nearly three hundred thousand people—including more "colored people" than Walter had ever seen or even imagined to exist.

He got a job working Saturdays (Ophelia wouldn't hear of him working on school nights or Sundays) bussing dishes at a club on

Beale Street, where he was awestruck to hear, up close and in the flesh, many of the great blues artists: W.C. Handy, Muddy Waters, Howlin' Wolf, Bessie Smith, and "Blues Boy" King, who would later be known as the great B.B. King.

Walter could hardly believe he was getting paid to haul dishes and hear the blues. He loved working in a big roomful of people where everybody's skin was the same color, more or less. And as long as you did your job, nobody looked down on you or made you feel like a plow mule, fit for nothing but doing their heavy lifting. He remembered, as little boy growing up in the mountains, running barefoot on a creek bank, squishing mud between his toes, chasing lizards and catching crawdads and feeling the sun on his face.

He couldn't quite put a name to that feeling back then, but now, as a young man, he knew exactly what to call it: freedom. He had felt it many places over the years. Always in nature. Often in his mother's kitchen. Sometimes in church on Sundays. And lately he had felt it just listening to the blues.

But Walter had rarely felt free with white folks. Mr. Pack and his wife were exceptions. And the McCallum brothers, who had pulled over that night on the road and stopped the beating that would surely have ended his life. There were other exceptions, too, folks he didn't know by name. He could sense it when he passed them on the street. Most white folks would look away, as if just seeing a colored person was somehow shameful. But once in a while, he would pass some old white lady, old enough to know she was running out of time, or a little white child, too young to have learned yet how to hate. And they'd look past his eyes into his soul and smile, as if to say, I'll be seeing you in the next life and we'll be friends.

Walter didn't want to wait for the next life. He wanted freedom in this life, here and now. Memphis wasn't everything, but it was a beginning, a movement, a step closer to that sweet taste of freedom. For Walter, there would be no turning back.

He would always miss his mother and the mountains he had called home. It pained him to think he might never see them again. Phone calls were costly, but he wrote to Effie every week. Effie treasured his letters. She even shared them—some, not all—with Loretta. Loretta said his stories about the music and the food down on Beale Street made her want to pack up and move to Memphis.

Walter wasn't sure what he'd do after high school. He knew someday he wanted to run his own store, but he had no idea where or how to start. His mother had always told him to just give each day his best and wait to see what door the Lord would open next. So he went to school and to work and to church every week and drove his grandmother all over town. He never saw the next door coming. When it finally flew wide open, it knocked him flat on his back.

Her name was Rosalinda Williams—a tall, smart, studious girl who sat next to him in their senior English class, and was, in his decided opinion, the most beautiful creature God ever put on the Earth. He spent weeks trying to get her to notice him. But she was always glued to the teacher's lectures, or lost in reading (usually a book of poetry), or writing feverishly in a journal.

He kept praying to God to please make her look at him. Finally, God laughed and knocked Rosalinda's pencil out of her hand onto the floor. When she reached down to pick it up, Walter reached, too. Then their hands met. And their eyes met. And their hearts met, all at once.

That afternoon, Walter walked Rosalinda home from school, carrying an armload of her books. When they reached her house—a small clapboard box surrounded by clumps of red roses and a white picket fence—they sat in the porch swing and talked. About school. And poetry. And the mountains where he grew up. And the blues he heard at the club. And the stories they read daily in the news about the war. They talked about everything and nothing.

The following Sunday, as Walter opened the Buick's door for Ophelia, he cleared his throat and said, "Grandma, would you mind if we give a friend of mine a ride to church? Her house is right on the way."

Ophelia rolled her eyes and chuckled, "Heh, heh, heh!"

Thereafter, Rosalinda rode to church with them, and sat with them, and worshipped with them most every Sunday. She often came over after church to stay for Sunday dinner and helped Walter with the dishes, while they discussed her favorite poet, Langston Hughes, or Walter's favorite minor league baseball team, the Memphis Chicks.

They graduated from high school in May of 1943, and celebrated with both of their extended families at a sumptuous barbecue in Ophelia's backyard. Loretta had urged Effie to attend, and offered to pay for her bus fare. But Effie had recently hurt her back hanging wash on the line, and dreaded the thought of such a long bus ride. Instead, she called to congratulate Walter and told him, fighting back her tears, how proud he had made her.

"Hold on, Mama," he said, grinning at Rosalinda. "Here's somebody I want you to know."

The next Sunday, sitting in church with his grandmother and his girlfriend, Walter tried to focus on the sermon, but kept wondering what his boss would say at the club when he got the nerve to ask for more hours. Suddenly, he heard what he would one day tell his children he believed to be the voice of God whispering in his ear, words that would forever change the course of his life.

The preacher was on a roll, delivering a powerful sermon in support of the war. He quoted from a speech by Franklin D. Roosevelt, in which the president had said, in effect, that the war was a battle to ensure for the world four basic freedoms: the freedom of speech and expression; the freedom of every person to worship God in his own way; the freedom from want; and the freedom from fear.

Those words winged their way from Walter's head to his heart and settled in his soul.

"Freedom," he thought, staring at a stained-glass image of Christ bearing the cross. "I will fight for it," he told himself and his God. "I will die for it, if need be."

That evening, after driving Rosalinda home, Walter wrote to tell his mother he had decided to join the army, and he asked for her blessing and her prayers. He enlisted the next day. Effie was devastated, but respected his wishes. Ophelia was heartsick to see him go, but assured him that he was making her proud. On his last night in

Memphis, before leaving for basic training, Walter wiped the tears from Rosalinda's beautiful face, confessed his boundless love for her, and asked if she could somehow find it in her heart to wait for him.

She kissed his hand and whispered the word he was praying to hear: "Yes."

27

THE COMPANY OF WOMEN

*A*ndrew was the first of Cora's boys to sign up. He had always wanted to beat his brothers at something, and so he finally did. On his nineteenth birthday—April 8, 1944—he enlisted in the US Army. At supper that night, he inhaled two helpings of peach pound cake, his favorite, which Cora had baked at his request. Then he stood, wiped his mouth on his sleeve, and tried, like a preacher at a funeral, to make bad news sound like good.

"I joined up today! I'm going over to Germany to fight those Nazi bastards!"

For a moment the room fell silent and still, as if God himself had reached down from Heaven and stopped the Earth from spinning. A breeze blew in off the creek and rattled the doors on the Hoosier cabinet. A mourning dove cried in the distance. Cora pushed her chair back from the table and stared at the wrinkles on her hands.

"Sorry for cussin', Ma." Andrew grinned, walked over to the sink, grabbed a bar of Lifebuoy soap, stuffed it in his mouth and waited for everyone to laugh. No one did.

A look passed between Frank Jr. and James. Cora saw it, and knew what it meant: they were silently agreeing, with only a slight nod between them, that Andrew's enlistment called for their own.

They would never let their brother go off to war alone. Frank Jr. would enlist the next day. James followed two days later, after breaking the news to Justine.

The morning they left to report for training, Justine refused to come out of the bedroom. She stood at a window staring at the mountains, the bones of her spine as rigid as a fence post.

"Justine?" James touched the back of her hair. She slapped at his hand, and he dropped his arms, letting them hang like wash on a line.

"I know you're mad at me," he said. "But my brothers want a goodbye kiss for luck."

"You kiss them!" she snapped. "You're the one that's leaving!"

James swallowed, pulling at his collar. When he spoke, the words clawed at his throat. "Justine? Please, just hear me out. I can't let my brothers go without me. Believe me, I would do that for you if I could, but I can't. It's not in me. I promise you I will come back."

Justine heard his words, but all she felt was an old, familiar sense of betrayal. James was the only man she'd ever known that she wanted to be with forever. She'd believed him that night by the pond, when he promised he'd never leave her. And now, because of his brother's harebrained decision, he was ready to run off and fight a war halfway around the world.

She spun around to face him. "Fine, James! Go! But don't count on me to be here when you come back. That's IF you come back!"

He had planned to say something more—some tender salve of words to ease the pain of their parting. He wanted to tell her what he had found in his heart, that in this world or the next, he would never love anyone more than he loved her. Not his mother or his brothers. Not even the land. He wanted to say it all out loud and make her hear it. But in the end, James just nodded. His brothers were waiting. Besides, there was no denying what he had seen in the depths of his wife's brown eyes, blazing up like the fires of hell: she was done with him.

"You've got a home here," he said quietly, "if you want it. I'll be seeing you."

Then he turned and left the room, closing behind him the door to her heart.

Grady had offered to drive them to the bus station. Cora didn't want to go stand in a crowd and see them off. She would say her goodbyes on the porch. One by one, she held her boys, pressing her face into their necks, memorizing the scent of their flesh, pleading silently to God to bring them home.

"Goodbye, Frank, Jr."

"Take care, Mama."

"Goodbye, James Harlan."

"Don't worry, Mama."

"Goodbye, Drew."

"I love you, Mama."

And with that, they were gone, her fine boys, leaving behind them an awful silence broken only by the rushing of the creek, the ticking of the clock and the wailing of her heart.

"Cora?"

It was dark on the porch. The sun had slid behind the mountain, leaving a pale lavender stain like a bruise on the western sky. A thin gray mist hung low above the creek. Swallows darted and swooped in the shadows around the barn.

Justine stood in the doorway dangling a cigarette between her fingers.

"What are you doing out here?"

Cora didn't look up. She sat huddled in the porch swing, like a bird taking shelter from a storm, with her arms tucked like wings about her chest and her eyes fixed on the gravel road where, that morning, the McCallum brothers had waved a last goodbye.

"Those boys," Cora said, finally. "They're all I've got."

Justine took a long drag on the cigarette and flicked it off the porch into the hydrangeas. Then she eased into the swing beside her mother-in-law.

"I know," she said, smoke curling from her nose. "They're all I've got, too."

They sat for a while, taking turns pushing the swing with their toes, watching the twilight fade to night. The stars came out, one by one, glittering like pinpricks in a paper lantern until they nearly filled up the sky.

Finally, Cora opened her wing and drew her daughter-in-law to her bosom. Justine closed her eyes and lay back, cradled in Cora's arms, limp as a sleeping child. No words were spoken. No tears were shed. None were needed. For the first time since they met, they simply took comfort in each other, in the healing company of women.

28

SALT PORK

Two weeks after James and his brothers shipped off to war, the morning sickness set in on Justine with a vengeance. At first, she tried to blame it on the salt pork Cora fried for breakfast.

"That meat was bad!" she said, pushing her chair back from the table. She stood for a moment, blinking at the salt pork. "God help me!" she groaned, clamping a hand over her mouth. Then she stumbled from the kitchen and down the back steps where she began retching and cussing, cussing and retching, into the creek.

Cora sat at the table, fork in midair. Through the window, she could see Justine doubled over the creek bank. A clap of thunder rolled down the mountain like cannon fire in the distance. It was the same sound Cora heard most every night in a dream, as she stood helpless, watching her boys run through flames that exploded all around them—James in the lead, Frank Jr. following, and Drew— dear God! where was Drew?—just a shadow, behind his brothers.

Shaking her head to clear the image from her mind, Cora rose from the table, wet a rag in the sink, and carried it down the back porch steps to Justine.

The next morning, when Cora served up another hunk of salt pork for breakfast, Justine bolted out the door and down the steps.

Cora followed to kneel on the creek bank beside her and held Justine's head with her hands. A blue-bellied lizard darted among the rocks, scrambling to avoid the bilious shower.

After a bit, Cora asked quietly, "When was your last monthly?"

Justine spat in the creek. "I'm two months late. And I'm never late."

Cora dipped a corner of her apron in the creek and wiped Justine's mouth.

"Do you think this means you're with child?"

Justine laughed. "You mean because I've missed two monthlies and I'm retching in the creek? I'd say it sounds fairly likely, wouldn't you?"

"Have you told James?"

Justine pushed Cora's hand away.

"No, Cora! Telling him won't make no difference. He'll still be just as gone."

A breeze rustled the leaves and the blue-belly darted behind a rock.

Cora spoke softly. "Doesn't a man have a right to know his wife's with child?"

Justine rose to her feet, raking her hair back from her face with her fingers. She gathered herself up, stiff and tall, and glared at her mother-in-law.

"Don't even try talking to me about that, Cora. I don't give a damn about James McCallum's rights. What about my rights? Mine! Have you given any thought to that? He's the one who decided to run off and play soldier. I'm the one who's left here retching my guts out over a creek!"

Cora reached out to touch her, but Justine took off running up the hill to the house. When the screen door slammed on the porch, Cora leaned back on the creek bank and felt the cool dampness seep through her dress. The blue-belly was back, sunning itself on a rock. The creek was busy washing itself clean.

"A baby," Cora said to the lizard. "My baby's baby. Thank you, Jesus."

In the kitchen, a plate shattered and Justine let fly a stream of obscenities.

"Old woman!" she shouted out the back door. "If you ever fry another piece of salt pork in my presence, I swear to God, you can just take me out and shoot me!"

Two long months later, just when Cora began to think her daughter-in-law might never eat again, the morning sickness lifted like a sour-smelling fog and Justine began to eat day and night and in between, as if she had never eaten before.

Come morning, when the sun washed through the bedroom window, and the smells from the kitchen crept in around the door, Justine would wrap her thickening body in a piecework quilt that Cora had made for her, and come padding barefoot out to the kitchen to inhale a half dozen of Cora's biscuits, hot from the oven, dripping with butter and sorghum molasses.

After breakfast, when Cora went to the garden to gather corn and beans and okra, Justine would follow along, picking ripe tomatoes, wiping one on the hem of her skirt, biting into its flesh and letting the juice trickle down her chin.

At noon, she ate every morsel Cora set before her—fried pork chops, boiled potatoes, chunks of stewed venison, green beans with ham hocks, collard greens with vinegar, thick slabs of cornbread, topped off with a cobbler, or on occasion, one of Cora's yellow cakes with chocolate icing and custard between the layers.

Come supper, when Cora usually just warmed up the leftovers and baked a fresh pone of cornbread to round things out, Justine would fill and refill her plate, then fold her hands in her lap and wait until her mother-in-law had finished eating.

"You plan to eat that?" she'd say, staring at the last hunk of cornbread.

Cora would laugh and slide the plate across the table. "Help yourself."

Justine loved the ritual of crumbling cornbread into a glass of buttermilk. She would break it into pieces with her fingers, then stir it all up into a thick soupy mess and devour it, every bite, scraping the glass with her spoon.

There would be hard, hungry days ahead for her—times when she would long for the taste of Cora's cornbread and the comfort of her kitchen. But on the worst of those days, for as long as she had breath, she would never eat another piece of salt pork.

29

A Candle in the Wind

*F*all lingered that year like a dying ember, with sunny skies and mild evenings into winter. But in the first week of January, Mother Nature awoke with an icy vengeance.

Cora shoved a log into the wood stove, stoking the coals to warm the kitchen and make breakfast for Justine, who in her ninth month of pregnancy had taken to sleeping later every morning. Cora heard a thump on the porch and looked out to see Grady hauling a load of firewood from the bed of his truck and stacking it in the woodbox. The sky was slate gray, thick with clouds. Wind whipped the trees, making them buck and rear and paw the air like horses. Cora pulled her mother's shawl about her shoulders and opened the back door.

"Grady Shields, have you lost your mind? Get in here before you catch your death!"

"Hey, Cora." Grady grinned and tossed another armload of logs on the wood pile. "Looks like it's fixin' to snow. I figured, with the baby coming soon and all, you'll have your hands plenty full enough. You don't need to be out here chopping and hauling wood."

Grady's bare hands were blood red, calloused thick as boot leather, like the hands of every mountain man Cora had ever known. Lord, how she loved the hands of a hard-working man.

"I sure 'preciate it, Grady. When you finish, come in and get some breakfast."

"Don't mind if I do."

An hour later, he was working on a plate of biscuits and gravy, along with his third cup of coffee, when Justine came stumbling barefoot out to the kitchen, blinking in the light, her belly bulging beneath the quilt Cora had made for her.

"Good God, Grady, what are you doing out in this weather?"

"'Mornin' to you, too, Miz Justine," he said.

Cora filled a mug and handed it to Justine. "Grady was kind enough to bring us a load of firewood, Justine. It's good of you to grace us with your presence. If you're hungry, we've got biscuits and gravy."

Justine sat down at the table, yawning. "Oh, I'm hungry all right," she said. "I could eat biscuits and gravy and about half the firewood that Grady brought, too."

They shared a good laugh over that.

After breakfast, Grady rose to leave. Cora followed him to the porch.

"How's Addie?"

"She's good, same as always. Oh, Lord, I almost forgot! I keep trying to talk Mama into getting a telephone—and Cora, believe me, you need to get one, too—but she won't hear of it. She said to tell you that when the baby's coming, just go out and shoot the shotgun three times off the back porch. We'll hear it, and I'll bring her over quick to help with the birthin'."

That evening at supper, after draining the last drop of a glass of cornbread crumbled in buttermilk, Justine looked over at Cora and shook her head.

"Sorry to leave you with these dishes, Cora, but I'm going to bed. I'm too tired to help and too pregnant to care."

Cora smiled. "Sleep well, Justine."

After the dishes were washed and dried and put away, Cora

banked the coals in the cook stove to be ready for breakfast come morning, and went out to the front room to sit alone reading, for the fourth time, a letter from James that had arrived yesterday. He had written, he said, while lying in a foxhole in a forest where it was snowing.

"It's not home, Ma," he wrote, "but it's sure beautiful. I wish you could see it."

James had sent a separate letter, as usual, to his wife, but Justine hadn't spoken a word about its contents to Cora. She never did. In the months since James left, Justine had written to him only a handful of times, never once mentioning her pregnancy. And she'd forbidden Cora from breathing a word of it to him. Cora had agreed to respect her wishes, but kept insisting that James needed to know.

Finally, two weeks ago, Justine had grown weary of Cora's urging and sent James a brief note announcing that she was with child, and due to give birth any day.

In his letter to Cora, James thanked his mother for persuading Justine to tell him. The news had meant the world to him, he said, and it would be of great help to him in the days ahead, until he could hurry home to his family and his child.

Cora kissed the letter, then tucked it away in a box where she saved every piece of correspondence from all three of her soldier sons. She looked in on Justine, who was snoring softly, and then headed off to bed. Before falling asleep, she would kneel for a long while on an old braided rug to pray: for a safe and speedy homecoming for her boys; for a fine and healthy delivery for Justine and her precious child; for peace and harmony and healing for the world; and for all the grace and strength and faith that she might need to do whatever might be required of her. Amen and amen and amen and amen.

The first snowflake fell just past midnight. An hour later, Justine awoke to a mild contraction. Her labor began, like the snow, lightly at first, with no hint of the storm soon to come. Justine waited, dozing, hoping the pains would pass. Finally, she could wait no longer.

"Cora!"

Rolling out of bed, Cora reached for the bare bulb that hung from the ceiling and flicked the switch. Nothing. Power's out, she thought, lines must be down. She padded barefoot down the hall to the room Justine had shared with James.

"Child?"

In the dark, Cora could barely see the shape of Justine's belly under the quilts.

"I think the baby's coming, Cora. It hurts like hell."

"You'll be all right," Cora said. "Power's out. I'll get a lantern and summon Addie."

"Well, hurry!" Justine called after her. "I can't stand being alone in the dark!"

Cora lit a kerosene lantern and flung open the wardrobe in her bedroom to dig out Frank's shotgun. She grabbed three shells and hurried out to the back porch.

Snow was falling fast, blanketing everything—the steps, the road, even the creek—piling in drifts three feet deep around the house. Cora was no stranger to childbirth. She had delivered her own babies into Ada's capable hands. But aside from her three and an assortment of livestock, she had never attended a birth. It would be different, she thought, being on the pulling end, rather than the pushing. Given a choice, Cora would prefer to push. But there was no choice in that now. She looked up at the road buried in drifts. No sense in waking Ada. It would take a miracle and a team of mules for Grady to get her here in this storm.

Cora felt her bare feet growing numb on the icy boards of the porch. She propped the shotgun in the corner by the screen door, gathered up an armload of Grady's wood, and went in the kitchen to stoke the stove.

In the bedroom, the lantern cast long shadows on the ceiling.

Justine was sitting up with the covers thrown back, staring at the bed. "I don't . . . I don't know what happened."

"Your water broke, honey. It's natural. Come on, let's get you a dry nightgown and put you in my bed. You'll be warmer in there. It's closer to the stove."

Cora sat in the rocker by the bed, keeping an eye on the clock out in the living room to time Justine's contractions. Her labor progressed quickly. Justine would drift off to sleep after each one, only to be roused by the start of the next.

At daybreak, Cora stopped timing long enough to wrap up in a quilt and go out on the porch to take a look. The sky had lightened a bit in the east, but the snow was still falling fast and the wind was starting to howl. Cora thought about the cows. After milking the previous evening, Grady had put them in the barn to shelter them from the storm. They would need to be milked soon or their udders would become painfully swollen and sore. But the storm had made the road impassable. And the shortcut through the woods would be shoulder-deep in drifts. There'd be no way Grady could get to the barn. And she prayed he'd have enough sense not to try.

She hurried back inside and found Justine at the end of another contraction.

Cora dipped a cloth in a basin of water, rung it out, and wiped Justine's brow.

"How long since your last one?"

"I don't know!" Justine snapped. "How much longer will I have to do this?"

"It will all be over soon," Cora said, "and you'll get to hold your baby."

"Soon is not . . . Cora, why are you wearing those boots? And that coat?"

She had pulled on a pair of Frank's old work boots and a heavy overcoat.

"I have to go milk," she said, tying a kerchief around her head.

"Are you crazy? You can't leave me! Why can't Grady do the milking?"

"Grady can't get here in the storm. I won't be long, I promise."

Justine began to wail, and Cora leaned down and pulled her close.

"I'm not leaving you," she said. "I'm just going to the barn. I'll be quick. But I need you to be strong, Justine. You can do this. You are stronger than you know."

Justine grew quiet. For the first time in memory, she found herself missing her mother. Most every Friday, she'd drive into town to eat supper and play cards with Loretta and Effie. She loved Effie's cooking, but she went mainly for the laughs. Loretta wasn't much as a mother, but she knew how to have a good time. In their years together, she had made Justine laugh almost as much as she made her cry.

Last Friday, as Justine had bundled up to drive back to the farm, Loretta had said, "I swear, girl, you look like you're ready to bust. I aim to be there for the birthin'. But how on earth will you let me know it's time when you still don't have a telephone?"

"I don't know, Mama. Maybe Grady can come get you."

"Well, figure it out!" Loretta had shouted, "because I've got a right to be there just as much as Cora McCallum!"

And once again, Justine had realized, as she had countless times throughout her life, that in Loretta's mind, everything that ever happened was always and only about Loretta.

Suddenly another contraction seized Justine's thoughts, shifting them back to her belly, and she grabbed Cora's hand and shouted, "Oh, Lord, here we go again!"

Cora sat on the edge of the bed, and whispered in Justine's ear, "Just keep picturing your baby, honey. You can do anything this baby needs you to do."

As the contraction eased, Justine lay back in Cora's arms and drew a weary breath. Suddenly she knew. What she missed was not Loretta. She missed the mother Loretta had never been. In that moment, on the brink of giving birth, in more pain and fear than she

191

had ever known, Justine looked into Cora's eyes and saw the mother she had always longed for—the kind of mother she hoped to be.

"Fine!" she said. "Go milk the damn cows! But git back here before this baby rips me apart!"

Cora smiled and smoothed the top of Justine's head. Then she buttoned up the overcoat and headed out. When she started down the steps, Blue began barking in the basement, scratching on the door to get out. She had put him in there last night with a pail of water and some scraps from supper to tide him over through the storm. This was not the Blue that replaced the one that was killed by intruders. It was getting hard, she realized, to keep them all straight. But she knew for sure this was the Blue they'd gotten as a pup when Andrew was in high school. Cora didn't hold with having dogs in the house. Drew would sneak that pup into his room and sleep with it every night, until he left to go off to war. Cora loved that dog, almost as much as Drew did, but not enough to let him in the house.

"All right," she said. "Come on out and do your business, but then you're going right back in the basement! You can't stay out here, Blue, or you'll freeze!"

Blue didn't argue. He hated snow. He found a bare spot under the overhang of the porch, relieved himself, and promptly trotted back into the basement.

"Good boy," Cora said. "I'll feed you later."

The snow was knee-deep on the path and still falling fast. Out in the pasture, it blew in swirls on the wind, like little white tornadoes. Cora plodded along, stumbling at times, until finally, she reached the barn and rolled back the door.

Samson, the mule, pawed the ground when he saw her. The Holsteins, Bertha and Delilah, stood side by side, swishing their tails, eager to be milked.

"Guess what, girls," she said. "Pretty soon, we're going to have us a baby!"

When she finished milking, the snow was deeper by half a foot. It pulled at her boots as she slowly made her way back to the house.

Passing the woodpile, she thought of Grady and felt her heart swell with thanks for his provision. By the time she reached the back steps to the porch, the milk in the two pails she carried had formed a slushy layer of ice.

Blue started barking and scratching on the basement door.

"Hush, Blue!" Cora said. "I'll deal with you soon. Right now, I've got bigger fish to fry."

In the bedroom, Justine lay curled up in ball. Hearing Cora in the hall, she moaned. "The pains are gettin' close! Don't know how much more I can take!"

"Close is good," Cora said. "It won't be long now."

Cora filled a basin with hot water from the stove and gave Justine a quick bath. She brushed the tangles from her hair and tied it back with a ribbon. Then she held Justine's face in her hands, smoothing her brow with her fingers.

"If this baby is smart," Cora said, "she will look just like her mama."

Justine closed her eyes and tried to smile. Then another contraction swept over her, the strongest yet, and she gripped Cora's arm so hard she drew blood.

An hour later, in a terrible, glorious racket like Joshua's trumpets tearing down the walls of Jericho—with the wind howling like wolves and Justine screaming blasphemies and Cora begging God to show a little mercy—a child was born.

Justine squinted, trying to see the baby. "What is it?" she said.

"She's a girl!" Cora laughed, wiping out the infant's mouth with a rag she had boiled on the stove. "You have a fine daughter to raise!"

Justine shook her head. "God help us both."

The baby looked nothing like Cora's memories of her own scrawny babies. She was fat and round and downy as a ripe peach, with deep red skin and thick tufts of auburn hair. But when she opened her eyes and fixed them upon her grandmother, no mistake about it, Cora clearly saw James.

In that instant, in the twinkling of a baby's eye, Cora lost her heart. She knew this child did not belong to her. But she would forever belong to the child. She draped the squirming infant across Justine's chest and began tying off the cord.

"What will you name your daughter, Justine?"

Justine ran a finger from the baby's forehead to her chin.

"Mama wanted me to name her Loretta, after her, as if I'd ever in a million years do that. If it suits you, Cora, I'd like to name her after you and your people."

Cora looked up. Justine was holding the baby close to her face, rubbing the child's nose against her own.

"What?" Cora said. "You mean, McCallum?"

"No, Cora. McCallum is her last name from her daddy. I want to call her Lacy after your family. And Grace for you. Lacy Grace McCallum. If you don't mind."

A draft dimmed the lantern. When the flame flared back, shadows danced around the room, shouting silent hallelujahs. Cora drew a breath.

"I don't mind," she said finally. "Not a bit."

While Justine wolfed down two bowls of stewed venison and half a pan of cornbread, Cora feasted on the baby, nuzzling the child's neck, feeling the warmth and weight of her body, inhaling the sweet, yeasty scent of her hair.

Justine wiped her chin. "Swear to God nothing ever tasted so good."

Minutes later, she fell asleep, lying on her side, with her newborn daughter nursing lazily at her breast. Cora slipped a pillow between Justine's knees, so she wouldn't roll over on the child, and another behind the baby's back to prop her close to her mother. Then she sat in the rocker, watching them sleep. Wind rattled the windowpanes and snowflakes slid down the glass. Out in the front room, the old clock on the mantel ticked away the seconds of a brand new life.

Cora looked at her grandchild. The baby, sound asleep, suddenly roused, sucking frantically. Then she drifted off again, with one tiny hand clutching at her mother's breast. Cora felt the lines around her weary eyes gather up into a smile.

Pushing up from the rocker, she took an old quilt from the wardrobe—a patchwork "Prayer Wheel" she had stitched as a child under Ada's close watch, with scraps cut from Cora's mother's old dresses. Thinking of Ada caused her eyes to well up. Addie would be heartsick at missing bringing this child into the world.

Cora shook the quilt, fanned it over the bed and watched it float, settling softly like a leaf falling to earth. She tucked it behind Justine's shoulders, folded it away from the baby's face, and leaned down to touch her lips to the child's downy head.

Picking up the lantern, she slipped out to the front room. The clock said half past seven, but the storm made it dark as night. Easing into a chair at the small pine desk where her father had once composed his sermons, she took out a thin sheet of airmail stationery, opened the ink well, dipped a pen, and began to write.

Dearest James,

I pray these words find you safe and well. I am writing with the happiest of news. Your daughter was born today, January 6, 1945, just after sunrise. She is perfect in every way. She has her mama's lovely face and her daddy's knowing eyes and what appears to be my hair—the auburn it was before it started turning gray.

Justine did well. You ought to be proud of her, as I am. I am sure, when she is rested, she will write to tell you all about it. She and the baby are sleeping now, safe and sound. The baby has already taken to nursing like a newborn pig.

We had a big snow last night. It prevented Addie from getting here for the birth, but we managed all right without her. Your baby pretty much birthed herself.

It is still snowing, but appears to be easing up somewhat. Grady, bless him, laid in a big load of firewood for us a few days back, so I won't need to chop wood for a while. Thank you for your recent letter. I have not had a word from either of your brothers in several weeks. I pray everyday without ceasing that the Lord will keep you all safe and well in the palm of His hand.

Oh, I nearly forgot. Justine said she wants to name the baby for my family. I trust that will set well with you. Lacy Grace McCallum. A fine name for a fine child. Come home soon, son. Your family needs you.

Your loving Mother,
Cora Grace McCallum

The weeks after Lacy's birth were the happiest Cora had known since the days when her boys were small. Justine took well to nursing, but was more than willing to share other responsibilities for tending to a newborn. Lacy woke every two hours around the clock demanding to be fed. Cora would drop whatever she was doing—cooking or washing or sleeping—to run and pick the child up from her cradle, change her diaper and kiss her nose before carrying her to her mother to nurse. After Lacy's belly was full, Cora would take her from Justine to burp her and rock her to sleep. She did this gladly and tirelessly, along with farm chores and housework that, before Lacy's birth, had somehow seemed to make her so weary.

Between chores and tending to Lacy, Cora made time every week to post a letter to each of her boys, telling them things of their own particular interests. She wrote to Frank Jr. about the latest news reports on the war and assured him not to worry, that thanks to Grady's help she was managing fine on the farm. For Andrew, she'd recount, with much embellishment, Blue's latest adventures chasing squirrels or getting sprayed by a skunk or tucking his tail and hiding under the porch when a bobcat screamed on the mountain. Drew so loved that dog.

But her letters to James were different. Cora always began them with a few lines of praise for Justine: how quickly she had recovered from being with child; how pretty she looked in a blue muslin dress that Cora had made for her; how she laughed when Lacy crowed like a rooster; what a fine mother she was turning out to be. But mostly Cora wrote to James about his daughter: The strength of the child's grip. The down on the back of her neck. How she furrowed her brow in a way that made her look just like her daddy. And oh, her first real smile, at barely two months! Cora had picked her up and whispered, "Hello, sweet girl!" and was amazed to see Lacy light up, moving Heaven and Earth.

Cora wrote her best stories, chose the finest and clearest words that she knew, to tell James all about Lacy. Words had often failed her, but for now—until James could come home and hold his daughter in his arms—words were all they had. So Cora filled her letters with all the joy the child brought to her heart. Then she sent them off across the sea, hoping somehow, when he read them, James might feel that same joy and know what a gift a child can be.

James longed to hear from Justine. But he took great comfort in his mother's letters. He read and reread them until he knew them by heart. In the midst of war, he recited them from memory to quiet his mind and find a measure of peace, while riding on the back of a tank through a village, shooting and being shot at. Crossing a field littered with bodies. Dodging bullets and landmines and mortar shells. Or lying half-frozen in a snow bank pinned down by artillery, listening to the screams of dying men he had known as brothers.

He kept his mother's letters, and the few he received from Justine, safe inside his shirt next to his heart where nothing, he told himself—not rain or snow or Hitler and his whole army—could touch them. He would do his duty for his country, whatever it asked of him. But he had another duty now, and somehow, God help him, James would live to see it through.

He had to get home to his daughter.

30

CROSSING OVER

*J*ames made it all the way to the Rhine. For a mountain boy who, before the war, had never been more than fifty miles from the farm where he was born, James considered it quite an accomplishment. Even so, after all the talk, all the miles, all the lives and limbs that had been sacrificed to get there, he was not much impressed with the Rhine.

In the end, it was just another river, with men on both sides fighting and dying to claim it. He would've gladly preferred to fight for rivers that he knew best and loved most, the French Broad and the Davidson, where the fishing was bound to be better. But foot soldiers seldom get to choose their battles.

They crossed the Rhine at St. Goar, shortly after midnight on the morning of March 26, 1945, moving silently in assault boats under cover of darkness, each boat carrying ten or so men, each man holding his rifle and his breath. James watched as the first boats crossed without incident. Then it was his turn.

The river at that point was some three-hundred yards wide. They were halfway across when the Germans began firing a barrage of mortars, machine guns, and small arms. James and his fellow soldiers returned fire as best they could until finally they reached the shore and rolled out of the boats.

It was that moment—that sweet taste of victory after months of bitter battle, finally at long last, getting to cross the Rhine and take the fight to the enemy's heartland—that James would remember the rest of his life. But the moment would be short-lived.

Soon after setting foot on the east bank of the Rhine, James was knocked to the ground by a German bullet. It entered the back of his left shoulder, puncturing his lung, stopping short of his heart and a thick packet of letters a medic would find inside James' shirt. The medic packed gauze in the wound, administered morphine, and lifted James onto a stretcher to be taken to a battalion aid station. At the station, he was given plasma and loaded into an ambulance to be transported to a field hospital for surgery. The driver of the ambulance was Pfc. Walter Washington.

Walter didn't make the connection until he saw the bloody packet of letters and caught a glimpse of a page with these words: "The mountains miss you, James. We all do. Hurry home—Your loving Mother." Curious, Walter carefully lifted the dog tags from James' neck and read the first and last lines: "McCallum, James . . . Rt. 1, Pisgah Forest, N.C."

He stared at the wounded man's face.

"James?"

Groggy from blood loss and morphine, James' eyes fluttered open, then squinted to focus.

"Walter? Is that you? You're a sight for sore eyes."

Walter grinned. "Don't worry, you'll be fine. I'm gonna get you to a hospital."

He checked James' vitals and changed the dressing on his back, packing it tightly to slow the bleeding. Then he jotted a note on the packet of letters and stuck it back inside James' shirt.

The assistant driver had been watching. "You know this fella?" he said.

Walter nodded. "He's a friend from back home. Stay with him," he said, climbing into the driver's seat. "And hang on. We'll be movin' fast."

>>>>

The field hospital was a bloody sea of stretchers bearing severely wounded men. Walter took a nurse aside and said, "The soldier I just brought in is in bad shape. He needs surgery. He won't make it unless you move him up the line."

"They're all in bad shape," she said. Then she nodded. "I'll do what I can."

Walter couldn't stay. There were other wounded men waiting for his help. Before he left, he placed his hand over James' heart and silently prayed, "Please, Lord, pour out your healing grace on this good man."

Then he patted James' head, climbed back in the jeep, and drove away.

After a quick examination, the field surgeon, a Yankee from Connecticut, decided the damage to James' lung was too extensive to be repaired. He was about to move on to the next patient, when the nurse asked him to take a look at something.

"The ambulance driver found this pack of letters in his shirt. Seems they knew each other back home. He wrote this note and asked me to give it you."

The note was short: "This man saved my life. I will count on you to save his."

The doctor frowned, studying James' face. Then he shrugged, handed the note back to the nurse, and said, "OK, move him to surgery."

Two hours later, to the surgeon's surprise, he had successfully removed the bullet from James' shoulder and repaired much of the damage. The rest would need time to heal.

The next morning, when he looked in on his patient, he found James awake, sitting up and eating scrambled eggs.

"You are one lucky devil to be alive," said the doctor.

"Thanks," James said. "That's what my mama's always told me."

The surgeon laughed and turned to leave.

"Doc?" said James. "I had some letters. You got any idea where they might be?"

The doctor glanced around, then stepped close to James' bed.

"I'll check with the nurses," he said. "I think they might be, uh, passing them around. They were from your mother, right? About your baby daughter, what is her name? Lacy? I'll see to it you get 'em back."

He turned again to leave, then stopped and looked back at James.

"Hey, soldier, we didn't mean to be nosy. It's just, those letters about your daughter . . . they made all of us feel better. If I could put 'em in a pill, I'd give 'em to all my patients. They shouldn't have been read without your permission. I apologize for that. But to tell you the truth? We didn't think you were going to live long enough to mind."

Two days later, James was transferred to a Red Cross hospital in France, where he would spend weeks recovering. He awoke the first morning to find a red-haired nurse standing at the foot of his bed, studying his chart.

"McCallum?" she said. "I don't see many of them."

"Me neither," said James. "Not since I left home."

"My name's Molly. I'm from Ireland. We're going to take good care of you."

"I 'preciate it," James said, smiling at the lilt in her voice. He thought it sounded almost like music, and somehow, it reminded him of home.

She stood for a moment, scratching her neck. "You know," she said, "there's another McCallum here just down the hall. Came in this morning in bad shape. Lost an eye and both legs."

James stared at her. "You know his given name?"

"No."

"What about his unit?"

She shook her head. "I can check, if you like."

James looked out to the hall where an orderly was mopping up a pool of blood. A wave of pain hit his shoulder, making him light-headed, as if he might pass out.

"Never mind," he said, closing his eyes. "I'll go see him when I can walk."

Molly nodded, turned to leave, then stopped. "You might want to be quick about it. He'll not likely last much longer. And . . . he looks a bit like you."

A moment later, when the fear in his heart screamed louder than the pain in his shoulder, James shuffled down the hall to the next ward, looking for a McCallum.

He found him. He didn't need to read the name on the chart. He knew him by the size of his body and the breadth of his shoulders and the look in the blue eye that stared up at him through the bandages, lighting up in recognition, like a prisoner who had just received a pardon.

"James? Is that really you?"

Too overcome to speak, James took his brother's hand.

"Hey, Frank," he said, finally. "How you doin'?"

Frank swallowed. "I reckon I been better."

James pulled up a chair and sat by the bed, trying not to look at the bandaged stumps that had once been his brother's legs.

"Grenade," Frank said. "Happened quick. Tore my legs off at the knees, cut me up pretty good inside. The feller next to me, just a kid, got blown all to bits. They said they dug a piece of his skull out of my eye. But I can't figure how they'd know what it was or where it came from."

James looked away.

"Hey," Frank said, drawing him back. "You heard anything from Andrew?"

James shook his head. "Last I heard, he was on some kind of special detail."

Frank grinned. "Sounds like Drew, don't it? What about Ma? Does she know about us, being here in the hospital and all?"

"I don't know . . ." James stopped to look at the soldier in the next bed, who was moaning, bleeding through the bandages wrapped around his head.

"I expect the army will tell her," James continued. "But I'll write and tell her myself, as soon as I can grip good enough to hold a pen."

He look down at his left hand and tried to flex his fingers.

"Does it hurt much?" Frank said.

"What, my hand? Naw. My shoulder hurts some. Kind of like the time when you flung that live coal out of the fireplace at me and damn near set me on fire."

Frank laughed so hard he had a coughing fit.

When the coughing eased, James said, "My hand don't hurt. It's just kinda numb. Doc says if I keep working it, it'll get better. I think mostly it's just tired of pulling a trigger."

They talked for an hour, as brothers and brothers-in-arms, about things they had seen and done and never wanted to see or do again. Then they fell into an easy silence, listening to the never-ending noise of the hospital, the clatter of trays, footsteps in the hall, cries of pain, bursts of laughter, the steady rise and fall of the voices of wounded men and the doctors and nurses and orderlies who worked tirelessly to care for them.

"James?" Frank's chest was rattling. "Will you do something for me?"

"Sure. Anything. What?"

"When you write to Ma, will you tell her I love her?"

"Like hell! You can tell her yourself when you get out of here!"

"Fine," Frank said. He grinned. "Will you tell her I said I always knew I was her favorite?"

It was an old joke, an ongoing debate among the brothers as to which of the three their mother favored most. They laughed until Frank started coughing again. When he stopped, he said, "'Member the time we switched ole Grady's mule to the other side of the fence and Grady thought the mule climbed through it?"

They kept at it, swapping tales, until finally Frank drifted off to sleep. James started to leave, but Frank held onto his hand. "Stay with me," Frank whispered. "Just a little longer. Just . . . help me cross over to the other side."

James wanted to go. The pain in his shoulder was agonizing. He wanted to sleep. He wanted a cigarette. He wanted morphine. He wanted to be back with his unit, getting shot at and killing Germans. He wanted to be anywhere on Earth but in this hospital, helpless and weak, watching his brother die. But each time he tried to pull away, Frank gripped his hand tighter.

Finally, James leaned down and rested his head on his brother's broad chest, and they drifted off to another world, a fine place of blue mountains and red dirt and all the people they loved, and the one thing they needed most of all: peace.

They dreamed it together, the way they'd often dreamed as boys, when they lay sleeping, curled up like foxes, with Andrew wedged between them. This was a dream of deliverance, a gift to them both. But only one of them would awaken from it.

Two days later, James was flexing the fingers of his left hand and staring out the window while Molly changed the bandage on his shoulder. She was cheerful by nature and usually talkative. James liked that about her. He loved hearing her stories about her homeland, and he found comfort, somehow, in the lilt in her voice and the way she chose, despite all the carnage she had seen, to view the world as a good and beautiful place. She reminded him, in many ways, of his mother. He felt sure that, if by some miracle they ever met, they'd be good friends.

But on this day, Molly was painfully mindful that James had just lost his brother. She had stood in the hallway two days ago, watching them cling to each other, as if somehow together their strength would be enough to overcome anything, even death itself.

Molly was shaken by how deeply the sight of it had moved her, how it had slipped so easily through all the walls she had built to survive, day by day, caring for men so damaged by war. She had learned in nursing and in life that there are times to talk and times to be silent. This day seemed to call for silence. So she worked quietly, carefully cleaning James' wound with an added measure of tenderness.

"It's looking quite well," she said finally, "you'll be out of here quick as a wink!" She adjusted the sling on his arm, patted him lightly, and hurried off.

Minutes later James heard footsteps hurrying down the hall, followed by voices whispering outside the door. Then he heard Molly's voice above all the others.

"No!" Molly shouted, "I'll not wait for the chaplain! He doesn't know the chaplain! He knows me!"

Molly walked into the room and stood at James' bedside. Her face was wet with tears. She reached over and took his hand.

"James," she said, "I'm so sorry. I have terrible news. We've had a message for you . . . it's about your brother . . . he's . . . he's been listed as missing in action."

James blinked, trying to make sense of her words.

"This is some kind of mix-up," he said. "My brother died two days ago, in this hospital, right down that hall. I was with him, Molly. I thought you knew that."

She drew a breath and made the sign of the cross. Then, instinctively, she cupped James' face with her hands, the way his mother used to do.

"I don't mean Frank," she said softly. "I mean your brother Andrew."

She watched James' eyes as the news became clear to him and confusion gave way to sorrow. He turned his face away from her to stare out the window. A sparrow was building a nest on the ledge, and he seemed transfixed, watching it.

Finally, she touched his shoulder. "Would you like me to stay for a bit?"

He kept watching the sparrow.

"Do you want me to get the doctor, James? Is there anything you need?"

He turned suddenly to face her, as if he'd remembered something.

"I'd appreciate some paper and a pen. I need to write my mother."

Molly nodded. "Of course. I'll be quick about it." She started to leave, then stopped. "The message came in a phone call to the front desk. The nurse who took the call . . . she was very busy, and she's not a bright woman, and she didn't write it down . . . anyhow, she mentioned two other things. She said the caller told her that there's a chance your brother was taken prisoner. And that the army is sending your mother notification on all three of you."

31

UNREFINED FAREWELLS

That Sunday, Cora planned to go to church as usual, catching a ride with Grady and Ada. She put a plate of biscuits and gravy, Justine's favorite breakfast, in the warmer on the back of the wood stove. Before leaving, she peeked in the door of the back bedroom. Justine lay sleeping with Lacy dozing at her breast. Cora smiled. Just looking at Lacy, seeing such God-given beauty, felt like an act of worship.

When she heard Grady's old pickup coming up the road, she hurried out the door, grabbing her coat and the Bible her father had used for his sermons.

John Allen, a young preacher, the latest in a series, was a local boy with an odd nervous tic that occasionally made it a little hard to take him seriously. Due to the tic, no matter what he said, whether preaching a sermon or eulogizing at a funeral, he sometimes appeared to be winking. The real problem, of course, was that he was no Harlan Lacy. Twenty years in the ground, Harlan was still the measure for any man who stepped into the pulpit and dared to try to fill his sizable shoes. Few measured up, including John Allen.

But John was blessed, or cursed, as some would say, with a pastor's heart. He was no orator, but everyone agreed he was a good and faithful shepherd for his flock. In return, they tried not to snicker at his tic.

That Sunday he awoke with a heavy heart. He sensed somehow that God was preparing him to help shoulder the burden of an unbearable grief soon to befall some poor soul in his congregation. John's mind raced with possibilities. So many families had sent fathers and sons off to war. Who would be the next to grieve?

During the opening hymn, his eyes scanned the room, looking for a sign of who it might be. Taking his sermon from the Gospel of Matthew, chapter seven, he began reading aloud, "Ask and it shall be given you; seek, and ye shall find . . ."

It was an exceptionally fine sermon, all would agree. But at the end, when John looked out once again at his beloved congregation, suddenly, he knew.

Cora had silently read the chapter along with him in the yellowed pages of Harlan's Bible. She knew the passage by heart. In the long months since her boys had gone off to war, she had often taken hope in its promise, asking God day and night to bring them safely home. But reading it this day, she felt a strange stirring.

When John raised his hand to call for the benediction, Cora looked up, met his eyes, and was stunned to see he was weeping. Yet his voice was calm and clear.

"May the Lord bless thee, and keep thee," he said, looking steadily at Cora. "May the Lord make his face shine upon thee, and be gracious unto thee. May the Lord lift up his countenance upon thee, and give thee peace."

And all God's people said, "Amen."

After the service, Cora felt a sudden yearning to get home to Lacy. She convinced Ada to cut short her usually lengthy fellowshipping, and Grady drove them back to the farm. He stopped at the mailbox and Cora climbed out, thanking them, as always, for the ride. As they drove away, Ada rolled down the window of the pickup and called, "Kiss that baby's toes for me!"

Cora waved and hurried inside. The house seemed strangely quiet. Were Justine and Lacy still sleeping? She hung her coat on the hall tree, placed Harlan's Bible back on the mantel and walked into the kitchen. That's when she saw the note lying folded on the table. She stared for a moment. Finally she picked it up.

"Cora, I am sorry. I cannot stay here waiting to hear that James is dead. Thank you for your many kindnesses. Lacy will miss you. I will teach her to be just like you. —Justine."

Cora stared at the words, trying to fix them in her mind, trying to make them stop swirling around on the page. "Justine?"

A gust of wind rattled the kitchen window. Cora dropped the note on the table and hurried back to the bedroom where, only hours ago, she had left Justine and Lacy sleeping. The bed was made. The cradle was empty. The blanket Cora had crocheted for Lacy was gone. There was no sign of them, nothing, as if they had never existed, never held any claim on her heart.

Then, on the floor by the bed, Cora saw the gown that she had pulled over Lacy's head the night before, after bathing the child's squirming body. Cora pressed it to her face, inhaling the sweet, milky, baby scent. Then she sat down on the bed and began to wail.

An hour later, a knock at the door sent her running, drying her face with her hands and praying to God that Justine had changed her mind and come back home with Lacy.

Instead, when Cora threw open the door, she saw a young man in a Western Union uniform, holding his hat in one hand, and in the other, a piece of paper.

Cora felt her breath catch in her throat. Two weeks ago, a neighbor, Dora Ingalls, had gotten word that her oldest boy, Luke, had been killed in France. The news had come in a telegram. At least a dozen other families had lost boys, too. The news always came by telegram. Why was this young man standing at her door . . . unless . . . dear God!

Cora shook her head, waved him way, and started to shut the door.

"Ma'am," said the young man, taking a half-step forward.

Cora stopped and raised her hand to silence him.

"Which one?" she said.

The young man blinked. "Ma'am, if you could just read this…."

Again, she stopped him, but this time with only the look in her eyes.

"Which one of my boys … .?"

She never finished the question.

Somewhere under the porch, Blue began to howl.

James' letter arrived nine days later. It was raining hard, a good spring soaking, when Cora heard a car pull up in front of the house. The news about her boys had spread through the valley. For days people had been stopping by to pay their respects. Cora appreciated their kindness, but she could hardly bear their company. Never in her life, since losing her husband, had she felt such a need to be left alone. Why did people not understand that? She stood at the window peering through the lace curtain and was relieved to see, not a visitor, but the postman. He leaned out of the car, wincing at the rain, and stuffed something in the mailbox.

When he drove away, Cora ran out bareheaded in the rain to fetch the letter, clutching it to her heart as she hurried back to the porch. She sat on the porch swing, soaked to the skin, took off her glasses, dried them with her apron, and settled them back on her nose.

Finally, she drew a long breath and studied the envelope. The handwriting belonged to James, but it was different somehow, written with a tremor, by the hand of a wounded soldier. Cora eased open the envelope, took out the single page and began to read.

April 6, 1945

Dearest Ma,

By now you have heard the awful news. I am sorry you had to hear it from strangers. I wanted to tell you myself. Here is what I know so far. I will try to tell you more when I can piece it all together.

Frank Jr. was wounded in battle somewhere near the German border on March 23, and was transported to a Red Cross hospital in France. By some miracle of God, I was there, too, in that same hospital, recovering from an injury to my shoulder that is now mostly healed. Doctors did all they could for Frank. He passed peacefully, no suffering, on April 4. I was with him at the end. We had a good visit. He asked me to tell you that he loved you. He also said to tell you that he knew he was your favorite. That was Frank, always looking to make me laugh.

This morning, I received word that Andrew has been listed as missing in action. For security reasons, they will not release the date and exact location of where he was last known to be. The important thing to remember, Ma, is this: missing in action means there is a good chance that he is still alive. If he was taken prisoner, he probably got sent to a POW camp. No church picnic for sure. But you raised him, Ma. You know how Drew is. He can do anything he sets his mind to. Besides, the war is winding down. The Germans are beat and they know it. It's just a matter of time until they surrender, any day now. Don't worry, Ma. POWs will be released first thing and Andrew, God willing, will be on his way home.

As for me, I am doing well, receiving excellent care, and hope to be released soon. It is not yet official, but it looks like I will not be required to return to active duty. If discharged for disability, I could be home pretty quick. Given a choice, I will ask to serve in some capacity until the war is officially over and the last shot is fired. Either way, Ma, I promise you I will be home soon. Give my love to Justine and Lacy. Tell Justine I will write to her soon.

I remain, as always, your loving son,
James Harlan McCallum

Cora read it slowly. Gusts of wind blew the rain onto the porch. She didn't notice how numb she had grown from the cold until her hands began to shake. Her mind raced to think of the words she would need that evening, after drying herself by the fire, to compose her reply to James. How could she possibly tell him that Justine had run off with Lacy? How could she admit she had no idea what had become of them or where they had gone? And even if she could find words to tell him, how would James, still suffering from the wound in his shoulder, bear the agony of losing his wife and child?

For the first time in her life, Cora vowed to tell a lie—a half-truth, which she knew perfectly well, as her father often said, was still just a lie walking around in fancier shoes. No matter. Somehow, she'd find a way to lie to James about his wife and daughter. She would wait until he was safe at home before telling him a truth that would be harder to face than anything he'd seen in the war.

She wouldn't need to wait for long.

James' shoulder healed surprisingly fast and his lung capacity soon returned to normal levels. But the numbness in his hand persisted, despite his nearly constant efforts to flex his fingers and regain his strength. He could write somewhat legibly with a pen, hold a fork, button his shirt, zip his fly, and even tie his shoes. The problem was his trigger finger. Firing an M1 rifle remained beyond his reach.

James wanted to go home. He ached to hold his newborn daughter, to see his mother's smile, and watch the sun set over those mountains. But more than anything, he longed to be with Justine. He could not stop thinking about her. The scent of her hair. The curve of her spine. The fire that flashed like lightning in her eyes.

He remembered her anger the day he left for the war, and how cold she had seemed in the few letters she had written. But, God help him, he loved her more than ever. Nothing—not even losing his father—had grieved him more than seeing how much his decision to go to war had hurt her.

Maybe he was a fool to think he could win Justine back. But he remembered something he'd once heard his father tell his mother. They were dancing in the kitchen, just the two of them, to music that played only in their heads. James was a boy, watching from the doorway. His dad whispered something in his mother's ear that made her laugh and say, "Frank McCallum, you are such a fool!" And his father replied, "Cora, my darlin', a man can do worse than be a fool for love!"

James would do anything to win Justine back. But first, he had to go home. His family had sacrificed enough to this war. No one would question that. But he and his brothers had vowed at the start to fight Hitler to the end—an end that was sure to come soon. He felt duty-bound to keep that vow, partly to serve his country, but mostly to honor his brothers. James requested to serve in any capacity. But his request was denied and he was honorably discharged from active duty and ordered to be sent home, pending release from the hospital.

The morning of his release, Molly was scheduled to be off duty. She had lain awake most of the night wrestling with her feelings for James. Nothing improper had passed between them. Neither of them would want that. But she had sensed something in him that she had never felt for anyone—a kind of strength and goodness and grace. The thought of never seeing him again filled her with a loneliness she had known only once in her life, at the age of seven, when her parents were killed in rioting in Belfast. She knew she had to let James go. But she couldn't bear to do that without a proper goodbye.

Molly showed up at the hospital, out of uniform, with her auburn hair in loose waves on her shoulders, wearing a pale green dress dotted with tiny yellow roses.

"James McCallum," she said brightly, "rumor has it you'll be leavin' us today!"

James sat in a chair by the bed, dressed, ready to go, waiting for a transport to take him to the train station. At the sound of her voice, he looked up in surprise.

"Molly O'Dea," he said, grinning. "You look . . . different."

She laughed. "I'm not always a nurse, you know. Sometimes I'm just ... me."

He nodded, then looked away.

She stepped closer, reached in a pocket, and handed him a piece of paper.

"It's grand you're going home, James. I'm happy for you and your family. I don't expect I'll ever see you again this side of Heaven. But some lucky day, if you decide to bring your lovely wife and darlin' daughter to see the glories of my homeland? I'd be pleased to offer you a place to stay. Just drop me a line. That's my aunt's address in Dublin. She'll know how to find me."

James stared at the slip of the paper, trying to think of what to say.

"So," she said, changing the subject. "You're going home to your mountains. I've read stories about them—the Blue Ridge, right? I'd love to see them someday. Are they really blue?"

He laughed. "Sometimes they look it."

"Well," she said, turning to go, "I'll be on my way. Take care of yourself, James McCallum."

She was almost out the door when he called after her.

"Pisgah Forest," he said.

She stopped and looked back. "What?"

"Pisgah Forest, North Carolina, USA. That's my home. If you visit the States, my family and I will be proud to put you up. You can write to me there. I'll get it."

James watched from the window as she walked out of the hospital and down the street. She stopped once to turn and wave up at him. Then she was gone.

He opened the paper she had pressed into his palm, and studied the address. The handwriting looked just like her, steady and hopeful. He refolded it and, without thinking, slipped it inside his shirt, where he had once saved letters from his mother and his wife.

Minutes later, the transport arrived. James McCallum was going home.

PART III

1950

32

I'm Here

*S*he was late. The birds were hungry, hopping back and forth from the feeder to the hemlock, perching on branches, bobbing and swaying in the wind. Finally they spotted her trudging up the hill from the farmhouse: an old mountain woman in a flour sack dress, with her bosom resting wearily on her belly and her long silver hair trying to break free from the bun at the nape of her neck.

Standing on her toes and reaching up with a weathered hand, she crumbled cornbread into the feeder, then stepped back to watch. All the regulars were there: an old jay, missing a tail feather from an ill-advised encounter with a bobcat; a pair of dainty, well-mannered Carolina wrens; and her favorite, the cardinal. She loved that bird the way some women love jewelry. Just to see it made her feel adorned.

Pulling her sweater tight around her, she looked out on another unseasonably cold April day. Trees were budding, but across the valley, the mountains had been hidden for days under a thick blanket of clouds.

"I swear," she said to the birds. "Feels like we're skipping spring and summer and going straight to fall. If any of y'all plan to head south before it snows, you'd best start packing."

Pecking greedily at the crumbs in the feeder, the birds paid her no mind.

"Just like my boys," she said, shaking her head. "More interested in my cornbread than in my advice."

The breeze blew a chill down her neck and she stiffened, sensing for the first time a sobering thought, coiled up and hissing like a snake in her path.

"This year," she said aloud to herself and the birds, "might be my last."

Cora McCallum was fifty-two years old. Cultured, some called her. Strong-minded, others would add. She wrote poetry on the backs of seed catalogs, painted watercolor sunsets on stones from the creek; grew dahlias as big and golden as a baby's head; baked biscuits so light you had to weigh them down with jelly. She churned butter and sold it in town; ordered stacks of *Reader's Digest Condensed Books* and read them cover to cover. Sometimes she read them aloud, sitting by the creek with her feet in the water, just to hear the sound of her own voice riding on the current, preaching to the wind.

As to the matter of her demise, she had weighed it carefully, the way she judged corn ripe for picking or a cow ready to calve. It had nothing to do with health. In all her years, she had never been ill, aside from a few months of the morning sickness that told her she was with child. She had always welcomed that.

There were times, days and weeks, when she had wanted nothing more than to hide—to crawl under the porch and curl up with Blue. But such times came from sorrow, not sickness. The two were different. Cora knew that difference well.

Her only physical malady was the arthritis that stiffened her joints and made getting out of bed at first light a bigger chore with each passing year. She figured anyone who survived a lifetime of farming in those mountains ought to expect a few aches and pains. Arthritis could make her suffer, but it would not end her life.

What would do that, she suspected, was one simple fact: she had no heart, no will, no reason left to live.

She still clung to hope and had prayed day and night since Andrew had been reported missing in action that he was safe and would someday come home. She also prayed for Lacy and Justine, and longed with all her heart to see them again. But her hopes had grown thin, hard to cling to, like wisps of smoke in the wind.

Cora had always believed that life is God's greatest gift, and she felt truly thankful, on most days, just to be alive. But feeling thankful was not the same as feeling needed. She missed feeling needed. Lately, she had felt only one reason to live: James. He'd come home from the war five years ago a decorated hero—gaunter, older, quieter—only to learn that his wife had run off and left him, taking their baby daughter.

For months, he'd tried to find them. Justine's mother had moved to Florida, with her maid, Effie. James found a letter Justine had left in a drawer with Loretta's address, and he wrote right away, hoping Justine might be there. Loretta wrote back to say Justine phoned now and then, but had never revealed her whereabouts.

Telephone lines had recently been extended to the mountains, so James had a line installed at the farmhouse and sent the number to Loretta, asking her to please give it to Justine, and to let him know the next time she called.

Other than Loretta, Justine had no living kin, no friends, no ties that James knew of. Still, he followed the slightest lead until finally he had to admit what he had known all along: the chances of finding someone who doesn't want to be found are often slim to none.

Since then, James had tried to make a go of the farm. Cora offered to put him in charge of the lumber operation, but he declined. Losing his daddy to a logging accident had caused him and his brothers to grow up wanting no part of the family business. But James was over that. He'd seen enough men die in the war to realize that it's not timber or bullets that kill you. You die because it's your time to go. But he didn't want to run the mill until he could log alongside the crew. His shoulder still hurt too much to do that. Instead, he took a job working shifts at the paper mill so he would never need to ask his mother for money.

Cora cooked their meals on the wood-burning stove that had

never cooled completely in more than fifty years. She loved that stove. When James' shoulder balked at chopping wood, he bought a newfangled electric range and set it up next to the old stove. He tried to show Cora how to turn it on and off, but she refused to touch it. Finally, three days later, when the woodbox stayed empty, Cora threw up her hands in surrender and learned to cook in a new-fangled way.

They looked after each other. It was a fair and pleasant arrangement. Both were grateful for the help and glad for the company. Yet Cora feared a day would come when she would need James more than he needed her. She had never been a quitter. But the thought of becoming a burden to her boy made her want to give up.

That chilly morning by the feeder, Cora closed her eyes and prayed, "Thank you, Lord, for the gift of life. May your will, not mine, be done. But, Lord, if you plan to keep me alive on this Earth, I surely would appreciate you showing me the reason why."

Opening her eyes, she noticed a new bird at the feeder, a thrush of some sort that seemed a mite greedy. She was about to shoo the bird away when she heard a car coming up the mountain, wheels growling on the gravel road. She heard only its approach, the slam of a car door, and a hasty retreat down the mountain.

A moment later, when the dust settled, Cora blinked, trying to make sense of what she saw. There on the road—clutching a paper sack of belongings in one hand, and an ugly doll in the other—stood a child.

Cora knew her at once. She was five, going on six years old, slight of build, scabby-kneed, with auburn hair that fell about her face in a glorious tangle of curls. She wore a Scotch-plaid Sunday dress, frayed about the hem; a red sweater missing two buttons; leather shoes with scuffed toes and no socks. She looked nothing like the baby Cora had pictured in memory and had prayed for night and day for more than five years. But two things were unmistakable: she had her father's green eyes and her mother's gorgeous face. A striking combination, it left Cora so breathless the child was forced to speak first. Scuffing lines in the dust with the toe of her shoe, she turned her head to one side and looked into her grandmother's eyes.

"Ma'am?" said the child. "I'm here."

A gust of wind brought the smell of rain, scattering birds from the feeder. In the distance, the 8:00 a.m. whistle sounded at the mill. Cora found the last crumb of cornbread in her apron pocket and dropped it on the ground.

"Child," she said finally, "where is your mother?"

Lacy stared down the road as if she might still see the car that had brought her. Then she rubbed her eye with the fist that clutched the rag doll.

"My mama's gone," she said. "She told me to stay here with you and my daddy until she comes back to get me."

"Did your mama happen to say when that might be?"

"Yes, ma'am. She said she'll come back soon as she can."

Cora nodded and looked up at the sky. "Well, then. I reckon you'd best come on in the house. It looks like it's coming a storm. Your daddy's working the graveyard shift. He'll be home soon from the mill and need his breakfast. I expect you might be hungry, too."

"No, ma'am," said Lacy. "I don't eat much." She glanced up at her grandmother and ventured a smile. "I hear you make good biscuits."

"Come on, then," Cora said, taking the sack from the girl, "let's go see if we can find one for you."

When James came home from the mill that morning he headed straight to the barn to milk. When he finished, he patted the cows rumps, put them out to pasture, then climbed the back steps to the farmhouse carrying two full pails of milk.

"Hey, Ma . . ." He stopped in the doorway of the kitchen, puzzled to see Cora sitting at the table with a child who appeared to be inhaling a biscuit.

Lacy looked up and met her father's eyes. A glob of jelly slid down her chin.

"Are you my daddy?"

For a moment, James was silent, hearing only the pounding of his heart.

"James," Cora said. "Speak up."

He took a step through the door, still holding the milk pails.

"Yes," he said, finally. "Yes, I am . . . your daddy."

Lacy nodded and looked at Cora. "My mama was right. I've got his eyes." Then she took another bite of biscuit.

James turned to look at his mother.

"Go wash up, son," Cora said. "Your breakfast is getting cold."

That night, as Lacy slept in the old feather bed that had once held her parents, Cora sat in a chair by the fire, rocking and humming, waiting for James to speak.

Finally, he cleared his throat. "Mama?"

"I'm listening, James."

"I doubt Justine will be coming back any time soon."

Cora stared at the fire.

"If she does come around," he said, "I'm not going to let her take Lacy again." He leaned forward, dangling a cigarette from his hand between his knees. "A child needs a daddy."

Cora gripped the rocker's arms and her eyes flew wide with fury. "In case you haven't noticed, James, a child also needs a mother. Maybe you need a wife?"

"I had a wife, Ma. She left me. What I need is a mother for my child."

Cora shook her head. "I'm sorry, James. I can't promise you that

I can stay alive and raise your child while Justine figures out what she wants."

"I know that, Ma. I'm just asking you to do what you can. Lacy needs you. So do I."

Cora studied her son's face, seeing for a moment not the man that he'd become, but the boy that he had been—a bright, tender child who loved people and animals and rivers and mountains, all with the same innocent, unfettered love. She sighed and felt her anger slip away, like the fiery heat of the summer sun when it finally sets.

"All right, son," she said. "I'm here. And I don't plan to leave."

James nodded and took a drag on his cigarette, then rubbed his mouth with the back of his hand. "There's one more thing, Ma. If Justine comes back and wants to stay, I aim to let her."

Cora closed her eyes and leaned back to rest in the old wooden rocker where she and her mother and her grandmother and Justine had each in turn nursed their babies.

"I know that, son," she said. "I've known that all along."

A month passed with no word from Justine. James heard a rumor from Earl Davis down at the mill that she was in Swannanoa, waiting tables and living with J.D. Allen. Whether that was true or not was anybody's bet. With Earl, it could go either way. Like most boys who knew her, he'd had a thing for Justine since he was old enough to admit it. He might have asked her out, had his daddy not made him quit school to take a job at the mill. After that, Earl let go of a lot of dreams, including Justine. People said it was a shame and all, but they didn't blame his old man, sick as he was with the cancer. The family needed the money. Besides, Justine had her mind set on marrying James. Any fool could see that. Any fool but Earl or James.

The mill whistle had just sounded 8:00 a.m., signaling the shift change, graveyard to first, when Earl caught up with James in the parking lot.

"Who says she's in Swannanoa?" James said, squinting into the sun, cupping his hands around a match to light a Camel.

"I ran into J.D. about a month ago. Hadn't seen him in ages. He was here to check on his family's old place. It's not much, but they're all gone now, and they left it to him. He said he'd moved up to Swannanoa to work construction about five years ago, and Justine's been living with him and waiting tables."

Earl nodded at the cigarette. "You got another one of them?"

James pulled the pack of Camels from his shirt pocket and shook one loose. "I never knew J. D. to work construction."

"He don't do it much," Earl said grinning, "only when he's sober."

James opened the door of the pickup and climbed in. "I got cows to milk."

Earl flicked a speck of tobacco off his tongue.

"J.D. says they're doin' all right. Says Justine's makin' good money in tips at the cafe. I guess she's still, you know, got her looks and all."

The engine caught in the pickup and James shifted gears. Earl stepped back and waved. As the pickup disappeared around a bend, Earl crushed the cigarette under his boot and mumbled to himself, "I bet she looks better 'n ever."

Cora wasted no time making Lacy feel at home. She woke the child each morning to help with breakfast, sent her out to gather eggs, called her in to set the table. She showed her how to skim the cream from the cows' milk and churn it into butter. Then she'd let her help pack it into a wooden mold, stamp it with a daisy shape, and wrap in wax paper to sell in town.

She taught her how to peel apples for a cobbler, stew venison until it fell apart, and bake biscuits that were lighter than angels' wings. She helped her to see beauty in ordinary things: to paint sunsets on stones, crochet lace one chain at a time, find roses blooming in the dead of winter, and play a fairly decent game of checkers.

She began teaching her to read by reading to her every evening before bed, first a passage from the King James, followed by a chapter from *Uncle Remus.*

Come morning, after breakfast, they'd take long walks on the mountain, leaning on the snake sticks that James had carved for them. Cora would call out in greeting the names of every plant and creature: "Hello, Hickory Tree, you're lookin' mighty tall today. Keep your distance, Mr. Skunk, we don't need what you're peddlin'!"

Lacy laughed and stored it all in memory.

One morning along a creek bank, Cora bent down to examine a find.

"Look at this," she said, digging up a small green plant with a slim, carrot-like root.

"It's called bloodroot. Did you ever see a plant bleed?"

Lacy shook her head.

Using her thumbnail, Cora pricked a hole in the root. A drop of red-orange sap welled up from the hole and slowly trickled downward.

Lacy's eyes grew wide. "Did you hurt it, Grandma?"

"What? No, child, it's just a plant."

"Is it going to die?" Lacy's lower lip was trembling.

Cora thought fast. "No, it won't die. We'll put it back in the ground, and next spring we'll come back and it will be blooming with flowers white as snow."

Lacy nodded. Cora dug a hole with a stick, inserted the root and packed the earth back around it. Still kneeling, she turned to Lacy. "You'll see. I promise."

"I don't like blood, Grandma. Blood scares me."

Cora rose to her feet, wiping her hands on her apron. "I know what you mean," she said. "I don't like it, either. Let's head on back home and have us a biscuit."

>>>

James had come home from the mill that morning, milked the cows, finished the plate of biscuits and gravy that Cora had left in the warmer of the wood stove, and gone straight to bed. Five hours later, he was just waking up, stepping out on the porch for a smoke when he heard them in the distance, Cora and Lacy, coming down the mountain, chattering like squirrels.

He spotted them on the path, Cora trudging, Lacy bouncing. A gust of wind blew a swirl of leaves around them and they dropped their sticks and lifted their arms, laughing and twirling like angels dancing on the head of a pin.

James was sure it was one of the most beautiful sights he had ever seen. Lacy's presence had been a healing balm on all his mother's ailments—body, mind, and soul. He could see Cora growing stronger, looking younger, taking pleasure in things she had long forgotten. It was like watching a movie of her life playing slowly in reverse. Picture that, he thought, a movie about his mama showing at the drive-in in town. Who in God's name could play her? Rita Hayworth? Vivien Leigh? Lucille Ball? And who would play him?

"Hey, Daddy!" Lacy had spotted him and started running. The sun caught her hair and set it to shining like a copper kettle.

James had heard it for years, but for the first time in his life, he was beginning to understand what his mother had so often said: children are God's best medicine. He had felt it from the start, after Lacy came back home to the farm, the first time she crawled up in his lap and fell asleep. Just like that, she had filled up a thousand empty places in his heart.

33

BAD RUBY

SUMMER

Cora could scarcely believe how quickly and happily each day had passed in the three months since Lacy's arrival. If the child missed her mother, it didn't show much. Sometimes Cora would see her standing on the hill, looking up the road, as if listening for a car. But Lacy never asked about Justine, or talked about their lives together.

Late one night, Cora woke to the sound of sobbing coming from the child's room. When she went to comfort her, Lacy blamed it on a nightmare. The next night the sobbing came again. This time when Cora went to her room, Lacy seemed to be talking in her sleep.

"No!" she said to the darkness, "please don't say that!"

"Child?" Cora said. "Are you having another bad dream?"

Lacy stopped crying, but couldn't stop shaking.

"I'm all right, Grandma," she said. "It's just . . . Ruby."

Lacy pointed to the rag doll on the pillow beside her—the same doll she had clung to on the road that day, and every day since. "She talks to me sometimes."

Cora frowned, puzzled. "What does she say to you?"

Lacy waited, studying her grandmother's face in the moonlight that came glimmering through the bedroom window. Finally, she poured our her heart in a rush.

"Ruby tells me bad things, Grandma. She says I'm ugly. And that my mama's no good. And that nobody wants me, not even you or my daddy. I ask her nicely, I say, 'Please, Ruby, let me sleep.' Sometimes she'll hush. But when she won't, it hurts my feelings and makes me scared, and I can't help it, Grandma. I cry like a big old baby."

Cora dried Lacy's face with her hand. "Do you want me to take Ruby away?"

Lacy drew Ruby close. "No ma'am, I have to keep her. She's all I've got."

Cora nodded. "All right. But I want you to listen hard to what I'm about to say. Ruby is wrong about you. She has no right to say those awful things. Not one of them is true. She's not all you have, child. You have us—your mama, even though she's not here, and your daddy and me. We all love you and want to be with you. You know that, don't you, in your heart?"

Lacy nodded and climbed into her grandmother's lap. Cora pressed her lips to Lacy's ear and whispered, "I promise you this: Ruby will say no more tonight, because I'll be here to stop her. You can rest easy now, child. Close your eyes and be at peace. I will pray you to sleep."

Tucking Lacy back in bed, Cora kissed the child's head and began to pray. First for Lacy, for healing and wholeness. Then for her boys: James at the mill, Frank Jr. in Heaven, and Drew in his faraway place. She prayed for herself, for wisdom and strength and time to be whatever Lacy might need. Finally, when Lacy fell limp with sleep, Cora prayed for Justine.

Then she slipped from the room, leaving the door ajar, asking God and the moon to keep watch through the night over the child who had completely stolen her heart.

An hour later, when James got home from second shift at the mill, he was alarmed to see a light in Cora's bedroom window. He bounded up the stairs and down the hall to her room, then stopped outside her door, hearing an old familiar sound—the humming of the Singer, her old treadle sewing machine. He started to knock, but instead turned and went to bed, leaving his mother to her mysterious late-night sewing.

34

GETTING BY

$\mathcal{T}$he taste of blood is a powerful force. It can turn an animal into a killer. It can turn a woman into a slave.

"James?" Cora shook him hard. "Wake up. Something's after the hens."

Lacy woke to the racket of squawking chickens and thumping feet. Seeing a light in the kitchen, she came down the hall rubbing her eyes to find her grandmother in her nightgown, peering out the window into the dark, and her daddy, barefoot and shirtless, running out the back door with a shotgun.

"Where's he going, Grandma?"

Before Cora could answer, two shots broke the night, echoing on the mountains. Cora looked at Lacy. "Go put your shoes on, child. You'll catch cold."

At the henhouse, James lowered the shotgun and cussed under his breath. He stood for a moment, squinting into the woods where a small red fox had run for cover, toting one of Cora's pullets in its mouth. The sun was inching above the ridge, sending the first rays of light reaching down into the valley like fiery fingers of God. Staring at the ground, he swore again. A trail of blood led from the back of the henhouse to the woods.

An hour later, at breakfast, Lacy played with her oatmeal and watched her daddy sop gravy with a biscuit.

"Why did that fox want to hurt Grandma's chicken?"

James popped the biscuit in his mouth. "'Cause he's a damn fox."

Cora shot him a look. He took a swig of coffee and set the cup on the table.

"He wasn't looking to hurt the chicken, Lacy," he said. "He was just looking for something to eat."

"Was he hungry?"

"If he's hungry," Cora said, "he can find plenty to eat besides my chickens."

James laughed. "Oh, he won't be looking for anything else to eat. You can count on that. He's had a taste of chicken blood. He'll be back for more."

Lacy's eyes got big. "Is he going to kill another chicken?"

"Not if I can help it," James said. "You want to help me set a trap?"

After breakfast, Cora cleared the dishes while James and Lacy set to work in the basement building a narrow wooden box about four feet long. Using chicken wire, James covered one end of the box and fashioned a trap door for the other, showing Lacy how the door would swing in, but not out.

"See?" he said, "When he gets past that door, he's done."

"What will we do with him, daddy?"

James set the hammer on the work bench and looked at Lacy.

"We can't let him keep killing our chickens, Lacy. You won't have to do anything. I'll take care of it."

For three nights, all was quiet in the henhouse. Lacy lay awake listening until the mill whistle blew at midnight and she couldn't keep her eyes open any longer.

Each morning, when James got home from working the grave-yard shift, he stopped at the henhouse to check the trap before milking. Nothing. On the fourth night, just before dawn, the chickens roused, clucking and squawking, and ran out of the henhouse. Then they settled their feathers and began pecking for worms on the ground in the pen. Cora and Lacy stirred in their beds and drifted back to sleep.

Come morning, Cora sent Lacy, as usual, to gather the eggs for breakfast.

Lacy hated gathering eggs. She hated the henhouse—a dark, dank, windowless box littered with nasty-smelling, black and white, swirly piles of chicken poop. Just to look at them made her gag. Most of all, she hated the chickens—the way they stared at her with their beady eyes, scratching the ground with their claws and making those awful sounds, like something evil was trying to crawl out of their throats. She had often heard about the devil in Sunday School. Now, whenever she pictured him in her mind, he was a giant rooster.

But Lacy didn't need to worry about Cora's rooster any more. That was a memory she'd never forget. One morning when Lacy had gone alone to gather eggs, the rooster was waiting, hiding behind a hay bale. As Lacy reached for an egg, he jumped on her back, sank his claws in her shoulders, and started flapping his wings about her head. When Cora heard Lacy scream, she came running, grabbed the rooster's neck, and wrung it. That night they ate stewed rooster and dumplings. Lacy swore it was the best meal she ever ate.

Every morning since the flogging by the rooster, Lacy had dutifully gone to the henhouse to gather eggs. But she never took Ruby. Ruby hated chickens even more than Lacy did. On this morning, Lacy stepped slowly into the henhouse and stood by the door, letting her eyes adjust to the dark. The hens were out in the pen scratching for the feed she had scattered. She liked to lure them out with the feed so she didn't need to lift them off the nests to get their eggs. But there was no need to lure them this time. For some reason, they were already out in the pen. She began working the rows of nests, gathering courage along with the eggs.

The first sound she heard was barely a whimper. Lacy stopped to listen, holding her breath. Turning slowly, she stared at the hole in the boards where James had positioned the box trap. Something was clawing, scratching hard inside the box. A sharp yelp pierced the air, and she jumped, crushing the egg she held in her hand. Wiping the yolk on her dress, she bolted from the henhouse, sending the chickens squawking around the pen. Then she flung open the gate, ran out of the pen, and slammed it shut behind her.

Halfway up the hill, she stopped to look back. The pounding of her heart began to ease a bit. In the distance, the eight o'clock whistle sounded at the mill. Her daddy would be home soon. She ought to wait for him. She ought to go tell her grandmother . . .

Another yelp and she flinched. Her heart began to pound so hard she thought it might fly out of her chest. Clinching her fists, she walked down the hill and went back into the henhouse, where she forced herself to kneel on the ground and peer into the trap.

When the fox caught her scent, he began thrashing, whining, writhing, within the narrow walls of the box. Lacy raised a finger to her lips.

"Hush," she whispered.

The fox grew still. Panting hard, with his red tongue lolling from his mouth, he slowly craned his neck and turned his head to face her.

There is a look that sometimes passes between God's creatures— the chosen ones that have had to suffer and fight to get by. That look passed between Lacy and the fox.

In the kitchen, stirring biscuit dough, Cora looked out the window to see Lacy skipping up the hill. Lacy waved and Cora waved back, sending a little cloud of flour dust floating on the air. Across the field, something caught Cora's eye. Squinting into the sunlight, she saw a bushy red tail snap like a whip and disappear into the woods.

The first time J.D. hit her, Justine didn't make much of it. She'd been hit by meaner and uglier men. One more didn't seem to matter. If you get knocked around enough, over time, you can develop a tendency to think it's normal.

When Justine was growing up, Loretta never hit her much, as long as Justine stayed out of her way. But Loretta's men—the truckers and loggers and millhands and drunks that she brought home and took to her bed night after night—they were a different story. As far back as Justine could remember, she had known the taste of her own blood. Most every man who stayed around for long had given her a sample. Until Bill Mason. The only other exception was James.

After they were married, Justine kept waiting for James to hit her, certain it would happen. When it didn't, she began to taunt him, saying things she had never dared say to a man. The more she goaded, the harder he laughed. The harder she pushed, the softer he grew. She had never known such tenderness, never felt such feelings. She had never, until James, known love.

In the end, he had hurt her worse than anyone ever had. The day he left to go off to war with his brothers, that was it, she was through. Call it pride or resentment or downright stupidity. The simple truth was this: Justine would rather take a beating from a man she despised than be left by the only man she ever loved.

It puzzled her why she'd thought J.D. Allen would be any different from most of the other men she had known. At the start—five years ago, when she saw him for the first time since high school, in the parking lot outside Pack's Store—he still had that easy, sleepy look about his eyes that had always made her think he might be worth getting to know a lot better. She remembered that day clearly. It went like this:

She had just loaded a sack of groceries in the back of James' pickup, climbed behind the wheel and slammed the door when she saw J.D. standing there in the parking lot grinning at her.

She rolled down the window and he came over and leaned on the door.

"Well, if it ain't the purtiest girl ever to set foot in these old mountains."

Justine smiled. "Hey, J.D. How you been?"

"I been all right. Hell, girl, I heard you married James McCallum and had a young 'un."

"Yeah, well, you heard right. James is off playin' soldier. I'm staying with his mama on the farm. My baby girl is three months old."

J.D. shook his head, chewing a toothpick. "You don't look like you never had no baby."

She looked away. "I best be going. Good seeing you, J.D."

"Hold on," he said, laying a hand on her arm. "I'm thinkin' 'bout going up to Swannanoa to find work. If you get bored with James' mama, call the Long Branch and leave me a message."

Justine didn't sleep that night. The next day, she left J.D. a message. A week later, while Cora was at church, she took Lacy and went to Swannanoa with J.D. That was five years ago.

The first time J.D. split her lip, Justine thought about leaving him. Truth was she had no place to go. Loretta would be willing to take her in, but Justine couldn't stand the thought of living with her crazy mother running her mouth day and night. And there was no way Justine could bring herself to go back to Cora and the farm. Besides, J.D. acted sorry for a while, and tried to make it up to her—the same way men had always tried to make it up to Loretta, before they started hitting her again. The longer Justine stayed with J.D., the harder it got to see a way out. She made good tips waiting tables. J.D. spent most of it on moonshine, but she didn't care. The drunker he got, the longer he stayed passed out.

Time passes in slow motion, unnoticed and unheeded by someone who feels hopelessly trapped. Like a prisoner on death row, Justine went through the motions of her life, taking care of her daughter and trying to keep J.D. happy. She told herself the beatings didn't happen all that often, only once a month or so, when she couldn't keep her mouth shut and made J.D. hopping mad. What hurt most was the anticipation—wondering when the next beating was coming and how bad it might be. Afterward, bruised and bleeding, she'd feel a strange sense of relief, knowing for now it was over, and it would be a while, at least, before he'd beat her again.

Some women, like Loretta, spend their lives waiting for the next beating. Justine told herself she wasn't one of those women. She wasn't like her mama. She swore that she would leave J.D.—just as soon as she could figure out how to get by without him. She would keep telling herself that for years to come. Nothing would change, until the day J.D. finally raised his hand to Lacy.

Lacy was five years old. She made a child's innocent mistake of sassing J.D. somehow, and he pulled off his belt, raised it over his head, and threatened to whip her with it. When Justine stepped between them, he whipped Justine instead. The next day, while J.D. was at work, Justine drove Lacy back to Pisgah Forest and dropped her off in front of the farmhouse. She promised Lacy she'd come back for her soon, but told her honestly, she didn't know when that would be.

In May, barely a month after Justine left Lacy at the farm, J.D. got fired and started talking about moving back home to look for work. Justine tried to think of some way to stay in Swannanoa on her own without him. But, no. If J.D. moved back to Pisgah Forest, she would go with him. She was hungering bad to see Lacy. And the baby was due any day.

35

BELONGINGS

*O*n a blistering hot August day, Lacy was wading in the creek, stacking stones to see how high she could pile them before they came crashing down. When she heard the whine of a pickup coming up the mountain, she knew it wasn't her daddy. He never drove that way. That was the way her mama drove, like she always needed to get away from something fast.

Cora stood at the kitchen sink peeling apples for a pie, keeping one eye on Lacy through the window. She saw the child climb out of the creek and go running up the hill to where the road swung around in front of the farmhouse.

Wiping her hands on a rag, Cora stepped out on the porch and shaded her eyes from the sun. A rusted-out pickup had pulled up and stopped next to the mailbox. Cora didn't recognize the truck, but she knew its driver.

"Hey, Cora." Justine climbed down from the driver's seat and threw an arm around Lacy, who had run up the hill to meet her. Then Justine reached into the truck and pulled out what appeared to a bundle of wash. Holding the bundle in her arms, she started up the path to the porch with Lacy hanging on her skirt.

As she drew near, Cora saw the bundle more clearly. It had a face.

"You look good, Cora," Justine grinned. "Same as ever."

Cora stared at the baby.

"He's mine," Justine said. "He's three months old."

Four months had passed since the day Lacy was left at the farm. Weeks before, when she asked about the bulge in her mother's belly, Justine had told her she was just getting fat. Lacy hadn't questioned it. She'd once watched a stray cat give birth to a litter of kittens. But the child had no idea where human babies come from.

Pulling the blanket off the infant's feet, Lacy laughed. "Look at his toes! They're so little! Where did you get him, Mama? Can we keep him?"

Justine stopped at the porch steps and held the baby out to Lacy.

"You can hold him. Just be careful. His name's Mason. He's your brother."

Lacy looked up from the baby to her mother, and then to her grandmother.

"Come on," Cora said, "Let's go in the house and get y'all something to eat."

In the kitchen, Cora spread a quilt on the floor to make a pallet for the baby. Lacy sprawled beside him, laughing at the way he gripped her thumb in his fist.

"He's strong, Mama! I can't make him turn me loose!"

Justine sat across from Cora at the kitchen table, crumbling cornbread into a glass of buttermilk and eating it with a spoon. "I've missed your cornbread, Cora."

"Well, Justine, I reckon it's missed you, too."

James' truck pulled up in the yard and Lacy scrambled to her feet to look out the window. "My daddy's back from the store," she said.

Justine rose to her feet and set the glass in the sink. "Thanks for the buttermilk and cornbread, Cora. It was mighty good. Lacy? Go get your stuff. We need to go."

"But, Mama . . ."

"Go on, I said."

"Wait, Justine," Cora said, reaching for Lacy.

Just then, James walked through the door carrying a sack of groceries. He stood for a moment staring at Justine and holding the sack as if he wasn't sure what to do with it. Her eyes had always done that, grabbed hold of him, swallowed him up, made him forget what he was doing.

The clock in the front room began to strike and everyone, even Mason, fell silent, listening, waiting for it to finish. At the stroke of ten, Lacy spoke up.

"Daddy, this here's my baby brother and he's real strong."

"Lacy!" Justine's voice snapped. "I told you to go fetch your belongings!"

James set the sack on the table. "No," he said. "She's not leaving here."

Justine whirled to face him. "Don't tell me what my child can do!"

Lacy began to cry, and Cora rose from her chair to rest a hand on Justine's shoulder. "Sit down, Justine. James? Pour Justine a cup of coffee. You take it with cream, right, Justine? Get one for yourself, too, son. Lacy's going to help me take Mason to see the cows. We'll be back directly. While we're gone, maybe you two can act like you've still got some of the brains God gave you, and talk this out in a civilized manner that won't make your daughter cry."

Thirty minutes later, after Mason had sucked all the life out of his fist and started howling like a hound, Cora and Lacy walked back to the farmhouse. James and Justine were sitting at the kitchen table with two half-empty cups of cold coffee.

"I swear the boy's hungry all the time," Justine said, taking the wailing Mason from Cora's arms. As she loosened the buttons of her blouse, she looked up at James and their eyes met, not in anger, but in longing. For a moment, there was no one in the room but the two of them as they had been at the start, crazy for each other's touch. Then James looked away, and Justine put Mason to her breast.

"I'm staying not far from here, Cora," Justine said. "You know the old Allen place? The farmhouse burned down years ago. They built a new place on it, small but not bad. Anyhow. You can see Lacy anytime you want. I got me a job, a couple of shifts a week, waiting tables at the Long Branch. If you wouldn't mind watching Mason once in a while, I'd be glad to pay you."

Cora nodded. "No need to pay me, Justine. Babies are easy," she said, glancing at James. "They wait until they're grown to give you fits."

Lacy climbed in James' lap and rested her head on his shoulder. She loved being with him and her grandmother. She loved life on the farm. But children who've seen their mothers abused often feel responsible for protecting them. Lacy would rather stay on the farm. But she would follow her mother to the ends of the Earth.

Cora excused herself to gather the child's belongings. When she returned, Justine was patting Mason's back to get him to burp. He did, and they all laughed.

Cora set the bag of Lacy's things on the floor and brushed her hand over the child's hair. "Your daddy will come fetch you soon for a visit."

Lacy kissed James' cheek and looked into his eyes. He tried to speak, but couldn't get the words out.

"Don't worry, Daddy, I'll be seeing you soon."

She climbed down from his lap and wrapped her arms around Cora's legs. Cora pulled her close and whispered in her ear the question she had asked her every night before bed.

"Where is your old grandma when you can't see her?"

Lacy answered, as always, by smiling and placing her hand on her heart.

"And how much do I love you?" Cora said.

"You love me ALL, Grandma," Lacy said, just the way Cora had taught her, "and that's as much as anybody can possibly love."

Then she picked up Ruby and the sack of her things and followed her mother and Mason out to the truck. James walked out with them. Stopping on the porch to light a Camel, he spit out a shred of tobacco.

"That looks a helluva lot like J.D. Allen's old pickup."

Justine opened the truck door and Lacy climbed up on the seat.

"Hold your brother," Justine said, handing Mason to Lacy. "Hold him tight."

Then she closed the door and looked back at James. "I forgot you knew J.D."

James flicked a spent match into the hydrangeas by the porch.

"Everybody in this county knows J.D. Allen," he said. "Especially the law."

Justine gave him a go-to-hell look. Then she climbed in the pickup, slammed the door, and drove off, slinging gravel. The last thing James saw was Lacy's small hand hanging out the window waving goodbye.

36

MASON'S LAUGHING EYES

NOVEMBER

$\mathcal{M}$ason was six months old, crawling like a box turtle on the porch of J.D. Allen's cabin. Justine sat in a rocker, snapping pole beans from her apron into a bucket. In the yard, Lacy was teaching Ruby how to catch a June bug.

"Lacy!" Justine pointed at Mason, who was making a break for the edge of the porch. "Don't let him crawl off of there! He can't see where he's going!"

Lacy dropped Ruby in the dirt and ran over to the porch, plopping down on the splintered boards to block Mason's path.

"Mason!" she yelled, "Stop!"

Hearing her command, he laughed and picked up speed, crawling faster until he rammed her head on. Then he rolled over and cackled, pleased with himself.

Lacy looked at her mother. "What do you mean he can't see where he's going?"

Justine kept snapping beans, tossing the bad ones to the chickens in the yard.

"Doctors said he was born too soon. They had to give him oxygen to keep him alive and . . . Lacy, take that stick out of his fist before he puts it in his mouth!"

Lacy wrestled the stick from Mason's hand and looked back at her mother.

"Anyhow," Justine snapped another bean. "He's blind."

J.D.'s mangy hound, Killer, covered in ticks, trotted up to the porch steps to lift a hind leg. Justine stomped her foot and yelled at the dog. "Get on out of here!"

Killer tucked tail and crawled under the porch. Lacy watched until the dog was out of sight. Then she turned to Mason, who crawled up into her lap. She waved a hand in front of his face and he reached out, grinning, as if to grab it.

Lacy shook her head. "He can't be blind, Mama. He laughs at my face."

Justine stood and fanned the apron, tossing the bean stems into the yard.

"He laughs at the sound of your voice, Lacy. He will never see your face."

A clap of thunder rumbled off the mountain, stirring a breeze that brought the smell of rain. Lifting Mason to her hip, Justine turned to go inside. "Bring that bucket of beans on in the kitchen. I've got to get cleaned up to go to work."

The screen door slammed as the first drops of rain began to pockmark the dust in the yard. Lacy looked out and saw something lying in the dirt. Ruby! She scrambled off the porch, snatched up the doll, and ran back to the steps. Holding her breath, she turned Ruby over, fearing the worst. Sure enough, both of Ruby's button eyes were caked with mud.

An hour later, Lacy lay on the floor holding a bottle for Mason and watching her mother stir a pot of beans on the stove. Justine had changed into a fresh blouse, pinned up her hair, and put on two coats of red lipstick. Lacy thought Justine always looked pretty, even when she stayed out late and woke up the next morning with purple shadows under her eyes. But red lipstick was magic stuff. It made her mama look even more special. Maybe she ought to try some red lipstick on Ruby?

Rain drummed a sleepy tune on the tin roof of the cabin. Mason drained the bottle with his eyes half closed, kicking his legs like a beetle and wrapping a fist in Lacy's hair. Resting her face on his belly, she breathed him in. Nothing, not even her grandmother's biscuits, smelled better than Mason's belly—except, of course, when he was sopping wet, or worse.

"Let go of me, Mason," she said, pulling her hair free from his grip. Seconds later, she was back with a dry diaper. "Stop kicking," she said, unsnapping a pin. He kicked harder and the pin pricked her finger, drawing blood.

Lacy sighed and sucked the blood. "Mama? Can me and Mason stay with Grandma tonight while you go to work?"

Justine tapped the wooden spoon on the edge of the pot and set it on the counter. "Not this time. You can watch Mason for me until J.D. gets home."

"Can I call Grandma and talk to her?"

"You don't need to bother her, Lacy. J.D. gets off work at four o'clock. He can bake y'all some cornbread to go with the beans. I'll be home by ten tonight."

A car horn sounded. Justine looked up. "That's Earlene," she said, turning the burner down on the beans. "Give these a stir now and then, Lacy, and take care of your brother. I gotta go."

37

A Short Drive Down
a Long Road

*T*he clock on the mantel had marked the passage of time for five generations of Cora's family, ticking minutes and striking hours with a hollow, clanging sound that brought to mind a silver spoon banging on a tin wash tub. It was a homely clock, but if properly wound, it kept good time. You could count on it. To Cora, there was a certain measure of beauty in anything you could dependably count on.

That night, as always, when the clock struck nine, Cora marked her place and closed the book that she was reading—Alan Paton's *Cry the Beloved Country*, a *Reader's Digest* condensed novel. Cora thought it was one of the finest and most beautiful books she'd ever read, next to the Bible, of course. Leaning back into the rocker, she closed her eyes, listening to the sounds of the night. Thunder rumbling on the mountain. Rain spitting on the roof. Frank whistling off-key in her memory.

When folks at church asked, "Cora, don't you get lonesome on that mountain all alone?" she would laugh and say, "Alone is not the same as lonesome."

But sometimes, like tonight, when the clock struck nine, she couldn't help but wonder. Was she a fool to be content with the company of nothing but birds and books and memories?

Two hours later, she was sound asleep when the phone rang. She leapt out of bed, clamping her hand over her heart to keep it from flying out of her chest.

"Lord, help me!" she shouted. "Good news never calls after dark!"

She switched on the light and stumbled to the telephone. On the fourth ring, she steeled herself and lifted the receiver.

"Grandma?" Lacy was crying.

Cora could hear Mason wailing in the background.

"Lacy, are you all right?"

"We're OK, Grandma, but—hush, Mason! I can't hear!—Mama's hurt bad!"

"Is J.D. there?"

"No, ma'am, he left," Lacy began to sob. "He . . . he told me not to call you!"

"Hold on, child," Cora said. "I'm coming over there."

"Grandma, wait, promise you won't tell Daddy! I don't want him to know!"

"Tend to your brother, Lacy. I'm on my way."

Out in the shed, Cora pulled the canvas off Frank's old Ford. James drove a pickup and had wanted to sell the Ford years ago, but Cora wouldn't hear of it. So James had kept it tuned up and drove it every Sunday to take Cora to church.

Cora opened the door and climbed behind the wheel. She could barely see above the dash. The smell of the leather reminded her of Frank. In all her years, she had never driven a car. But she had watched Frank and the boys drive plenty of times. A person could learn a lot by watching. How hard could it be?

"Lord, help me!" she prayed again, and fired it up. Frank was probably spinning in his grave.

Twenty minutes and a few minor mishaps later, Cora and the Ford crossed the bridge over the river. The moon was just rising over the top of the mountain, kicking back the clouds like quilts on a feather bed. She followed the road along the river for almost two miles until she came to a clearing that had once been the Allen farm. The original house had burned to the ground years ago, leaving nothing but the stone chimney. Beside it, J.D. had built a three-room shack surrounded by a half circle of scrub pines. The door hung partly open, crooked on its hinges, spilling light out into the yard. No sign of J.D.'s pickup. Cora set the brake on the Ford, and climbed the warped steps to the porch.

"Lacy?"

In the dim light of a single bulb dangling from the ceiling, Justine lay in a heap on the linoleum, limp as a load of wash. Lacy sat on the floor, dabbing her mother's face with a bloody rag and holding Mason, who had fallen asleep in his sister's lap.

At the sound of Cora's voice Lacy burst into tears. Mason startled and began to wail. All in one movement, Cora hoisted Mason onto her hip, then reached down to turn Lacy's face up to the light. Her lower lip was bleeding.

"What happened to you, child?"

Lacy looked at her mother. "I'm all right, Grandma. Just help my mama."

Cora reached for the rag, but Lacy clung to it, wiping Justine's brow.

"Let it go, child. You can go fetch me a clean one."

Lacy didn't move.

"Go on now. Your mama needs your help."

Lacy dropped the rag and ran out to the kitchen.

When Mason heard his sister's footsteps, he began to wail again. Cora gathered him up against her neck and clucked into his ear. He was sopping wet, smelling of soured milk.

"Hush now, little man. I'll tend to you soon. First I've got to see to your mama."

She laid Mason on a quilt on the floor, wrapped him in a blanket, and helped him find his fist. Then she turned and knelt on the floor beside her daughter-in-law.

Justine was conscious, barely. Her lip was split, a tooth broken, and one eye was swollen shut. But she managed a bloody grin.

"Hey, old woman, what brings you here?"

Cora pressed a palm into Justine's abdomen. "Does that hurt?"

"Hell, yes!" Justine moaned, rolling her eyes. "I'm all right. Leave me be."

Cora heard Lacy running water in the kitchen. She looked at Justine.

"Justine, you are bleeding on the floor and your babies are crying. You are not all right. Not one bit. But I reckon you will live."

Justine looked away. "J.D. didn't mean to hit Lacy, Cora. I told her to stay out of it, but you know how she is. She got between us. And J.D. had been drinking."

Cora's lips tightened in a line. "Are you blaming this on him being drunk?"

Justine laughed, her teeth showing red. "No, ma'am, he wasn't nearly drunk enough. If he'd been a little drunker, I could've killed him."

Lacy returned with a clean rag. "I put soap on it. Is my mama OK?"

"She will be," Cora said, pushing Lacy's hair back from her face, "but your brother is hungry. And he surely needs somebody to change his diaper."

While Cora worked on Justine, Lacy heated milk on the stove and changed Mason's diaper. Then she lay beside him on the quilt, holding a bottle that he quickly drained. Cora heard Lacy singing softly, "Jesus loves me, this I know, for the Bible tells me so. Little ones to him belong, we are weak but he is strong." A moment later, both children lay sleeping, wrapped up together like petals on a rose.

"I'm grateful you came here, Cora. You didn't need to do it on my account."

Cora daubed salve into the cut on Justine's lip. "I didn't come here on your account, Justine. I came on account of your children."

Justine licked at her mouth, tasted blood and camphor.

"All the same, even more for them, I'm grateful."

Cora wrung out the rag in a basin of water and pressed it against Justine's swollen eye. A gust of wind blew rain like a shower of gravel on the window.

"How did you get here, Cora? Where's James?"

"James is at work at the mill. I drove myself here in Frank's old Ford."

"You did what?" Justine snorted. "Since when did you start driving?"

Cora looked at her. "Since when did you start letting J.D. Allen slap you and your daughter around?"

"Oh, he'll be sorry," Justine said. "I'll guarantee you that. Soon as he sobers up, he'll be sorry that he was born."

Cora threw the rag in the basin, washed her hands, and dried them on her skirt. "I don't care if J.D. is sorry, Justine. Just tell me where to find him."

Justine studied her mother-in-law's face.

"What are you gonna do, Cora? Beat him with your rolling pin?"

"Tell me where he is."

Justine laughed, then winced in pain. "You are one crazy old woman, Cora McCallum. I've always liked that about you."

Shortly before midnight, Cora eased the Ford into the parking lot of the Blue Moon, a honky-tonk on the road to town. Mistaking the clutch for the break pedal, she slammed accidentally into the side of an empty pickup. Shaken by the impact, she swore to God that she would never try to drive again. Then she recognized the pickup. It belonged to J.D. Allen. Cora caught a glimpse of her face in the rearview mirror. Who was that woman? And why was she smiling?

She nodded, put the Ford in reverse, backed up and rammed the pickup again. "The first one was an accident, J.D.," she said. "The second one was for Lacy!"

When Cora stepped into the bar and showed her face to the room, the crowd stopped drinking and smoking and laughing and spitting and stared at a sight they never expected to see within these walls—an old mountain woman who most of them knew, or would soon figure out, and would never, after this night, forget. On the juke box, Hank Williams wailed, "Your cheating heart will tell on you."

J.D. was in the back of the room at the pool table, falling down drunk, with a few of his buddies. Cora recognized one of them: Ray Brown came to church with his mama, when he wasn't too hung over.

The bartender was Virgil Evans, one of Andrew's old friends. He had gone off to war along with Cora's boys, and come back with a bad limp. He was drying beer glasses behind the bar when Cora walked in. His eyes grew wide when he saw her.

"Miz McCallum? What on Earth . . . is there something I can do for you?"

Cora straightened her back and tried to make her hands stop shaking. She turned and looked at a roomful of faces staring back at her.

"You all know me," she said. Some of them met her eyes. Others looked away.

"Your people and mine have been farming this valley longer than most of us can remember. You know how I lost my men—my husband Frank to logging, and two of my boys to the war. You all know my boy James. He's all I've got left . . . him and his little girl."

She waited, studying their reactions. Every ear in the room was listening.

"James would be here in my place, if he knew about it. But I aim to put it to rest before he finds out. I don't want him going to prison for killing J.D. Allen."

"Go home, old woman!" J.D. shouted, slurring his words.

Cora gave him a steady look, then turned her eyes back to the room.

"I've come here to ask you all to do right by my family. Tonight, this man nearly killed my daughter-in-law. Justine might deserve some of what she gets in this life. But no woman deserves to get beaten half to death by a coward twice her size. And her babies surely don't deserve to be left on the floor crying over their mama's bleeding body."

A mutter rumbled through the crowd. Heads shook. Eyes stared at J.D.

"Shut your mouth!" J.D. dropped his pool stick and staggered toward Cora, but stopped when Ray Brown reached out and placed a hand on J.D.'s arm.

"You want to beat on me, J.D.?" Cora said. "Come on then, I'm here. But take a look around you first. You see all these people? They are my neighbors. Our families have leaned on each other for more years than you can count. If you ever raise another fist against my family—against my daughter-in-law or her children—these folks and their kin are going to stop you. If need be, they will make you cry the way you made those babies cry tonight. If you don't believe me, J.D., just ask them. Go on. Ask your buddy Ray there."

Cora looked at Ray. He stared at the floor, but kept his hand on J.D.'s arm.

Cora nodded. "And if these folks can't stop you? God in Heaven will strike you down. It's time for you to move on, J.D. Leave tonight, son, before my boy comes looking for you. Go with God. I will pray for you and your soul."

She turned to leave, but stopped to face the crowd once more.

"I'm grateful to all of you for doing right by my family. It will be a blessing to you and your children and your children's children, as much as it will be to me and mine. If any of you want butter, you can have it for half price. Next time I come to town, I'll bring money to buy you all a round of beer. Now go on home to your families. Tomorrow I hope to see you all in church."

That night the demons that tormented J.D. Allen's soul faced an army of wingless angels dressed as millhands, farmers, and mountainfolk. It was no match. At daybreak, J.D. left town.

38

THE DEAL

The morning after what some were calling "Cora's Show-Down at the Blue Moon Saloon," James finished the graveyard shift at the mill, got in his pickup, and drove over to the Long Branch Cafe for a cup of coffee before heading home to milk. Ducking through the door, he took off his cap and was puzzled to see every face in the place turn to look at him, nodding and grinning like it was Christmas and he was pulling Santa's sleigh.

He spotted Jubal Avery sitting at the counter drinking coffee and reading the paper. The only empty seat was at the other end of the counter. James headed over to grab it, laying a hand on Jubal's shoulder in passing. "Mornin', Jubal."

Jubal looked up. "Mornin', James. Long night at the mill?"

"Not bad." James took the empty seat and hung his hat on his knee. Before he could speak, the waitress—Doris Bradley, who'd had a crush on him since high school and still held out hopes—poured him a cup of coffee, passed him the sugar shaker, and proceeded to fill him in on the details of his mother's encounter last night at the Blue Moon.

The diner fell silent as every neck in the room craned to catch

James' reaction. He sat frozen on the barstool, squinting at Doris as if she had just sprouted horns.

"I'd give my last dollar to have seen it!" Doris hooted. "I heard J.D. took off this morning and he told Ray Brown he ain't never coming back. You ought to be proud of your mama, James. That old woman is something!"

James studied his coffee.

"Is that getting cold, hon?" Doris said. "You want me to freshen it up?"

James rose from the stool, dropped a dime on the counter, and slapped his hat on his head. "Thanks, Doris, I got cows to milk."

Every head turned to watch as he walked out the door and crossed the parking lot to his truck.

Earl Davis sat in a booth by the window, eating a plate of grits and red-eye gravy. He waited until James was out of earshot to call after him, "Hey, James, if you see J.D. Allen, tell him your mama's looking for him!"

The crowd laughed, and Earl grinned, all full of himself.

Jubal Avery rose from his seat at the counter, dug some change out of his pocket and left it under the rim of his plate for Doris.

"Earl," Jubal said, tipping his hat as he passed the booth.

"Sheriff." Earl nodded and looked down, stirring his grits.

Jubal stopped in the doorway, adjusting the brim of his hat.

"You know, Earl, folks around here don't give you enough credit. You were mighty smart to wise off the way you did, behind James' back, and not to his face. I gotta hand it to you. I reckon you're not quite as dumb as you look."

At the farmhouse, James slammed the door of his pickup and bounded up the back steps to the kitchen. Cora was frying a pan of fatback and eggs.

"Ma?" he said, breathing hard.

"'Morning, son. Breakfast is almost ready. Pour yourself some coffee."

James filled a cup and took a long swig. Then he took another.

"You want to tell me what happened last night?" he said.

Cora flipped the fatback and basted the eggs.

"Sounds to me like you've already heard. What more would you like to know?"

James reached for her shoulder and turned her to face him.

"Well, Mama, for starters, I'd like to know what in God's name ever possessed you to think you could take on the likes of J.D. Allen?"

Cora brushed his hand away, picked up the skillet, slid the food onto a plate, and set the plate on the table. Turning back to face him, she raised herself up tall to look him in the eye. Then she waited, staring him down, until he blinked.

"All right," she said, "here it is. I did it because it had to be done. If I'd left it to you, you'd be dead by now or on your way to prison. Your child would've lost her daddy, and I'd have lost another boy. I did it because it was my business to do it. Mine. Do you hear me? It's finished, James. Done. Now sit down and eat your breakfast before it gets cold."

He looked at the eggs. The yolks were broken, sliding across the plate.

"What about Lacy?" he said. "Is she all right?"

Cora refilled his cup and set it sloshing on the table. "Lacy called a while ago. She's fine. The baby, too. Justine's doesn't look real pretty, but she'll get over it."

She turned to leave the room, then stopped. "In the future, James Harlan, I'd appreciate it if you'd refrain from using the Lord's name in vain in my presence. I'm your mother. You need to show me and the Lord a little more respect."

After breakfast, James milked the cows and did the chores before pulling off his boots and going to bed. Cora waited, listening, until the bed stopped creaking. Then she crept down the hall and leaned her ear to his door. He was snoring, the way he did when he was a baby, puffing his breath like the sound of wind rustling through a cornfield.

Minutes later, she was wiping the breakfast dishes dry when Jubal Avery's pickup pulled up in front of the house. "Lord have mercy," she muttered, drying her hands and smoothing her hair.

"Hey, Cora!" Jubal climbed the steps to the porch grinning like a mule eating briars. "I hear you had a little excitement last night."

Shielding her eyes from the sun, Cora looked at the pasture. The cows were milling about, swishing their tails and looking glum.

"People sure like to talk," she said.

Jubal laughed. "Yes, ma'am, they sure do. Especially if you give 'em something to talk about."

Cora shook her head. "I'm glad to know I can still be of interest to somebody."

Jubal took off his hat and raked his hair with his fingers.

"You've never been short in that department, Cora."

He remembered a day, some thirty-five years past, when he almost got the nerve to tell her just exactly how interesting she was to him. He had waited, unable to make the words come out of his mouth. And then, one day, there she was, sitting in church with Frank McCallum and smiling like the morning sun. Jubal held that thought for a minute, as he had held it for all those years, turning it over in his mind. Then, once again, he let it go.

"Why didn't you call me last night, Cora?"

She sat down beside him and gave the swing half a push.

"It was late, Jubal. I didn't want to wake Margaret. How's she doing?"

He straightened his back, turned the brim of his hat around with his fingers, and looked out across the farm. The wind was playing with the leaves on the poplars, making them glitter with little flashes of silver and green.

"Margaret has her good days and her bad," he said. "We've been going up to Durham to see a cancer doctor. But . . . well, it don't seem to be helping much yet."

Cora rested a hand on his shoulder. "I'm sorry, Jubal. I didn't know it was that bad. If there's anything I can do to help, you know it would be my blessing."

He took her hand and pressed it against his face. "You should've called me last night, Cora. That would've been my blessing."

She pulled away, feeling the heat rise up her throat. "I know that," she said. "I've always known it." Then she turned to meet his eyes. "Any woman would be proud to have a man like you stand up for her. I'm grateful. You know I am. But no matter who we are—me or Margaret or my little Lacy or even you, Jubal. Sooner or later, we've all got to stand alone before God."

They sat for a spell swinging together, two old friends, no need to talk, content to study the shapes of clouds and hear the wind whisper memories in the pines.

She was not, Jubal realized, the girl he once knew, the one who still danced in his dreams. But as God was his witness, she had never been more interesting.

Cora planted her feet and stopped the swing. "Can I get you some coffee?"

"Thanks, darlin'," he said, plopping his hat on his head, "but I best be going. Hiram Edwards claims his pig was stolen and he thinks it's my job to get it back."

He pushed himself up from the swing. "Before I go, I want to say this. I'm here, Cora. If you need me, call. Any time, day or night. You hear?"

She nodded, and he helped her to her feet. Wrapping her in his arms, he held her to his heart. Then he patted her head and stepped off the porch.

"By the way," he said, grinning back over his shoulder, "if you plan to keep driving, you'd best get a license. I'd hate to have to give you a ticket."

The next knock, a pounding at the door, came soon after Jubal drove away. Grady had been buying tobacco at Pack's Store when Buford Pack filled him in on Cora's appearance at the Blue Moon. Grady nearly blew the engine in his pickup high-tailing it over to Cora's place.

"Cora!" he said breathless, when she opened the door. "Are you all right?"

"I'm fine, Grady! Why are you beating down my door? James just got home from work and he's trying to sleep!"

"I heard what happened. I'd have gone after J.D. Allen, if you'd let me!"

"I know that, Grady, but it's over. You don't need to worry. Just go on home."

"I'll go," he said, "if you promise to let me know if you need me."

"I promise. Say hey to Ada for me. But don't tell her about the Blue Moon!"

"I won't have to tell her," he chuckled, "I guarantee she's already heard!"

Cora watched him drive away. Minutes later, she was sweeping the kitchen when she heard yet another knock at the door. She thought Grady had come back.

"Grady," she said, opening the door, "I told you . . ."

Justine stood on the porch with Lacy and Mason. Her eye was purple and swollen, and she had tried to hide the cut on her lip with a coat of red lipstick.

"Hey, Cora," she said, with a grin. "I thought you'd be out driving."

An old Chevy sat idling on the road, black smoke swirling from its tailpipe. Cora couldn't see the driver. She reached down to run a hand over Lacy's hair.

"Come on in," Cora said, stepping back from the door. "Let me fix you all something to eat. I've got some biscuits left from breakfast . . ."

"What, no salt pork?" Justine laughed, then looked back at the Chevy. "I can't stay long," she said, handing Mason to Lacy.

"Take your brother to see the cows, Lacy. I need to speak to your grandma."

Lacy gathered up Mason, wiped his runny nose with her sweater, and said, "We'll have a biscuit when we get back, Grandma. Mason loves your biscuits."

Cora watched as Lacy trudged down the hill carrying Mason like a sack of potatoes. Then she turned and put her hand on Justine's arm.

"How are you, child?" she said. "I'll clean that cut for you, if you'll come in and sit a spell."

"You've done enough, Cora. Thanks, but I've got to be going."

The Chevy's engine cut off, and they both cast a glance in its direction.

"Who's that?" Cora said.

Justine shrugged her shoulder. "It don't matter," she said. "You don't know him. But I can tell you who he's not. He's sure as hell ain't J.D. Allen."

"Come on in the house," Cora said. "Let me wash that cut. It won't take long."

"I'm leaving, Cora, going to Florida to stay with my mama. They got doctors down there that might be able to do something for Mason's eyes. I don't plan on coming back here."

She sat down in the porch swing and Cora sat beside her. Justine gave it a push, tapping her toe on the porch, and Cora lifted her feet to let it glide.

"I've come to ask you for something," Justine said.

An autumn breeze filled the air with falling leaves, red and gold, that danced to music drifting up from the pasture, a duet of Lacy's voice and Mason's laughter.

Justine drew a long breath and turned to face her mother-in-law.

"I want you to keep Lacy for me. She needs to go to school. She should've started this fall, but . . . well, I didn't take care of it. She's smart, she'll catch up. Anyhow. She needs her daddy. And he needs her. But mostly, Cora? Lacy needs you. She'll have . . . a better chance at life with you than with me."

Justine fell silent, watching a spider spin a web up in a corner of the porch. Then she continued. "I'll call her when I can, and I'll try to come see her every chance I get. But . . . I don't rightly know how often that will be."

Cora looked down at the barn. The cows had spotted Lacy and Mason by the fence and came lumbering up, hoping for the apples Lacy often fed them. No apples this time. Instead, Lacy held out Mason's hand to let him feel the cow's slobbering muzzle and he shrieked.

The Chevy's engine turned over twice and fired up.

Justine stopped the swing. "Guess I best be going."

Cora reached over and drew her in, as she had done that day, nearly six years ago, when her boys went off to war. Now, as then, no words passed between them. What more could any words say? After a moment, Justine pulled away, looked into Cora's eyes, and nodded. Then she walked up to the road and took a paper sack out of the back seat of the Chevy.

"Lacy!" she called, "bring Mason on back up here!"

Cora stood on the porch, watching as Lacy carried Mason up the hill to his mother. Justine took the baby in her arms then leaned down to bring her face close to Lacy's, speaking soft and low. When Lacy shook her head, Justine pulled her close and whispered in her ear. Cora didn't need to hear what was said. When hearts are breaking, they cry out in old familiar tongues that need no amplification.

As the Chevy pulled off, Lacy stood in the road waving until the car pulled out of sight and the sound of its tires faded away. Cora waited on the porch.

A crow cawed in the distance, a calf bawled from the barn. Lacy raised her hand to wave one last time. Then she picked up the sack and walked up the path to her grandmother.

"Grandma?" she said. "I'm still here."

In the kitchen, Cora poured a glass of milk, buttered two biscuits from the warmer box on the back of the wood stove, and sat down at the kitchen table to watch Lacy eat. The child ate as if she had never eaten in her life.

"Would you like another biscuit?"

"No, ma'am, I'm full. Thank you, Grandma."

Cora nodded, then turned and looked out the window. "You know, it's such a fine day. I could use a good long walk up on the mountain. How 'bout you?"

Lacy nodded. "I'll go get our snake sticks."

Cora heard James flush the toilet in the bathroom.

"All right," she said. "You go get our sticks and I'll be out directly. I just need to have a word with your daddy."

Lacy clattered down the back steps, where Blue was wagging his tail, waiting for her.

"Hey, Blue!" she said, scratching the dog's ears. Then she stood in the basement doorway, staring into the dark abyss. Above her head, the floorboards creaked and she followed the sound of her daddy's footsteps as he moved from the bathroom to the kitchen. Then the footsteps stopped and she heard the muffled rise and fall of voices as her daddy and her grandmother spoke softly in the kitchen. There was a moment of silence, no footsteps, no voices, just the rushing of the creek, the wind in the poplars, and the bickering of blue jays.

When Cora called to her from the porch, Lacy grabbed the snake sticks from their leaning place in the corner and ran out of the basement into the light. She looked up and saw her daddy standing on the porch with her grandmother.

"Hey, Daddy," she grinned. "I thought you was gonna sleep the live-long day."

James laughed at the old joke. "Nope," he said. "Got to go into work directly."

Cora started down the steps, taking them slowly, one at a time. "Don't forget to take your lunchbox. It's sitting on the counter packed and ready to go."

"Thank you, Ma," James called after her.

Lacy waved up at him, and he grinned and waved back. Then he watched as they headed off, his mother and his daughter, trudging up the hill, chattering like two magpies about everything and nothing. He knew they would talk—or rather, Lacy would talk and Cora would listen—all the way up the mountain and back. Just the thought of it made him glad. For Lacy, of course, but for everyone.

James had always been grateful for his mother's kindness to him and his brothers, to Grady and Ada, to any and all. That's just how she was. Everybody said so. He'd been especially appreciative of Cora's goodness to Justine, a kind of mercy and grace that some folks could never muster, or even understand. But it was a whole different feeling, a far deeper level of gratitude than any he had ever known, this feeling that he'd had lately watching his mother with his daughter. He prayed Lacy would grow up to be just like Cora. Except maybe a little less hard-headed.

When they turned on the path out of sight, James went inside to Andrew's old room and stretched out on the cot. He'd slept there every night since coming home from the war. He couldn't bear to sleep in the bed he had shared with Justine.

For five years, he'd carried the weight of her leaving him, wrestling with it day and night, refusing to let it go, the way a drowning man struggles to save another.

Lacy's return in recent months had been a godsend. She belonged here on the farm with him and Cora. She gave them reason to wake up each day and smile. James had clung to the hope that he and Justine would find a way to stay together, if only for their daughter. Lying there on Andrew's cot, he suddenly realized that every trace of that hope was gone, as if it never existed. The realization did two things: First, it broke his heart. Finally, when he stopped weeping, it set him free.

James opened a drawer in the dresser and took out a cigar box that held a few keepsakes. There was not a lot in it: his ribbons and medals from the army, a purple heart and a bronze star; a lock of Justine's hair; a tooth he'd dislodged from Andrew's mouth, on accident, though Andrew clearly had it coming; the hook from the line on which he'd caught his first fish; and the letters his mother had written to him in the war, along with a few from Justine.

He sorted through the contents of the box, thinking something was missing. There ought to be more to show for his thirty-five years. Finally, he took the lock of Justine's hair and held it to his nose. Nothing. No scent of her. She was gone. For the first time since they were married, James removed his wedding band. He turned it slowly in his calloused fingers full circle. Then he dropped it in the box.

That's when he noticed it: a folded slip of paper. He couldn't recall what it was or why he had saved it. When he unfolded it he saw the address Molly O'Dea had given him on his last day in the hospital.

The only letters James had ever penned were to Justine and his mother. The army had posted those for him. He had never bought a postage stamp, let alone used one. If a person wanted to post a letter to a place like, say, Ireland, how exactly would that person go about it? His mother might know, but he sure as hell was not about to ask her. Then it dawned on him, a thought bright as day: a postal question might likely get answered at the US Post Office in Pisgah Forest.

Dear Molly O'Dea,

I do not know if you will receive this letter. I am sure by now some smart, lucky feller has snatched you up in matrimony. Please give him my heartfelt congratulations.

I came home from the war to find my wife had left, taking my daughter, Lacy, the baby I so often told you about. I searched all over, could not find them. I did not see them for almost six years, counting the year I was off at war. A few months back, Lacy showed up at my mother's door, no longer a baby, a sweet little girl, pretty as her mama and smart as a whip. She is the light of my life. And my mother, I swear, is ten years younger for the pleasure of having Lacy here.

I wanted to write and tell you all of that because I knew that it would make you and your good heart happy to know that we are doing well. I also wanted to thank you for your kindness and excellent care, both for me and my brother Frank. I do not know what else to say, Molly. I will always be in your debt. I wish you and your loved ones all God's best.

Your friend,
James Harlan McCallum

39

DROWNING RUBY

A week after Justine left for Atlanta, Lacy took Ruby to the creek to work on the stones. She liked to stack them in piles instead of leaving them scattered about untended, as if nobody cared about them. They looked happier, she thought, stacked together, not scattered.

The night before, she had lain awake once again, just as she had all week, missing her mother and worrying about Mason. Who would sing him to sleep when he was weary? Who would hush him with stories when he cried? Who would tell him she had not forgotten him? Around midnight, a storm had come raging over the mountain, flashing lightning, rolling thunder, pouring buckets of rain, turning the trickle of the creek into a torrent. Lacy had heard the water come rushing over the banks, and worried about the stones she had stacked the day before.

Sure enough, this morning, they were all scattered along the banks. The creek had calmed some, but it was still swollen and rushing, all full of itself.

"Lacy!" Cora stood on the porch, peering through the screen door. "Keep your distance from that creek! It's still running high from the storm!"

"I'll be careful, Grandma!"

"The butter's done churning," Cora called. "You want to come stamp it?"

Lacy liked the job of packing the clots into an old wooden press that had belonged to Cora's mother, pushing a plunger to stamp a design—two delicate eight-pointed shapes—on the top of each pound of butter. Cora called them daisies, but Lacy saw them as stars. She glanced at the creek stones.

"I'll be up directly, Grandma!" she called. "I need to clean up this mess!"

Cora turned to go inside. "Well, all right then. But don't you fall in there!"

"No, ma'am, I won't!"

Lacy waited to hear the back door close. Then she set Ruby on the bridge over the creek, propping her up with a rock so she could watch Lacy work. The doll never liked to let Lacy out of her sight. She'd been in an especially foul mood of late, blaming Lacy for Justine's leaving and swearing this time Justine was gone for good. But she'd been quiet all morning, and Lacy had no desire to get her riled.

"Stay here, Ruby, I won't be long." One of Ruby's button eyes was smaller than the other. The big button looked mad. Lacy patted Ruby's leg. "It's all right. I'll hurry." Then she went to work on the stones, stacking piles along the bank.

After the fourth pile, she looked at Ruby and smiled. "Don't they look nice?"

Ruby didn't answer. She just glared at Lacy with her big mad eye. A crow flew down from a hickory tree and landed on the bridge next to Ruby. It cawed twice and pecked at Ruby's head. And then, very slowly, Ruby fell, toppling over head first, tumbling through the air, and splashing into the creek.

Lacy stood on the bank watching, holding a stone in each hand, as the current caught Ruby and dragged her downstream, whirling and spinning and bumping over the rocks. When the doll raced past her—face up, arms wide, with her matted hair floating like a halo about her head, and her big button eye bigger than ever—Lacy threw down the stones and ran after her.

The summer before Cora was born, Edward Lacy had marched his brothers through the woods a hundred yards or so from the farmhouse to a small, pretty clearing where the creek opened wide. Under his able direction, they spent weeks, every day after their chores were done, rolling stones and shoveling mud to build a dam that slowly turned the creek into a swimming hole. It was there, some years later, where Edward taught Cora to swim.

The McCallum brothers, in turn, had expanded on the design, adding stones and deepening the pond until the creek barely flowed beyond it. The Shields' place sat a few miles downstream. When Grady mentioned to Cora that it was getting harder by the day to water his mule, she made the boys loosen the dam to let the creek keep flowing. But even after twenty years of gathering silt and decaying leaves, the pond was still plenty deep for diving.

Cora had taken Lacy to the pond once when they went for a walk, and told her stories about the good times she had spent there as a girl with her brothers, and later, as a mother with her boys. She had promised to teach Lacy to swim in the pond next summer on one condition: Lacy was never to go to the pond alone.

Lacy loved her grandmother, and would never want to betray her trust. But on this day, she could give no thought to promises. Her only thought was for Ruby. She could see the doll just ahead of her, riding the current downstream. Lacy ran through the woods, stumbling over rocks, her heart pounding, knees bleeding, face stinging from the lashing of the branches of the wild rhododendron that grew along the bank.

At first, Grady thought she was a deer. Or maybe, if he was lucky, a bear. Raising his rifle, he closed one eye and sighted with the other, waiting. When she came bounding out of the woods into the clearing, his finger tightened on the trigger—then it froze. Lord help me!

Grady had often watched Lacy from afar as she stacked stones by the creek or fed apples to the cows or went for walks with Cora. He especially liked watching the two of them together. But he was surprised to see Lacy at the pond alone.

The sun broke free from a cloud and struck the water with a blinding blaze of light. For a moment, he couldn't see her. He only heard her crying. Then he spotted her kneeling on the bank stretching an arm out to something in the creek. Leaning farther, she seemed to grab it. Suddenly, the bank beneath her gave way.

Cora had cleaned out the churn and set the butter on ice waiting for Lacy to come pack it into the press. When she walked out on the porch to summon the child, she saw someone laboring up the hill from the creek.

"Cora! Come quick!"

Grady Shields was carrying something. It took only a moment, the skip of a heartbeat, for Cora to realize that the offering Grady was bringing this time was not Frank's bloody cap.

"Dear Lord!" Cora stumbled down the steps to meet them. "Is she alive?"

"She's breathing!" Grady said. "She fell in the pond and I pulled her out!"

Cora led them to Lacy's room and Grady lowered the child's body, soaking wet and shaking, onto the bed. Then he turned his head, as Cora began stripping off Lacy's wet clothing.

"Grady, grab some quilts out of that chest and bring them over here!"

When he handed her the quilts, she saw that he was dripping.

"Good Lord, Grady! You're going to catch your death! Go in my bedroom and look in the wardrobe. There's some of Frank's old things in there. Help yourself."

He shifted on his feet, blinking his eyes, but didn't move.

"Go!" she shouted. He went.

Cora dried Lacy head to toe, rubbing her feet to speed the flow of blood, and began covering her with the quilts. But first she had to pry Ruby out of Lacy's grip.

"Give her to me, child. I'll take care of her for you."

Lacy opened her hand and Cora took Ruby, wrapping the doll in a towel and setting her on the dresser. Then she bundled the quilts around Lacy and gathered her up in her arms, rocking back and forth, singing low: "O they tell me that He smiles on His children there, and His smile drives their sorrows all away . . ."

By the end of the hymn, Lacy had stopped shaking and had fallen limp, sound asleep. Cora looked up to see Grady standing in the doorway barefoot, wearing one of Frank's old flannel shirts and a pair of Frank's overalls. He started to speak and she put a finger to her lips to hush him. Then she slipped Lacy onto the bed and tucked the quilts around her.

Motioning Grady to follow, she went to the wardrobe and rummaged around to find a pair of woolen socks and Frank's old boots. "Here," she said, "put these on. I think they'll fit."

Grady didn't argue. He waited to speak until they walked out on the porch.

"I'll have Ma wash Frank's clothes and I'll bring 'em all back to you."

Cora reached up and brushed a strand of wet hair from Grady's forehead. "You don't need to bring them back. They fit you fine. And besides," she said, as she straightened the collar on the shirt, then waved her hand as if fanning away a fly, "I've got no use for them."

He nodded and stepped off the porch.

"Wait," she said. He turned to look back her.

"There's something I've been meaning to talk to you about."

He took a step closer and cocked his head to one side, listening.

She studied him for a moment, thinking of how best to speak her mind. Finally, she crossed her arms and just let it loose.

"Grady Shields, if you know what's good for you, you will not go hiding up under that hemlock, smoking cigarettes and watching my house any more. You hear me?"

Grady's eyes got big.

"I mean it, Grady. I check up there every few days for cigarette butts and there's fresh ones every time I check. So don't even try to deny it. One of these days you're going to catch that tree and yourself on fire, and then what would I do without you? If you want to see me, you can knock on my door anytime, day or night, and I will let you in. Matter of fact, I want you to come for Christmas dinner. I want Ada to come, too. Tell her to bring one of her pound cakes."

She whirled to go back inside, calling over her shoulder, "And you might as well bring your banjo and your fiddle. Lord knows we could use a little music around here."

For a long while after she closed the door, Grady stood like a fence post, feeling his heart swell up inside his chest and thinking about the fool he had been. Then he headed up the road, humming a brand new tune that had popped into his head the way the best tunes always did, unexpected and undeserved as the gift of God's grace. Maybe he would play that tune at Christmas dinner, while Cora served up Ada's pound cake?

Kicking up his heels, he danced a little jig and the lines on his face crinkled up in a grin. Frank's boots, he decided, felt mighty fine on his feet.

40

COMPANY'S COMING

In mid-December, an early morning snowfall dusted the valley in much the same way that Ada liked to sift sugar on her pound cakes. Cora smiled to herself, thinking about that.

James stomped up the back steps onto the porch, kicking snow off his boots, then came in the kitchen and dropped a load of firewood by the stove.

Cora handed him a cup of coffee with a lot of sugar, the way he liked it.

"Cold out there?"

"Not bad."

They stood together, sipping coffee, looking out the window to the top of the hill, where Lacy—swallowed up in James' hunting jacket and Cora's red scarf—stretched tiptoe, crumbling cornbread into the bird feeder.

"She's going to be tall like her mama," James said.

Cora nodded. "And hard-headed like her daddy," she said with a wink.

James grinned, but kept his gaze on Lacy, who had fished another hunk of cornbread out of the pocket of his jacket and fed it to Blue.

"We'll be needing a tree soon," Cora said. "For Christmas."

James swallowed a mouthful of coffee, then looked at his mother. She had not asked for a tree since before the war. He remembered it well. It was the first Christmas after he and Justine were married, and the last one they were all together. They went up on the mountain, he and his brothers, as they did every year, to find the best tree. Andrew picked it out, a cedar, because he so loved the smell.

They took turns chopping it down. While James and Frank dragged it down the mountain, Andrew chucked snowballs at their heads, until they threatened to strip him naked and leave him tied to a tree. It was no hollow threat, and he knew it. When they got home, they stopped in the basement to take a few quick swigs of moonshine from a jug they kept hidden behind the tool bench. Then they carried the cedar in the house and thawed their feet by the fire, while Cora and Justine adorned the tree's branches with old glass ornaments, strings of popcorn, crocheted snowflakes, and tinsel.

James doubted he would ever know another Christmas as fine as that one.

"You don't need to fool with a tree, Ma."

"A child needs a tree, James. I always had one for you."

"It'll just make a big mess . . ."

They heard clomping, and turned to look out the window as Lacy came up the steps to the porch with Blue on her heels. She stomped the snow off the old boots that her daddy had worn as a boy, then took a rag from a hook and started drying Blue's paws.

"James?" Cora said. "When you go to get the tree? Make sure you get a good one."

He rolled his eyes. "Fine," he said. "I suppose you want me to go out and shoot a turkey for Christmas dinner, too?"

"Well, now that you mention it . . ."

"Mama, we don't need a whole turkey for two and a half people!"

Cora pushed the coffee pot to the back of the stove.

"I've been meaning to talk to you about that," she said.

He looked at her. "About what?"

"Christmas," she said. "I've been thinking that this year, with

Lacy being here with us and all, we ought to do something a little special. You know, to celebrate."

His eyes narrowed.

"Nothing big," she said. "Just, well, a little company for Christmas dinner."

"Company?" The last time James heard that word, he was in the army. "Like who?"

Cora dried her hands on her apron. "Like Ada and Grady."

James nodded slowly, trying to get a fix on the idea that, for the first time in five, no, six years, his mother wanted a tree and a turkey and company for Christmas dinner.

"Well," he said, "all right then. Ada and Grady are like family anyhow."

He poured another cup of coffee and starting stirring in the sugar.

Then Cora added, quickly, "And Jubal."

He stopped stirring.

"Jubal? You mean . . . Jubal Early?"

"Yes, James! How many Jubals do we know?"

"Won't he have . . . family plans? I mean, I know he just lost his wife, rest her soul. When was that? A month ago?"

"Two weeks," Cora said. "Margaret was buried two weeks ago. You drove me to the service. I can't believe you don't remember."

"Two weeks? Well, isn't it kind of soon for Jubal to be . . . socializing?"

"It's Christmas dinner, James. It's not a square dance."

"All the more reason he should want to be with his own family. Doesn't Jubal still have a sister somewhere up around Waynesville?"

Cora set her cup down hard on the table, sloshing coffee left and right.

"He has no one, James. He's alone. He was your daddy's best friend. He taught you boys how to hunt and fish and stand up to bullies. I've known him all my life, and I know how much he's hurting. I asked him to Christmas dinner, and he's coming, and that's that!"

"Ma, you know I love Jubal just as much as you do, but . . ."

The kitchen door flew open and Lacy came running in with a gust of icy wind to ask the same question she always asked several times a day.

"Grandma, can I pleeeeese bring Blue in the house?"

Cora gave her the same answer as always. "Blue is fine to stay right where he is, Lacy, either on the porch or under it. He's a dog. That's what dogs do."

Lacy looked at James.

"Don't look at me," he said. "She never let me bring the old Blue in, either."

Lacy wrinkled up her nose. "You had another Blue?"

"Yes," James said. "We've had five dogs in this family since I was your age, and thanks to your grandma, every last one of them was named Blue."

Cora shrugged. "Blue's a good name for a dog."

"Five dogs?" Lacy said.

"More than five," Cora said. "I can't recall the exact number. Every dog I ever fed was named Blue. Your great-grandpa Harlan started it. Or maybe his great-grandpa. Anyhow, go get out of those wet clothes before you catch your death."

Lacy trudged off to her room mumbling something about dogs and colors.

When she was out of hearing distance, James cleared his throat.

"Ma," he said, "I need to talk to you about something."

Cora set a pot of beans on the stove and gave him a look.

"Let me guess," she said. "Does it have anything to do with all those letters you've been getting from that Irish girl?"

The question hit him like an ambush. James took his time, thinking about the best way to answer it. Finally, he quit thinking and just went on and told her.

"Her name is Molly," he said. "She was a nurse at the hospital where Frank . . . where me and Frank met up. She's come over from Ireland to visit a cousin in Atlanta. I've been thinking, maybe, I mean, if it's all right with you, I'll ask her to come up and see us on the farm."

Cora's eyes got big. "On the farm? You mean this farm?"

James laughed. "Yes, Ma, this farm. How many farms do we own?"

Cora took a rag and wiped up the coffee she had sloshed on the table.

"When would she be coming?"

"She's been in Atlanta at her cousin's for about a week, plans to stay for a spell, six months or so. I was thinking she might like to come up here in the spring when, you know, the dogwoods and everything's in bloom. But, hey, as long we're having us a crowd for Christmas, one more won't make much difference, will it?"

He grinned, and turned to leave.

She called after him. "James? When you go huntin' for a turkey? Get two!"

41

ROOM IN THE INN

On Christmas Eve, while Lacy and Cora strung popcorn and cranberries, James hiked up on the mountain to chop down a seven-foot cedar and dragged it home in the snow. He was sorry the jug of moonshine in the basement had long since gone dry. Exhausted, he fell asleep by the fire, until Lacy climbed up in his lap and lifted his eyelids with her fingers.

"Wake up, Daddy. We got cows to milk."

Grady and James took turns with the milking chores, depending on which shift James worked at the mill. This week was Grady's turn, but the mill was closed for Christmas, and cows don't take days off, so James had said he'd do it instead.

Lacy always insisted on helping him. She helped Grady, too, on occasion, but she never missed a chance to help her daddy. They walked down to the barn together, holding hands, each carrying an empty pail, with Ruby riding shotgun in the pocket of James' coat. Lacy loved watching James milk, seeing his big hands pat the cow's rump, hearing his voice, smooth and low, "Steady, Bertha, easy, girl."

To keep Lacy from spooking the cows when she chased the cat or tried to toss hay with a pitchfork, James had given her a job, which she treated as a matter of great importance: while he sat on the stool to milk, Lacy stood beside him, clutching Ruby with one hand, and with the other, holding Bertha's tail so it didn't swish around and swat James in the face.

James wiped the cow's udder with a clean rag, then set to work, pulling the teats, sending sprays of warm milk striking the pail in a rhythm that sounded to Lacy like music, like the piano in church playing "Away in a Manger."

"Daddy," she said, "Baby Jesus was born in a barn like this."

James squirted a stream of milk in her direction. "Where'd you hear that?"

She dodged and laughed as the milk missed her leg and hit the cat.

"I heard it in Sunday School. I learned Bible verses, too. The teacher said I'm smart." Lifting her chin and straightening her back, she recited: "'And she brought forth her firstborn son, and wrapped him in swaddling clothes, and laid him in a manger; because there was no room for them in the inn.' Luke, chapter two, verse seven."

James grinned. "That sounds right to me. You know what it means?"

Lacy looked at Ruby. "Yes, sir, I do. It means Baby Jesus had to be born in a barn because nobody wanted him and his mama."

James stopped milking midstream. "Your mama took you to Sunday School?"

Lacy rolled her eyes. "No, Daddy, Mama never went to church. But she made me go. She said just because she was a heathen didn't mean she was about to let me be one, too."

James finished the milking, patted Bertha's rump, and set the pail of milk aside. Then he swung around on the stool to face his daughter.

Lacy was running about, swinging Ruby and trying to catch the cat.

"Lacy," James said, "come over here."

She wrinkled her nose at the cat, then skipped over to stand before her father.

He covered her bird-like shoulders with the palms of his broad hands and looked into her eyes until, slowly, the cat and the cows and the barn disappeared, and there was nothing left in the whole wide world but just the two of them.

"Listen to me," he said. "This will be hard to hear, but you need to hear it."

Her body stiffened, and she turned away to look down at Ruby.

"Lacy?" he said. He waited. She looked back at him.

"Your mama loves you. You know that, don't you?"

Lacy nodded. Her eyes began to shine.

"She's got some things to figure out," he said. "And the thing is . . . well, it might take her a while."

Behind the barn, Blue started barking, sending an owl flying off in search of another perch.

James reached up and combed Lacy's hair with his fingers. Her hair felt almost as thick as her mother's. He swallowed hard, and rested his hand on her head.

"Lacy? I don't think your mama's coming back any time soon."

Bertha swished her tail and Lacy reached over to grab it. She studied it for a moment, using the tip like a paintbrush to make little swirls on Ruby's face.

"No, sir," she said, swirling harder, "I don't expect she will."

James looked out into the pasture. The snow was falling faster, sifting in through the barn door, softening the muddy tracks they'd left behind them.

"If she comes back," he said, "she's welcome to stay. Mason, too. For as long as they want. But you need to know this, Lacy. I'm not going to let her take you away from me again. Not unless you want to go. You are home now, you hear?" Then he repeated the word like the chorus of a hymn: "Home."

Lacy searched James' face, as if looking for something she had lost or had maybe never known. When she found it, there in the barn, on a snowy Christmas Eve, in the light that shined from her father's eyes, she dropped Ruby in the straw and wrapped her arms around his neck.

"Home," she whispered in his ear. "Yes, sir. That sounds right to me."

Back at the farmhouse, Cora was busy making cornbread stuffing for two wild turkeys that she had picked clean and left soaking in a tub of brine on the back porch. Tomorrow, on Christmas Day, she would stuff them and roast them to serve alongside a dozen other delicacies: mashed potatoes and gravy, sweet potato casserole, green beans canned from her garden, spiced apples and pickled beets and buttermilk biscuits and home-churned butter and blackberry preserves and sorghum molasses. And for dessert, Ada's pound cake with a generous whipping of Bertha's cream.

Crumbling cornbread into a bowl, Cora thought it all through, once again, the plan for Christmas day: James' Irish friend, Molly, was due into the bus station in Brevard around noon, Lord willing, if not delayed by the snowstorm that was forecast for the area. Cora and Lacy had fixed up the spare room, covering the bed with the first counterpane that Cora had crocheted years ago, and decorating the bedside table with Cora's mother's crystal vase, filled with sprigs of cedar and holly that Lacy had picked from the yard.

James would drive into town to meet his guest and bring her back to the farm to introduce her to Cora and Lacy. They'd all have an hour or so to get acquainted before Jubal and Ada and Grady were to arrive for Christmas dinner around three.

That was assuming, of course, that Ada got her pound cake in the oven before imbibing in a little too much muscadine wine. Ada was often known to run late, blaming it on what she called the "imprecise science of pound cake baking." Cora didn't mind. Ada and her pound cakes were worth waiting for.

Amidst all the other preparations, while James and Lacy were out at the barn, Cora had worked magic on the tree, covering it with old glass ornaments, crocheted snowflakes, and sprigs of red holly. Then she'd added strands of silver tinsel and garlands of popcorn and cranberries that she and Lacy had strung together.

After finishing the tree, Cora went to her bedroom to the sewing closet, climbed up on a footstool, and took down from the back of the highest shelf her Christmas gift for Lacy. No wrapping paper or ribbons. She placed it under the tree, rearranged it a bit, then stood back smiling, like God on the seventh day of Creation, admiring her handiwork.

She took it all in—the tree, the smell of the cornbread in the kitchen, the gift she had made for Lacy. She thought of the guests who'd come tomorrow and the time they would share, and the phone calls she would get from her brothers and their families, wishing her a merry Christmas, and promising to visit soon, maybe in the spring. All of it. It was good.

When she heard James and Lacy coming up the back steps, she hurried over to the fireplace and sat down in her father's old rocking chair to wait.

Out in the kitchen, Lacy was begging.

"Daddy, it's Christmas! Can I pleeeeese bring Blue inside?"

"Lacy," James said. "Go find your grandma."

Cora smiled. Those two were quite a match.

Lacy came stomping into the front room. When she saw the tree, she froze. Then she shrieked so loud James and Cora both had to cover their ears.

She ran to the tree, then stopped, awed by what she saw peeking out at her from beneath its branches—a small, delicate face with two cornflower blue eyes.

Cora glanced at James. He stood in the doorway watching, holding his hat to his chest the way he did whenever the National Anthem played on the radio.

They waited. Lacy just stared. Finally, Cora got up from the rocker, walked over to the tree, and bent down to pick up the gift she had worked on in secret for months and had saved just for Christmas—a muslin-faced doll with hand-stitched blue eyes, tiny red lips, and long threads of coal-black hair, wearing a flour-sack dress just like one that Cora had also made for Lacy.

"Go on," Cora said, holding the doll out to Lacy. "Take her. She's yours."

Lacy slipped Ruby under her arm and took the gift, holding it lightly in her hands, the way she'd hold a butterfly, as if expecting any minute it might fly away. She began tracing with one finger the delicate stitches that formed the features of the doll's face, her nose, her mouth, the curve of her neck, the hem of her skirt.

The clock on the mantel ticked away, twenty seconds, then twenty more.

Cora looked at James. He shook his head.

Finally, Cora lifted Lacy's chin and looked into her eyes.

"From now on," she said, "even when you're an old woman like me, this will be your doll, and you will be her girl. And she will say good things to you, only good, never bad. Things you need to hear. But you'll have to listen hard to hear her. Go ahead, try it, hold her up to your ear."

Lacy looked over at James.

"Go on," he said, grinning. "I'm dying to hear what that doll's got to say."

Slowly, Lacy lifted the doll to her ear. Suddenly her face it up with surprise.

"Well," Cora said, "What did she tell you? Is it a secret?"

Lacy laughed. "No, Grandma, it's not a secret. She told me to say thank you!"

"You're welcome," Cora said. "What do you think of her?"

"I think . . . I think she's the best doll in the whole wide world. But . . ."

Lacy looked at Ruby, who lay on the floor at Lacy's feet, glaring up at her.

"It's just . . . I'm not real sure, Grandma, how well Ruby will take to her."

Cora picked Ruby up and smoothed the tangles in the doll's matted hair.

"Don't worry about Miz Ruby," Cora said. "We discussed it, she and I. At first, she wasn't happy. She said some ugly things. You know how she is. But I told her, 'Miz Ruby, you will get along just fine with Lacy's new doll. Or you will find yourself sleeping in the barn.'"

Lacy blinked, picturing Ruby in the barn with Bertha. Then she burst into laughter. Her father and grandmother, Blue under the porch, her new doll and even Ruby, they all laughed, too.

"Will you give your new doll a name, child?" Cora said.

"Yes, ma'am," said Lacy. "I will call her Justine."

42

CHRISTMAS

*L*ate that evening, in Hendersonville, NC, George Morgan had a sudden change of heart. In early December, after George declined her invitation for Thanksgiving, his sister Emmaline had written in the strongest of language to insist that George spend Christmas with her and her family in Brevard, some twenty miles away.

George had written back with a polite, if thin, excuse about how busy he was at the auto shop and that, as much as he appreciated her kind invitation, he did not want her to worry about him, because, really, he was doing just fine.

Emmaline didn't buy it for a minute. She knew George too well. Besides, how could any man claim to be "just fine," after the kind of suffering her poor brother had endured—the loss of his only son to the war, followed by the death of his dear wife, the love of his life, who had been so overcome by her grief for their son that she had chosen to end her own life? Emmaline wrote back and flat-out ordered George to come for Christmas.

George had set her note aside, determined to ignore it. But on Christmas Eve, he closed up shop early to give his help some time off to spend with their families. Then he came home, as usual, to an empty house, a make-do supper, a lifetime of memories and a whole lot of lonely.

Next thing George knew, he had phoned Emmaline, packed a bag, gassed up his '49 Ford, and was on the road to Brevard, in what would soon prove to be a blinding snowstorm.

It was late when he left. The storm slowed his progress to a crawl. It would be midnight before he made it to Brevard. Emmaline and her family would all be fast asleep. George wasn't worried. He knew his sister. She'd leave a light on for him.

What he didn't know and couldn't have imagined when he set out on that cold, dark night, was that this was going to be the most memorable Christmas of his life.

A few miles out of Hendersonville, on a deserted stretch of US 64, George was taking it slow, trying hard to keep the Ford on the road. He was tired and hungry and had brought only about a half pack of Camels, barely enough to last him to Brevard. Suddenly his headlights picked up the outstretched arm of a hitchhiker.

Passing him by, George slowed to a crawl to get a better look. Not much more than a kid, bareheaded, wearing an old army field jacket. What the hell. George pulled over and waited for the kid to catch up.

The hitcher opened the passenger door, stuck his head in, and grinned.

"Merry Christmas, sir! 'Preciate you stopping!"

"Where you headed, son?"

"Not far, sir, just up the road."

"All right then, get in."

George cranked up the heat to thaw the kid out and they drove on.

"What are you doing hitchhiking on a night like this, especially on Christmas?"

"Just trying to get home to my family, sir. How 'bout you?"

George fished the half pack of Camels and a lighter out of his pocket.

"Care for a smoke?"

"Don't mind if I do, sir."

"Here," George said, handing him the Camels, "light one for me, too, will you?"

The hitcher tamped two Camels out of the pack, lit one, handed it to George, then lit the other for himself, and set the remaining pack and the lighter on the seat.

They rode for a while, enjoying the smokes, listening to rhythm of the wiper blades scraping snow off the windshield.

George glanced over at the field jacket. "Were you in the war, son?"

The question was simple. The answer was not.

"I served for a while, sir," he said. He took a drag on the Camel, held the smoke, then watched it curl slowly from his nose.

George nodded. "I can understand how you might not want to talk about it."

"Not that I don't want to. There's just not much to tell."

They rode for a mile in silence.

"My boy was in the navy," George said, finally. "David. We called him Dave. He went down with his ship at Pearl Harbor. His mother never got over it. She . . . passed away last year."

Twenty yards in front of them, the Ford's headlights caught a glimpse of the broad wings of a barn owl gliding across the road.

"Sir," said the hitcher, quietly, "I am sorry for your loss."

George thanked him and handed him the Camels. The young man lit one for each of them, took a long draw, and began telling his story.

He'd been taken prisoner by the Germans, spent some time in a POW camp.

"I can be pretty hard-headed," he said, with a laugh. "The Germans tried to cure me of it. You get hit in the head enough times with a rifle butt, it gets hard to remember much of anything. My dog tags were gone. I didn't know who I was or where I'd come from."

After the war, he spent a few months in a hospital in San Diego.

"It took 'em a while to figure out who I was. When they told me my name, it didn't register or nothin'. They might as well have said it was Jesus H. Christ. They wanted to contact my family, to let 'em know I was alive, but I told 'em to wait. At the time, I didn't feel much alive. I had no memories. Those people they were calling my family—they were strangers to me. I didn't want 'em to know I was alive, until I knew it myself."

George listened, asking no questions. He'd learned to do that long ago with Dave. But after a while, when the young man stopped talking and started studying the falling snow, as if the snow knew things that he didn't, George couldn't resist.

"So, what happened?" George picked up the Camels, shook out two more and handed them to the boy to light. "When did you start remembering?"

He lit the cigarettes and handed one to George.

"After I was discharged, I got a job in Long Beach in the ship-yards. My memory started coming back in pieces. I was walking down a street one day and passed a bakery and all of a sudden, I could taste my mama's biscuits. But for the life of me, I still couldn't picture the hands that had made them. Then the pieces started coming faster. Like a jigsaw puzzle that didn't want to fit . . ."

Suddenly, George hit the brakes hard. The Ford fishtailed, slid half off the road and stopped just shy of a deer. The deer stared. They stared back. Then the deer trotted off into the woods.

"Well," George said, easing the Ford back on the road, "I'm awake now."

Two miles later, the young man spoke up. "It ought to be coming up any time now, the road where you can drop me off."

"Think you'll remember it?" George said.

"I hope so," he said, thinking on it for a bit. "I'm pretty sure I will. Seems like the road home is just something you ought to know when you see it."

George nodded. "Why now?" he said. "I mean, after all this time. What's it been, five years since the war was over? What made you decide to come home tonight?"

"Don't know," the boy said, lifting his shoulders. "A couple of weeks back, I was in a store in Long Beach, that was all done up for Christmas. They had a big fake tree with all kinds of fancy decorations made out of metal or plastic. But the thing was, it made me remember the smell of cedar. And . . . wait, sir, I think that's the road . . . yeah, that's it. I'll get out here."

George looked at the snowy turn-off that wound up the mountain out of sight.

"No," he said, "I'll take you on up to your house."

"You've done enough, sir. I can walk. You might get stuck. It's a hard road."

"Not as hard as the one you've been on, son."

George slowed to make the turn, then gunned the engine like spurring a horse. The Ford slipped and slid, but made it up the mountain without getting stuck.

They stopped in front of a mailbox, and the young man stepped out in the snow. A hound barked on the porch and a light came on at the back of the house.

"I'm much obliged to you, sir, for your kindness. If you'll come in and stay the night, you'll be more than welcome. I guarantee it."

"Thanks," George said, "but my sister's expecting me."

The porch light came on and in the doorway, in her nightgown, stood an old woman with long silver hair, peering out at them through the darkness. For a moment, the young man stared up at her in silence. Finally, he thanked George again, and turned to go.

"Wait, son!" George called after him. "Do you have a name?"

"Sorry, sir," he said, reaching back into the car to shake George's hand.

"My name is Andrew McCallum," he said. Then he nodded toward the porch and grinned. "But my mama calls me Drew."

The screen door slammed and the hound came running for him.

"Hey, boy!" he said, scratching the dog's ears. "I missed you, too!"

Blue licked his face and for the first time in years, Andrew laughed his old boyhood laugh. On the porch, when she heard that laugh, his mother raised her arms to Heaven and came running barefoot in the snow, weeping and laughing along with her boy.

This was no ordinary, everyday kind of laughter. It was the kind that's heard only in the most joyful of moments, when words fail and gratitude pours like tears from the soul. It danced out of their hearts and took wing across the farm, rippling over the valley, echoing on the mountains.

And every creature, every plant, every rock and hill and stream, all the stars in the sky, all the fish in the rivers, all the snakes in their holes, all the foxes in their dens, all the birds in their nests, all the limbs on all the trees, all the snowflakes swirling, all the angels singing, and even God Himself smiling down from on high—they all heard the sound of that laughter and shared in that perfect joy.

And suddenly, it was Christmas.

Epilogue

September 5, 1963
Berkeley, California

Dear Grandma,

Here I am in that place you call "California of all places!" I'm sorry you couldn't hear me when I called to tell you I'd arrived in Berkeley. I'm sure Daddy filled you in on all I said, but I wanted to tell you myself. So I am writing what I promise to be the first of many letters (I know how you love to get mail!) to assure you that I am safe and well, trying to behave myself, settling into my dorm room and slowly finding my way around the campus and this strange new world.

Oh, Grandma, I wish you could see it! There are all sorts of people, different races and nationalities and persuasions, all walking around looking as if they feel right at home. I don't feel that way yet, but I know I will soon. I keep remembering what you told me when we said goodbye on the porch: home is a place inside of us that we carry with us wherever we go.

People here are friendly, but they talk so fast it hurts my ears. They say I sound funny, but you ought to hear them! The cafeteria can't touch your cooking (what I wouldn't give for one of your biscuits!) but the scholarship covers meals, so if I don't eat, I've got no one to blame but myself. Classes start next week and my new roommate is due to arrive tomorrow from New York. I hope we hit it off. I've not shared a room with anybody since Mason was a baby! Speaking of Mason, he's grown an inch in the month since I last visited them in Florida. Pretty soon he'll be taller than I am. Mama called this morning with good news. She had trouble finding work after they moved down there to live with Grandma Loretta and Effie. But she just got hired to wait tables at some fancy resort where she is required to wear, of all things, a bathing suit and high heels!

Mason didn't want to change schools, but he likes his new teachers (and the food!) at the school for the deaf and the blind in St. Augustine. He's still full of the devil and fighting with the deaf boys! When Mama called, Grandma Loretta was out getting her hair dyed, but I got to speak with Effie, who said to give you her best. Her boy, Walter, was discharged from the army and lives near Fort Ord, in Seaside, where he owns his own grocery store! Effie said not to tell Grandma Loretta, but she's thinking about moving to California! She said if I'm ever down that way, Walter and his family would love to meet me. Wouldn't that be something?

It's late, Grandma. I can hear you saying, "Child, you ought to be in bed!" Tell Daddy and Molly I'll call Sunday. Give my love to Uncle Drew and Jubal and Addie and Grady, and scratch old Blue's ears for me. I miss you all something fierce.

Promise me that you won't worry. You taught me well, Grandma. You gave me all I need. I'll be fine in "California of all places." I'll write you every week and call every Sunday. Even if you can't hear me, I need to hear your voice. I love you the way you have always loved me, with all the love in the world, and then some.

I remain, as ever, your devoted granddaughter,
Lacy Grace McCallum

ACKNOWLEDGMENTS

$\mathcal{T}$o acknowledge everyone who contributed to this novel would fill more pages than the novel itself. Please forgive me if I fail to remember anyone who should never be forgotten.

The book is dedicated to family, but I want to add this: my husband, my children, their spouses, and my grandchildren are the sun, moon, and stars in my sky. They make everything possible, including the love and encouragement I needed to complete this work.

I was honored and grateful to have the expertise of Colonel Dino Pick, USA, Ret., and Commander Richard Pagnillo, USNR, Ret., who read and approved the wartime passages.

Though I've written a weekly column for thirty years, I knew nothing about publishing a novel. Fortunately, I had the help of Heather Lazare, who assembled a team of incredibly talented people: designer Laura Duffy did the gorgeous illustration for the cover; copyeditor Sasha Tropp made me look like a better writer; proofreader Sarah Sarai caught every little thing we missed; and interior designer Elina Cohen brought all the pieces together for a perfect fit.

Finally, I want to thank Cathie Spindler. In 1992, when I was a reporter at the Monterey (California) *Herald*, Cathie asked me to meet with her daughter, Heather, a budding writer in sixth grade, to talk about writing. Heather and I met and talked and laughed, then went our separate ways. Twenty-five years later, out of the blue, Heather wrote to tell me she'd grown up to be an editor at a publishing house in New York. She and her husband were starting a family and had moved back to California, where she had recently started her own editing and publishing business. So we met again and talked and laughed. And I hired her to edit my novel. Then I hired her as project manager to publish it. I wish I could hire her to run my life. Thank you, Heather. This book—and my great joy at seeing it in print—would not have happened without you.

ABOUT THE AUTHOR

SHARON RANDALL is an award-winning writer whose work has been syndicated for more than twenty-five years to newspapers around the country. It has also appeared in *Reader's Digest, Carmel Magazine,* and other publications. A frequent speaker at conferences and fundraisers, she receives thousands of letters and emails each year from readers who say her stories are their stories, too.

Born and raised in the Blue Ridge Mountains of North and South Carolina, Randall has spent most of her adult years in "California of All Places." She began her career at the *Monterey Herald* in 1982, starting in the newspaper's library before she became a feature writer, covering a wide range of topics that included violence in schools, the lives of cloistered nuns, the Loma Prieta earthquake, the Clinton inauguration, and the kidnapping of Polly Klaas.

In 1991, Randall began writing a column about "everyday people and ordinary things." The column, "Bay Window," became extraordinarily popular and was picked up for syndication in 1994. A collection of her columns, *Birdbaths and Paper Cranes,* was published in 2001 and is still in print. Selected by a group of more than 1,100 independent booksellers for the prestigious 2002 "BookSense 76" list, the book includes an introduction by her son, actor Josh Randall.

While her professional work has been honored with numerous awards from journalism organizations, including AASFE, APNEC of California and Nevada, and "Best of the West," Randall proudly notes that she has also "scrubbed a lot of toilets, washed a lot of towels, and burned a lot of cookies." From 1972, when her first child was born, until 1982, when her third child entered kindergarten, she was "a full-time homemaker, Sunday School teacher, Little League scorer, and PTA volunteer." Her first husband, a teacher and coach at Monterey High School, died in 1998, following a lengthy battle with cancer that she often wrote about in her columns.

In 2005, Randall married her former editor and moved to "Las Vegas of All Places," where her husband worked for newspapers. After he retired, they moved back to California in 2018 to be nearer to their growing family. They now make their home on a hill in Carmel Valley, where she continues to write a weekly syndicated column. She credits her training as a writer to "thirty years as a reporter and columnist, some forty years as a wife and a mother, and a lifetime as a daughter, a sister, a friend . . . and now a nana!"

The World and Then Some, her debut novel, was inspired by countless stories—factual, fabricated, or both—that she cut her teeth on as a child, growing up in a family of incorrigible storytellers, who refused to be hushed until all their stories were told. She can be reached online at SharonRandall.com.

Made in the USA
Monee, IL
09 October 2021